THE BONE IS POINTED

THE
BONE IS
POINTED

Arthur W. Upfield

CHARLES SCRIBNER'S SONS
NEW YORK

First Charles Scribner's Sons paperback edition published 1984

Copyright © 1947 by Arthur W. Upfield
Copyright renewed 1974

ISBN 0-684-18247-5

1 3 5 7 9 11 13 15 17 19   K/P   20 18 16 14 12 10 8 6 4 2

Printed in the United States of America.

Contents

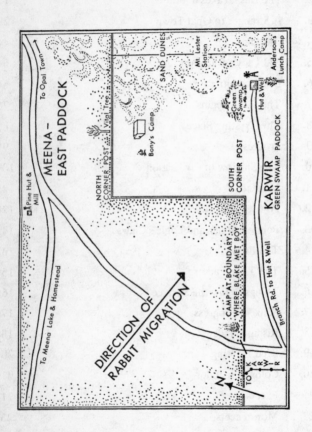

MEENA-EAST PADDOCK

To Opal Town

Pine Hut & Mill

To Meena Lake & Homestead

SAND DUNES

Mt. Lester Station

Vital Tree

NORTH CORNER POST

Bony's Camp

Green Swamp

Hut & Well

Anderson's Lunch Camp

SOUTH CORNER POST

KARWIR
GREEN SWAMP PADDOCK

Branch Rd. to Hut & Well

DIRECTION OF RABBIT MIGRATION

CAMP AT BOUNDARY WHERE BLAKE MET BOY

N

TO KARWIR

CHAPTER ONE

Suspense

HISTORY repeats itself!

It was dreadful how the phrase recurred in her mind, as though in it there dwelt an imp determined to torture her with its incessant repetition, as though the imp knew that this night would be one of tragedy as that other night had been twelve years ago.

Twelve years ago, almost on the same date of the year, Mary Gordon had walked about this pleasant room in the rambling homestead of Meena Station waiting for her husband to come home. The same clock on the mantelshelf was chiming out the quarter-hours as it had done that night twelve years before. The same calendar had then announced the date, the nineteenth of April, as to-night it announced the date, the eighteenth of April. It was raining this night as it had rained that other terrible night of suspense, and the sound of it on the iron roof annoyed her because it interfered with the sound she longed to hear—hoof beats on the sodden ground.

Eight times the hammer struck the gong within the clock.

The dinner table was set out for three persons. The spoiling dinner was being kept warm on the oven shelves and on either side of the stove. Eight o'clock, and the dinner had been waiting two hours!

Twelve years before, Mary's husband had not come home. Was her son, John, not to come home this night?

The Bone is Pointed

Mary found it impossible to sit down, to read or sew. The rain maintained a steady thrumming on the roof, and within this major sound were others, the hiss of falling rain on the leaves of the two orange-trees, just beyond the veranda, on the roofs of more distant outhouses. The early darkness was accounted for by the low rain clouds that had begun their endless march from the north-west shortly after noon.

"What on earth's keeping them?"

Standing at the open door of this large kitchen-living-room, Mary strained her hearing to catch the sound of hoof beats beyond the sound of the rain, but beyond the rain she could hear nothing. This rain coming after the hot and dry months of summer had filled her with a kind of ecstasy and, breathing the warm, moisture-laden air, she had stood often and long on the west veranda watching the rain falling upon the great empty bed of Meena Lake. The rain held no significance in the long-delayed appearance of her son, but its first music was now a noise preventing her hearing the sound of hoof beats.

History repeats itself!

Twelve years ago she had stood in this same doorway, listening for hoof beats and hearing only the rain on the roof, on the leaves of the orange-trees, then so small, and on the roofs of the distant, night-masked outbuildings. She had waited hour after hour till the dawn had paled the sky. There were four hands employed on the station then. She had wakened them, given them breakfast, and sent them with two of the blacks to find her husband. He was lying beneath the body of his horse that had broken a leg in a rabbit burrow, and they had brought him home all wet and cold and smeared with mud. Now no men were working on Meena save her son and Jimmy Partner, and this night they were both somewhere out in the darkness and the rain when they should have been with her.

8

Well, perhaps she was worrying herself unreasonably. Her husband had ridden out alone to look over the cattle in South Paddock. John had gone to look at the sheep in East Paddock, and with him had gone Jimmy Partner. If anything had happened to John, there was Jimmy Partner to help him. And it might be the other way round. Still, for all that, what on earth was keeping them out so late, especially when it was raining and had been raining ever since two o'clock?

Tall and gaunt and grey was this Mary Gordon, a woman ill-fitted to counter the hardships of her early life, hardships suffered with the dumb patience of animals. Like an old picture, her face was covered with tiny lines. Her hair was thin and almost white, but her eyes were big and grey, wells of expression.

Life had been particularly hard upon Mary Gordon, but it had given her the love of two men to compensate for the years of unnatural harshness when, as a teamster's girl, she had accompanied her father on the tracks with his bullocks and the great table-top wagon, doing the cooking, often hunting the bullocks in the early morning, sometimes even driving the team when her father was too drunk and lay helpless atop the load. After he had died—beneath one of the wheels—she went into service at the station homesteads until John Gordon married her and took her to Meena, his leasehold property of three hundred thousand acres.

She had never become quite used to John Gordon's affection, for when one is thirty-four, and has never known affection, affection never ceases to be strange. Of course, she had paid life for it, paid in anguish over years which had begun when they brought home the poor body and the minister from Opal Town consigned it to rest beside John the First in the little station cemetery.

John the Third was at school down in Adelaide, a mere boy of sixteen. He had at once returned home and demanded to stay at home to learn the management of sheep and the affairs of this small station property. Like his father in so many things, the son was like him in his steady affection for her.

History repeats itself! Time to pay again!

Ah, no! No, no, no! It won't! It can't! It mustn't! Oh, why don't they come home?

No longer could Mary support the intolerable inactivity. Turning back into the room, she slipped on an oilskin coat and lit a hurricane lamp, and with this small light to assist her she stepped off the veranda down to the wet ash path of the small garden and traversed it to the low gate in the wicket fence. Away from the iron veranda roof the night was less noisy and permitted the little sounds to reach her ears—the pattering of the rain on the gleaming coat, on the trees, on the ground. It thudded on her hands and on her face like the tips of nervous fingers urging her to go to him she loved. Besides those made by the rain there were no other sounds, no sound of creaking saddles, of hoof falls, of jangling bits in the mouths of horses eager to be home.

No longer hesitant, she walked across the open space to the out-buildings of which one was the men's hut. In this there were two small rooms. In the outer room was a rough wood table, a form and several cases serving as chairs. On the table were weekly journals, a cribbage board, a hurricane lamp. Within the inner room stood two beds, one without a mattress, the other with a mattress and with blankets tossed in disorder on it. It was Jimmy Partner's bed.

Mary's mind seemed partitioned to-night and one pàrt of it noted that the interior of this room smelled clean despite the fact that its tenant was an aboriginal. But then Jimmy Partner was an unusual aboriginal.

Again in the rain and hemmed by the menacing darkness, Mary walked to the wire gate in the low wire fence enclosing the whole of Meena homestead. She was unable to see it, but to her right stretched away the great bed of the lake that she had seen thrice filled with fifteen feet of water, giving life to countless water birds and heavy blackfish. Passing through the wire gateway, she began to follow a path winding away beneath the wide riboon of box-trees bordering the lake's shore, and now into the lamplight came wide-eyed rabbits to stare at her approach and vanish to either side. The rain was to give the rodents another lease of life.

Without a flicker the light went out; unexpectedly, because there was no wind. The night's blackness struck her eyes like a velvety blow; and, her mind momentarily confused, she halted, the rain drops on the leaves and on the trees like the footsteps of gnomes.

But Mary knew exactly where she was on this path made by the naked feet of aborigines connecting their camp with the homestead, a path first formed more than sixty years ago. Gradually the blackness waned to become faintly luminous, and when her eyes became accustomed to the night light, she continued along the path she was unable to see but on which she was guided by the shapes of familiar trees.

She had walked slowly for five minutes when a ruddy glow illuminating the trees ahead indicated the camp. Presently she was able to see the red eyes of several banked fires and one that burned brightly before a humpy constructed with bags and canegrass. On either side of this fire stood an aboriginal. Its roseate light revealed further rough humpies but no other inhabitants of the camp.

He who stood with his back to the humpy was short of stature. His body was thick with good living, but his legs were astonishingly thin. His hair and straggly beard were white, and the look of him belied the power he held over the entire Kalchut tribe. Nero was an autocrat.

The other man Mary also instantly recognized. In his elastic-sided riding boots he stood six feet in height, with his arms folded across his white cotton shirt, now all steaming from the heat of the fire. The sight of him made Mary Gordon falter in her slow walking. He was Jimmy Partner for whose return with her son she had been waiting.

In heaven's name why was he talking to Nero at this hour? Nine o'clock is a very late hour for aborigines to be outside their humpies. To be sure, only Nero was outside now in the rain, but something most unusual must have happened for Jimmy Partner to have come to the camp at nine o'clock at night, and in the pouring rain, and to have got Nero to come out of his humpy to talk with him in the light of a replenished fire.

It is doubtful if any woman in all this wide district of western Queensland knew the aborigines better than did Mary Gordon. To her they were not children; nor were they semi-idiots or mere savages. Why, she had raised Jimmy Partner in her own home, and Jimmy Partner had grown up to be a brother to John in all save birth and race. He was a member of this Kalchut tribe, fully initiated, and still he was apart from it, electing to live in the men's hut, to eat with John and herself in the kitchen-living-room, to work for wages and to be always loyal and trustworthy. Early that morning he and John had left to ride the fences of East Paddock, and now, at nine o'clock at night, he was here talking to old Nero and John was not yet home.

Her mind accepted the extraordinary situation even whilst she made nine steps forward towards the fire. Then its possible significance burst in her mind like a bomb exploding. Jimmy Partner had come to seek Nero's aid—as she had come to do —to find and bring in her son—alive, perhaps dead.

History repeats itself!

She began to run, her gaze directed to the face of Jimmy Partner, and the face of Jimmy Partner showed alarm. He was speaking rapidly but softly, and he was emphasizing points with the index finger of his right hand. Nero was relegated to an inferior position in this conference. She could not see Nero's face, for his back was towards her, but she did see his round head constantly nod in assent to what Jimmy Partner was saying.

Now the camp dogs heard her flying feet and set up their chorus of barking. The men on either side of the fire drew farther apart and stared about, becoming tense in attitudes of listening. She saw then that Jimmy Partner saw her. He came swiftly to meet her.

"John! What has happened to John?" she demanded, pantingly.

Now the firelight was behind Jimmy Partner and she was unable to read his face although she did see the white of his eyes when he drew close to her.

"Ah—Johnny Boss is all right, missus," he replied, his voice deeper than the average aboriginal voice and even more musical. "He left me to put a mob of sheep out of East Paddock 'cos of the rain makin' the Channels boggy. He sent me on home. He's all right, missus."

Relief surged like a tide from her heart to her weary mind, to banish the numbing terror. Yet it seemed to draw strength from her legs and she swayed forward and would have fallen had not Jimmy Partner quickly placed his great hands beneath her elbows.

"I tell you Johnny Boss is all right, missus," he said, now more confidently. "He'll be back home any minute. We been droving small mobs of sheep away off the Channels all afternoon."

"Yes, yes!" Mary cried. "But why didn't you come home and tell me, Jimmy? What are you doing here when you know the dinner's getting cold and I'm so anxious?"

"Well, missus, I didn't think. True. This morning we found over beside Black Gate a sign message for Nero from Mitterloo saying he wanted the tribe to go across to Deep Well where poor old Sarah is very crook and looks like dying. So I rode this way home to tell Nero about it, and the tribe's going off on walkabout first thing in the morning. Better go home,

13

missus. I'm coming now. Perhaps Johnny Boss is there already. Here, let me light the lamp."

Thank God that that imp was a liar to keep shouting that history repeats itself. Consciously now she noted Jimmy Partner's flimsy shirt again drenched by the rain.

"You hurry home," she said with her old time authority over two boys who would regard their bodies as though they were made of wood or iron. "No hat on your head, as usual. No coat; just a cotton shirt over a vest. And standing here in the cold rain."

"I'm all right, missus. I'll get me horse and be home before you."

Nero had vanished inside his humpy and now the dogs were quiet. With the lamplight to give her feet confidence, Mary hurried back along the natural path, feeling the urge to laugh and knowing the emotion for hysteria. Back again at the wire gate she was joined by two dogs as she was fastening it, and she then wanted to cry out her joy, for they were John's dogs. Over by the harness shed she heard the clink of stirrup-irons and, with the dogs escorting her, she ran across to the dark form of a horse.

"John! Oh, John!" she cried. "I've been so worried about you. I—I thought you were lying out hurt."

She saw his slim form beside the greater bulk of the horse, halted when the animal moved between them, shaking itself, to trot to the trough beside the windmill. Then she was clinging to her son, and he was saying, the school-given accent still in evidence: "I'm all right, mother. I wanted to get the sheep away from the Channels. What a rain, dear! We must have had an inch already. Let's hope it'll rain six inches and fill the lake."

A dull tattoo of hoofs preceded the arrival of Jimmy Partner who ground his feet before his horse could stop. Quick fingers began their work of removing the saddle.

"I told Nero about the message at Black Gate," he said.

"Oh!" responded John Gordon a trifle vaguely, then hastened to add: "Oh, the message! Yes, that's right, Jimmy. The tribe will start off for Deep Well first thing in the morning. Old Sarah is due to pass out. She must be the oldest lubra of the Kalchut. Now hurry along and get washed and change those clothes. Have you got clean shirt and vest and pants?"

"Too right, Johnny Boss."

Mother and son began the walk across to the house, marked in the void by the light in the kitchen-living-room.

"I'm sorry we're so late," John Gordon said, slipping an arm about the gaunt figure. "Didn't think this rain was coming when we left this morning, and I would have worried all night had I left the sheep on the Channel country."

"But I've been so anxious, dear, so terribly anxious," she complained. "I couldn't help thinking of that night twelve years ago."

The arm about her increased its pressure.

"I know," he said, tenderly. "You are a bit of an old worry pot, aren't you? The fact is that you have been too closely associated with the blacks, especially the lubras, and have borrowed much of their belief in the supernatural. Because poor dad failed to come home one night, you needs must imagine that I won't turn up. It's piffle when you come to think of it, isn't it? Anyway, I'm home safe and sound, and it's raining good and hard and looks like raining all night, and perhaps it will rain for a week and we'll have feed and water for years. I don't see anything to worry about, but everything to dance about."

He opened the wicket gate for her and she hurried on into the house to look to the dinner, the fire, and then to take up airing underclothes and lay them on his bed beside his second best trousers and coat. She was humming a little tune as she passed back again to the kitchen, but the humming gave place to a cry of concern when she saw on John's throat a wide bluish mark.

"It's nothing, and it doesn't hurt," he quickly told her. "I was riding under a mulga-tree in the dark when a low branch gave me a knock. There's no damage done, so don't worry about it or I'll have to take you in hand and talk to you seriously for being a bad woman. Now, what's for dinner? I'm hungry. And here's Jimmy Partner."

The cloud in her big eyes passed, but she followed him with a bottle of embrocation, to fuss about him until he applied some of it to the bluish mark.

When they sat down to dinner it was still raining.

CHAPTER TWO

The Bush Takes a Man

BILL THE BETTER began his day's work at seven in the morning when he rode out into the horse paddock to bring in the working hacks for the stockmen stationed at the homestead of the great Karwir cattle station.

He was a shrimp of a man, this Bill the Better. Scanty hair failed to cover a cranium that would have delighted Cesare Lombroso who, it will be remembered, determined criminals by their heads. A long nose appeared to divide the gingery moustache which he constantly pulled down by the ends, and watery blue eyes invariably contained an expression of great hope of a brighter future.

On this morning of the nineteenth of April the alarm clock awoke Bill the Better as it did every weekday, and instantly the quiet of the iron roof announced to him that the rain had ceased and that the horses would be wanted.

Only the two station cooks were astir thus early, and uttering a lurid curse that he was the unfortunate third, Bill the Better set off for the stable, at the side of a maze of cattle and horse yards, for the night horse. It was then he saw the big, jet-black gelding, bridled and saddled, standing beyond the gate spanning the road to Opal Town.

"Crummy!" he said loudly. "That there's Handerson's 'orse. Ha! Ha! I might win that two quid off Charlie yet."

The Karwir groom swerved from the line he was following

to the stable to follow another line that brought him to the hardwood gate. There, resting his arms on the top rail, he regarded the horse whilst a smile played over his irregular features. Raising his voice, he said directly to the gelding:

"Ha! Ha! So you didn't bring Mister Blooming Jeffery Handerson 'ome? So you left 'im somewhere out there in Green Swamp Paddock, did yer? Well, I'm hopin' you broke his flamin' neck, and then I'm hopin' you turned back to him and kicked the stuffin' outer 'im. Then I wins a coupler quid and does a chortle, rememberin' that time that Mister Bloomin' Jeffery Handerson took to me."

Turning away from the gate, Bill the Better walked across to that gate in the canegrass hedge surrounding the big house, washing his hands with invisible soap and blithely whistling. It being a part of his duties to keep tidy the garden within the canegrass fence, as well as to clean the many windows of the rambling house, he knew the room occupied by Mr Eric Lacy who was known over an enormous area of country as Young Lacy, the son of Old Lacy.

Bill the Better tapped vigorously on the window of Young Lacy's bedroom until the window was raised and beyond appeared a tousled red head and a pair of keen hazel eyes. Once again the groom was washing his hands with invisible soap, and he said with satisfaction somewhat extraordinary:

"The Black Emperor's standing outside the Green Swamp gate. Mr Handerson's saddle and bridle still on 'im. Lunch bag looks empty. No tracks made by Mr Handerson showing as 'ow he left the animile there and come on acrost to 'is room, or any tracks showin' that 'e came as far as the gate on The Black Emperor's back."

The clipped voice of Young Lacy issued from the room.

"Wait there, Bill. I'll be out in a second."

It was five seconds and no more when Young Lacy joined Bill the Better. He was arrayed in a wonderful dressing-gown of sky-blue with scarlet facings. His deep red hair was unbrushed and unruly. Of medium height and yet robust of body, his feet protected by yellow slippers, he did not speak until they were outside the garden gate. Bill the Better was continuing to wash his hands with invisible soap and was still whistling a lively tune.

"Doesn't it strike you that Mr Handerson may be lying out in Green Swamp Paddock seriously injured?" inquired Young Lacy, deliberately prefixing the name with an aspirate. Some twenty-five years old, he looked a bare nineteen.

"Too right!" replied Bill the Better. "I got a coupler quid on 'im being dead, and a quid on 'im being that busted up that 'e's got to be taken to the hospital at St Albans. As I lost seven and a tray over the flamin' rain, I'm sorta wanting to make a bit over on Mr Handerson."

"I suppose you'd bet on your funeral?"

"Yes, any time you like, Mr Lacy. I'm game to bet you a level fiver you dies first outer us two. We can put the money in an envelope wot can be kept in the office safe and handed out to the winner."

"Tish, man! You're a ghoul."

Arrived at the gate giving entry to Green Swamp Paddock and the road to Opal Town, Bill the Better swung it open sufficiently to permit them to pass and then reclosed it. The great black gelding now stared at them with wide, white-rimmed eyes, his ears flattened and his legs iron-stiff, a beautiful horse and yet the devil incarnate. Without hesitation, Young Lacy walked to it and caught up the broken and trailing reins.

"Didn't The Black Emperor have a neck-rope on him when Mr Handerson left yesterday morning?" asked Young Lacy.

" 'Anged if I know. Mr Handerson usually put a neck-rope on this little dove."

Two pairs of expert eyes focused their gaze carefully to examine the horse.

The Bone is Pointed

"Only damage I can see is the reins," said Bill the Better. "'E musta chucked Mr Handerson clear and then, most likely went back to finish 'im orf with 'is teeth and 'is hoofs. Ah well! Them that arsts for it generally gits it sooner or later. Betcher a quid, even money, Mr Handerson's lying quite cold."

"You don't like Mr Handerson, do you, Bill?" Young Lacy said it more as a statement of fact than a question. He was looking into the saddle-bag at the folded serviette that had been wrapped about the missing man's lunch.

"Oh, I like 'im well enough when I'm liable to make money outer 'im. Other times I don't feel particular brotherly."

"Well—no good standing here. You nip out for the horses, Bill. I'll put The Black Emperor into the yards and then call the boss."

"Righto, Mr Lacy. Better leave me outer the search party, 'cos if I seen Mr Handerson lying hurt I might pass 'im with me eyes shut."

"Pleasant little blighter," murmured Young Lacy, crossing back to the house after having put the gelding into the yards. He found his father drinking coffee in his room preparatory to dressing and going to meet the men gathered outside the office waiting for their orders. A tall, well-set-up man despite his seventy years, his keen grey eyes bored into those of his son.

"Any sign of Jeff?" he demanded, his voice resonant and containing a faint burr.

"No, but The Black Emperor was found standing outside Green Swamp gate by the groom. I've just put him into the yards. He's undamaged, and so are the saddle and bridle, except the reins which are broken at the buckle end. Jeff isn't in his room. He must be lying out hurt."

Old Lacy caressed his prominent Roman nose with the fingers of his left hand. His right held the coffee cup. The clear eyes indicated a quick brain.

"Ha-um! Jeff must be getting childish," he said. "I'll have

20

a look-see at the horse. Confound Jeff! He's upset the day's routine."

Young Lacy nodded that he heard and then went to the kitchen where the only maid on the house staff gave him a cup of tea.

"Mr Anderson's not in his room, Mr Lacy," she said.

"I know that, Mabel. His horse is back. Mr Anderson must have met with an accident. Have you taken tea to Miss Lacy?"

"Yes. She was wanting to know if Mr Anderson had come home during the night."

"Then you slip along and tell her about the horse coming home without him."

"You there, lad?" called Old Lacy from the hall, and Young Lacy hurried out to accompany the older man to the yards. Having circled the suspicious horse, the old man said:

"Must have thrown his rider long before the rain stopped. No mud on him. Any idea when the rain did stop?"

"No. I didn't put my light out till after one, and it was still raining then."

Old Lacy continued to inspect the horse, and then he said:

"Ah-um! We'll take a look for tracks beyond the gate."

Together the two men walked to the right of the two gates in the six-wire fence running parallel with the creek. The sun was making diamonds of the water lying in the claypans and in the wheel tracks far along the road. The subdivision fence separating Green Swamp Paddock from North Paddock ran to a hair stretched to infinity across the grass plain. Having passed beyond the gate and come to halt on the road to Opal Town, the old man spoke with conviction in his strong voice.

"The Black Emperor got to the gate long before the rain stopped last night," he said, staring at the ground. "See, his tracks are almost but not quite wiped out by the rain. He came home following the road. You'd better get your breakfast, lad, and I'll put every available man up on a horse.

You'll have to organize a muster of the paddock. Pity the 'drome's too boggy to let you get the plane aloft. I'd better ring up Blake. We might want his tracker out here."

Sergeant Blake was breakfasting with his wife when the telephone shrilled a summons to the office, one of the two front rooms of the station building which fronted the only street in Opal Town. The senior police-officer controlling a district almost as large as England and Wales was dapper but tough. His weathered face emphasized the grey of his well-brushed hair and carefully trimmed short grey moustache. His wife, a large woman his own age—forty-six—made no remark on this early call, and silently placed her husband's half-eaten breakfast chops into the open oven.

Correctly dressed in uniform, the Sergeant thudded along the passage to the telephone. From beyond miles of mulga forest and open plain a deep, booming voice spoke.

"That you, Blake? Lacy here. Sorry to ring you up so early. I fear that Jeff Anderson has met with an accident somewhere out in our Green Swamp Paddock. May want your help later."

"What's happened?" asked Blake, his voice metallic.

"I sent Anderson into Green Swamp Paddock yesterday morning to ride the fences. He hadn't come home last night, and we thought it likely enough that he had camped for the night at the hut out at the swamp, seeing that it was raining and that we always keep a few rations at the hut.

"Knowing Anderson, we didn't worry much about him, but this morning the groom found his horse with saddle and bridle still on him waiting outside the paddock gate. I have looked the animal over. It hasn't been damaged nor has the saddle or bridle, except the reins which the horse had been dragging and treading on. It looks as though Anderson was thrown. I've sent every available man with the lad to muster the paddock."

"I understood that Anderson was an exceptionally good horseman. What's the horse like?"

"The worst on Karwir, Blake. The Black Emperor."

"Humph! I've heard of him. Horse and man a good match, eh?"

"You're right," agreed Old Lacy with some reluctance. "Still, Anderson likes that type of horse and he could well manage The Black Emperor. Now the position this morning is this. The ground is too soggy for the lad to take the plane up, so he can't make a search from the air. The road is so wet that I don't think a car could be driven far without becoming well bogged. It's on the cards that Anderson was parted from his horse yesterday afternoon at some point at the northern end of the paddock. If that happened late in the afternoon he would be almost sure to make for the hut if he could manage it, or even if he wasn't hurt—in which case the men would meet him walking home this morning. The chances are in favour of his having been thrown, then, unhurt, camping at the hut last night and now walking home. On the other hand he may be lying seriously hurt and suffering from exposure."

"Yes, that may be," Blake agreed. "What d'you want me to do?"

"Nothing just now. But I thought that later on, if the men haven't found Anderson, you might send a constable and your tracker out—even come out yourself. Or you could ring up the Gordons and ask John Gordon to ride over with a couple of the blacks. If Anderson doesn't turn up, or can't be located by two o'clock, we can be sure he's come a cropper."

"It might be better to get Gordon to take a couple of the Kalchut blacks over to Green Swamp Paddock than to attempt to get there from here by car," Blake stated. "Ring me up after dinner. I'll be on hand all day. Been a good rain, hasn't it?"

"It has that. We had an inch and seventy points. Let's hope

it means the beginning of a good wet winter. All right, I'll ring you again early this afternoon. Good-bye."

Again seated at the breakfast table, Sergeant Blake related the story to a news-hungry wife who was, too, a devout Methodist. She quoted:

" 'He that taketh up the sword shall perish by the sword.' A violent man will surely meet with violence."

"It's not yet proved that Jeff Anderson has met with violence," her husband pointed out.

"No, but it will be proved some time if not now. As I've often said, you'll be taking Jeffery Anderson before he's much older, mark my words. Where's Abie this morning? He hasn't come for his breakfast."

"He's lying in, I suppose. And the horse waiting for a feed. Abie's getting that way that I'll have to shake him up. They all go the same in time. Can't keep away from the tribe more than a month."

Breakfast over, Blake rose and lit a pipe. Without hat he stepped down into the yard at the rear of the building and crossed it to the stables on the far side. Here a horse was always kept ready for duty, although Blake ran his own car and one of his two constables owned a motor cycle outfit. It was the tracker's main duty to exercise, feed and groom the horse, and he camped in one of the vacant stalls.

To Blake's astonishment the stretcher provided for the tracker was not occupied, nor were there lying about it any articles of spare clothing or the stockwhip of which he was so proud. The sleek brown mare in the adjacent stall whinnied her request for breakfast, and, with a heavy frown between his eyes, the Sergeant took her out to water at the trough. He shouted several times for Abie. There was no reply. Blake was now convinced that the tracker had left to rejoin his tribe. He had been at the stable at ten o'clock the previous night. Out in the yard Blake met one of his two constables.

"Seen Abie this morning?" he asked, grey eyes glinting.

"No, Sergeant."

"Must have cleared out. Nothing belonging to him now in his quarters, and Kate neither watered nor fed. I've just attended to her. You'd better groom her, and then you can ride her out to Mackay's place and get that return fixed up."

Throughout the morning Blake worked in the station office, having for companion his other constable who pounded on a typewriter with his index fingers. After lunch he called Meena Station.

"Gordon speaking."

"Good day, Mr Gordon. You seen anything of Abie? Not in his quarters at breakfast time."

"No, I haven't. The tribe cleared out for Deep Well early to-day. I didn't see them go. Abie might have been with them."

Gordon described the message at Black Gate.

"Well, Abie's not on hand to-day. Did the tribe go on walkabout to see old Sarah?"

"Oh yes. Jimmy Partner went, too. Grandma Sarah is dying out at Deep Well, and they've all gone there to do the usual thing when she's dead. Nero is the only black left here in camp, and he's having a gum-leaf bake for rheumatism. At least he was when I went to the camp after breakfast. Could see nothing of him but his head. How much rain did you get in town?"

"A hundred and fifty-two points. What did you have?"

"A hundred and forty-eight. Must have been a general rain. Did you hear what Karwir got?"

"Yes. Karwir got a hundred and seventy. Old Lacy rang me up early this morning to say that Jeff Anderson is missing. His horse was found outside the paddock gate this morning, and all hands, led by Young Lacy, are out mustering the country for him."

"Strange!" exclaimed John Gordon. "Anderson is a pretty good rider, you'll admit. What paddock was he working in?"

"Green Swamp. Left to ride the fences yesterday morning. Old Lacy says it's too boggy for the plane to get off the ground out there."

"Jimmy Partner and I were working in our East Paddock which is as you know north of Karwir's Green Swamp Paddock. We were getting small mobs of sheep away from the Channels on account of the rain making bogs of them. We were often in sight of the boundary fence but we never saw Anderson. Let me know when you get news from Karwir, will you? I mayn't be here, but mother will."

Shortly after four o'clock Old Lacy again rang Sergeant Blake. He reported:

"The lad has sent Bill the Better home to say they haven't come across Jeff Anderson. They back-tracked The Black Emperor along the road for about a mile to where the hoof marks were wiped out by the rain. There are no signs that Anderson reached the hut and camped there overnight. They've found no track or sign of horse or man. D'you think you could send out or come out with your tracker? Road ought to be drying by now. My girl took me out to the boundary gate in the car this afternoon."

Blake reported the disappearance of Abie, and its probable cause.

"I'll get in touch with Gordon and ask him to ride after the tribe and bring over a couple of trackers. They ought to be on the job first thing in the morning—if Anderson hasn't been found before nightfall."

For several seconds Old Lacy was silent and Blake was beginning to think the squatter had hung up his instrument when the booming voice spoke.

"Funny that those blacks went on walkabout this morning and that your tracker left to go with 'em. Did you know anything about old Sarah dying?"

"No. Gordon said he and Jimmy Partner came across a sign message at Black Gate yesterday, and that when they got home Jimmy Partner told the tribe of it, saying that Sarah was pegging out. Gordon also said that he and Jimmy Partner were working sheep off the Channels in his East Paddock, and were often close to the boundary fence but didn't see Anderson. I'll ring him up about going after a couple of trackers. Let me know how your men get on, will you?"

When Blake did ring Meena it was Mrs Gordon who answered the call.

"John has gone riding round to the west side of the lake to see if any water has come down Meena Creek into the lake," she said, adding eagerly: "Have you had news yet of Mr Anderson?"

"No, they haven't found him, Mrs Gordon. You see, the rain has blotted out all tracks to be seen by white men. Will you ask Mr Gordon to ring me immediately he gets home?"

John Gordon rang Blake at five minutes past seven.

"No, they hadn't found Anderson at six o'clock when the men came home for dinner," Blake told him. "They're all leaving again to-night to camp at the hut at Green Swamp so's to be out on the job again in the morning early. Will you get after the blacks first thing and bring a couple of 'em to hunt for tracks?"

"Certainly. I'll have to take horses because the road to Deep Well can't be used for two or three days. Too many deep water-gutters to cross. But I may not succeed all the same. The blacks haven't forgotten how Anderson treated Inky Boy, you know."

"Humph! Well, that can be understood," Blake agreed. "Still, you might try 'em."

"Oh yes, I'll go after them. I'll leave before daylight."

"Good enough. Old Lacy is talking about foul play, or hinting at it. Seems to think the blacks might have killed Anderson for his treatment of Inky Boy."

"Oh, I say! That's all rot," Gordon said warmly. "Why, you know, Sergeant, that if the blacks wanted revenge for what Anderson did to Inky Boy they would not have waited all this time to take it. And, if they had killed him, I'd have known of it by now."

"I'm more than inclined to agree with you on that score, Mr Gordon," Blake said with unmistakable candour. "They'll find Anderson with a broken leg, probably. If they don't I think we can search for him elsewhere. Good night!"

"Good night, Sergeant. I'll get a tracker or two across to Karwir as quickly as I can. I can be almost sure of Jimmy Partner."

But Jeffery Anderson was not found by the Karwir searchers or by the blacks brought to Karwir by John Gordon three days after The Black Emperor was seen at the gate by Bill the Better.

May passed and June, and still the bush held Jeffery Anderson.

Old Lacy openly accused the Kalchut tribe of murdering him and burying the body, and the Gordons, mother and son, stoutly defended them. Sergeant Blake and his constables visited many people and obtained statements from them, but no two statements could be correlated and all of them together failed to provide a clue. Then Old Lacy took to writing to the Chief Commissioner, candidly giving his views on police systems in general and the Queensland force in particular.

June passed, and August gave way to September, and still the bush kept Jeffery Anderson.

CHAPTER THREE

A Stranger to Opal Town

THE mail car from St Albans arrived at Opal Town every Tuesday about noon, weather permitting, and the twenty-third of September being fine and warm, it arrived this day on time. A shock-headed youth relinquished the wheel, backed out of the car, surveyed the township, saw Sergeant Blake standing before the door of the post office, and called, cheerfully:

"Good day-ee, Sergeant!"

Sergeant Blake, wearing civilian clothes, returned the greeting and transferred his interest to the passengers. The two young men who were obviously stockmen he greeted, each by name, but the third and last passenger caused him to narrow his eyes. This third passenger was plainly stamped as a city man by his clothes and heavy suitcase. Of average height and build, he was remarkable for the dark colouring of his skin, which emphasized his blue eyes and white teeth when he smiled at something said to him by the driver who was delving for the half-dozen mail-bags.

The stranger stood a moment at the edge of the side-walk, regarding the hotel across the street, while the other passengers and the driver moved past the Sergeant to enter the post office. When slim, dark fingers began the manufacture of a cigarette, Blake thought the time opportune to learn something of this stranger's business in a town so situated at the end of one of the long western trails that but few strangers ever came there, even swagmen.

"Staying long in Opal Town?"

The stranger turned to regard him with eyes containing a distinct twinkle.

"I hope not," he replied, lightly. "Are you Sergeant Blake?"

"I am," was the cautious reply, followed by a further examination of the stranger's face and clothes.

"Then I hope you will be pleased to meet me. I am Detective-Inspector Napoleon Bonaparte."

Blake was only just in time to prevent his lower jaw sagging and his eyes widening in astonishment. Napoleon Bonaparte! The man of whom he had heard so much indirectly and semi-officially! The man who, it was said, had never known failure! The man who had so often proved that aboriginal blood and brains were equal to those of the white man! Automatically the Sergeant's right hand flashed upward in a salute.

"I am more pleased to see you, sir, than you might think," he said warmly. "Your coming is quite unexpected, sir. I haven't been notified of it."

"I dislike advance notices," Bonaparte murmured, and the Sergeant, seeing that his superior was glancing over his shoulder towards the post office, also lowered his voice when he spoke.

"Will you be putting up at the hotel, sir?"

"That, I think, we shall decide after we have had our conference. I could leave my case with the post office official meanwhile."

Blake carried out this suggestion, and then together they walked along the street to the police station at its western end.

"I think already that we will be able to work well in harness, and enjoy an official association," said the stranger to Opal Town. "But, please, Sergeant, kindly omit the 'sir' and call me Bony. Everyone does. When I am home, my wife often says: 'Bony, the wood box is empty.' My eldest son,

Charles, who is studying at the university I myself attended, most inconveniently says: 'Can you lend me a quid, Bony?' The rising generation is, I fear, contemptuous of the correct use of words. But to revert. Being addressed as 'sir' or as 'Inspector' causes in me a sensation of discomfort. Even our mutually respected Chief Commissioner calls me Bony. He shouts: 'Where the so and so have you been, Bony?' and 'Blast you, Bony! Why don't you obey orders?' "

Blake glanced sideways at the detective, strongly suspicious that he was being fooled. Consequently he was careful to make no comment. Bony flashed a glance at him and marvelled at the stiffness of the Sergeant's body.

"Are you married?" he asked.

"Oh yes."

"Then, perhaps, your wife might be persuaded to make us a pot of tea. Cups of tea and cigarettes make me a brilliant man when normally I am quite ordinary."

At the police station, Bony was shown into the office and left there for a moment whilst the Sergeant interviewed his wife. He returned to find the detective studying the large-scale map of the district.

"The wife says that lunch is quite ready," Blake said, a little of the stiffness gone out of him. "We'd be glad if you would join us."

"That is, indeed, kind of you," Bony said, smilingly.

So the Sergeant took him to the bathroom, and from there to the pleasant veranda beside the kitchen where the meal was set out and where Bony was presented to his hostess.

"If you will sit here, Inspector," Mrs Blake said, indicating a chair.

"Dear, dear!" Bony exclaimed. "I forgot. Forgive me, Mrs Blake. Now do I look like the Governor-General?"

Mrs Blake became still, and then, since Bony was obviously waiting for an answer, she made it a negative one. She experienced a growing feeling of wonder when he smiled at her and said :

"Thank heaven for that, Mrs Blake. My friends all call me Bony. May I account you one of them ?"

It became quickly apparent that he could and when they found a common subject of interest in the welfare of the aborigines, her husband was ignored. Mrs Blake became almost vivacious, and Bony suspected that Sergeant Blake could have been less a policeman to his wife.

Back again in the office, Bony once more studied the wall map.

"This Karwir Station is quite a big holding, Sergeant," he remarked. "I'm going to ask you a great number of questions which you may think unnecessary seeing that I have read your report on this case. As the man vanished on Karwir Station, we will make it the pivot around which shall revolve influences that may or may not bear on Anderson's disappearance. However, first put me right if I am wrong on these several points.

"Anderson left Karwir homestead to ride the fences of Green Swamp Paddock on the eighteenth of April. The next morning his horse, still with its saddle and bridle, was found standing at the gate. A hundred and seventy points of rain had fallen, and, in consequence, the horse could be back-tracked for only a mile along the road. That day a search was made for Anderson by mounted men. On the twentieth the horsemen again searched, and, during the afternoon, Mr Eric Lacy, accompanied by his sister, flew his aeroplane over the same ground. On the twenty-second Mr Gordon arrived with three trackers. By this time two constables and yourself were added to the body of searchers. The search was continued until the twenty-ninth, when it was abandoned. No clue to the man's fate was found. You know, Blake, it is all quite remarkable."

"It is that," agreed Blake. "I no longer think that Anderson

A Stranger to Opal Town

was merely thrown from his horse and killed or even injured. Either he was murdered, or he wilfully vanished for some reason unknown."

"I think you are right Sergeant, and I shall establish one or other of your alternatives. Two weeks only did the Commissioner give me to complete this case, but I always refuse to be hurried or to give up an investigation once I begin it. I am not sure, but it is either five or seven times that I have been sacked for declining to obey the order to return to headquarters before I have completed a case. So many people in our profession, Blake, insist on regarding me as a policeman. Well, now—

"Let us first visualize this Green Swamp Paddock on Karwir Station. It is situated on the north-eastern extremity of the run, almost due south of Opal Town from which it is distant only ten or twelve miles. In shape it is roughly oblong and it is bounded on the north by the netted boundary fence separating Karwir from Meena Station. In area it is about fifty thousand acres. The southern half is plain country; the northern half is covered with mulga belts and dry water channels culminating at a swamp backed on the east and north by sand-dunes. To the south of Green Swamp Paddock is the Karwir homestead. To the east of it is Mount Lester Station. To the north of it is Meena Station.

"Let us begin with the people at Karwir. Describe to me the Lacys. Then the Gordons, and then the Mackays. Give a rough outline of their history."

Not until he was satisfied that his pipe was drawing properly did Blake comply, and it was evident that he intended to choose his words carefully.

"I'll begin with Old Lacy," he said. "For many years and over a wide area, he has been known only as Old Lacy. He created Karwir in the eighties, and for years didn't do much with it, since he hadn't much money and was forced to make a living bullock and camel driving. Then he married a woman

2—TBIP

33

who had a little money, and he settled down to the cattle business. He's rough, tough and just according to his lights. To-day, though he's more than seventy, he looks and acts like a man of fifty. It is whispered that he must be worth a million, and if you want to see him riled just hint that he ought to retire and live in a city.

"Every week he comes to town and sits on the bench. His fellow justices simply don't count. Old Lacy fines everyone presented at the flat rate of two pounds, no matter if the fine ought to be five shillings or fifty pounds. You'll like him. We all do.

"He's got two children. Eric is twenty-five and probably the most popular man in the district. Old Lacy dotes on him, gives him lashings of money, but the young fellow has kept his balance. He learned to fly a plane several years ago, but was dished somehow for the Air Force. Flies his own plane about here now and keeps the station books. Diana, the daughter, is just twenty years old. She's been back from school two years and now runs the homestead. If you've got an eye for beauty she'll make you happy.

"So much for the Lacys. About the time Old Lacy took up Karwir, a John Gordon made a station north of it that he named Meena, the homestead being situated on the east shore of a fine lake of water. This year it's bone dry. He and Old Lacy had a struggle for the possession of Green Swamp, and when Old Lacy got it, the first Gordon was embittered for life. His son carried on after him until twelve years ago when he was killed by his horse. The son's wife, a fine type of woman, then carried on the place until their son, the present John Gordon, was old enough to take his father's place. They are respected people. They don't mix much with local people, but they have maintained a kind of tradition begun by the original Gordon who made himself a protector of the blacks out there, the Kalchut tribe, an off-shoot of the Worgia nation. They will have no interference with the blacks, and because

34

Meena is at the end of the road, and a desert lies beyond it, they and their aborigines are most favoured.

"The Mackays are different from either the Lacys or the Gordons. Their place is about the size of Meena, only three hundred thousand acres, but their land is much poorer. Mackay himself was stricken with paralysis fifteen years ago, and his wife died four years ago. There are three boys and two girls in the family, ranging from twenty-five to sixteen. The boys are wild and they seem always to have more money than the place could provide them with. That's about all I can tell you, I think."

"Quite good, Sergeant. Now we have the background against which Anderson lived. Tell me about him."

"All right. When Anderson disappeared he was about thirty-five years old. He came to Karwir to jackeroo when he was fifteen or sixteen, and he's been a jackeroo ever since. Old Lacy was always a bit hard on him, and he gave him his biggest knock in refusing to promote him to the overseership a few years ago when the overseer left. When Young Lacy came home it was expected that the old man would sack Anderson, but he didn't.

"Anderson was a wonderful horseman, a big, fine-looking man spoiled by a vicious temper and a cruel disposition. The first trouble with him was over a young aboriginal whom Mrs Lacy employed as maid. There was hell to pay over that. The present Gordon's father and Mrs Gordon created ructions, and refused to permit any female aboriginal to tread on Karwir ground. Then followed another trouble when Anderson beat up an employee named Wilson, known as Bill the Better. Wilson was in the hospital for nine months. Old Lacy paid all the expenses, paid compensation to Wilson, and when the money had been spent, took him again into his employment. Bill the Better is the Karwir groom to-day.

"There was an affair concerning a horse that had to be destroyed, but I never got the rights of it and it was hushed up. Then came an ugly business concerning a blackfellow named Inky Boy. It happened two years back. Inky Boy was employed to look after the Karwir rams. For years Karwir has been running sheep as well as cattle. Anderson one day found half the rams perished in a fence corner, and Inky Boy asleep in his hut. He took Inky Boy out to a tree, tied him to it, and flogged him with his stockwhip until he was almost dead.

"No report of this affair reached me until it was all settled up. Young Lacy was sent to St Albans in his plane to bring out the doctor. The Gordons went over and demanded the carcass, and after the doctor had done what he could they took Inky Boy to Meena and nursed him back to normal. After that no black was allowed by them to work on Karwir.

"You see, the Gordons were just as keen to keep this affair from me as were the Lacys. They feared that if it leaked out the busybodies down in the cities, who think they know all that's to be known about our blacks, would agitate for official interference with the Kalchut tribe, probably to the extent of having them moved to strange country on some reserve or other.

"And so Anderson got off scot free. As Inky Boy made no complaint to me, and as I didn't get to know of it until months after, I decided to let sleeping dogs lie."

"In those circumstances, my dear Blake, you acted wisely," Bony interjected. "Proceed, please."

"Well, as I said, Anderson was a fine horseman, a good cattleman, and a passable sheepman. As far as his job was concerned, he knew it. But—Old Lacy knew him. Besides being a good horseman, Anderson was a wizard with a stockwhip. He used it to satisfy his sadistic lust, to give and to witness pain. No one in the district liked him. No one could understand why Old Lacy allowed him to stay on Karwir. After the miss over the vacant overseership, Anderson became sullen, and drank more than was good for him or any man."

"What is your private opinion about Anderson?" Bony asked.

"Well, as the man is probably dead—"

"I appreciate your reluctance, Blake, to answer my question; but we have to get down to the foundation. Character if often a pointer."

Still Blake hesitated, filling his pipe and lighting it before replying. Then:

"I think that had life been easier for Anderson he might have turned out differently. From what I've heard from time to time, I think that Old Lacy was always too hard with him. Anderson had the right to expect promotion when the overseer left, and, after it was refused, he followed the downward road. When a big man, as Anderson was, becomes governed by passion he is an ugly proposition. I never liked to see him come to town; I always liked to see him leave it. He never gave us any trouble, and that is about all I can say in his favour."

"He must, then, have had many enemies?"

"That's so," Blake replied. "But I've never heard of any threats against his life, and I haven't seen the finger pointing to any particular person who might have engineered his death."

Abruptly Bony left his chair again to study the wall map. On returning to his seat, he manufactured one of his badly made cigarettes, exhaled a cloud of smoke, and said:

"You mentioned in your report that on the morning of the nineteenth of April you discovered that your tracker had gone back to the tribe. Also that it was learned that he had accompanied the tribe to Deep Well where an aged lubra was dying. Did she die?"

"No. She got better. Still alive and now with the tribe at Meena Lake."

"About what time did you, or one of the constables, last see the tracker the previous day?"

"I saw him at ten o'clock on the evening of the eighteenth, the day Anderson rode Green Swamp. I went as usual to the stable to see that the horse kept there for duty had been properly fed and bedded. Abie—that was his name—was then asleep on his stretcher in the adjoining stall."

"How did he receive word about the sick lubra?"

"I don't know. Mulga wire, I suppose."

"This Meena Lake is how many miles from here?"

"Twenty-eight."

"You missed him the next morning, at what time?"

"Half-past seven."

Bony looked beyond the Sergeant and out the open window. For nearly a minute neither man spoke.

"I suppose that the old lubra out at this Deep Well was really ill. Did you ever check up on that point?"

"Well, no."

"We'll have to. An old lubra is reported ill at Deep Well which is forty-two miles from this place where Abie is employed as a tracker. During the vital night it is raining hard, and Abie walks twenty-eight miles to Meena Lake, and a further fourteen miles to Deep Well to find the woman not dying. On the face of those facts the blacks made an extraordinarily bad mistake. You know, my dear Blake, I am already becoming interested in this case. There is another point.

"It was never established that on the morning that Anderson last rode Green Swamp his horse was carrying a neck-rope. The next morning when the groom found the animal at the gate there was no neck-rope, though it was Anderson's custom to have one with him. We mustn't lose sight of the probability that the horse carried a neck-rope on that fatal day, and that when the man vanished the neck-rope as well as the stockwhip vanished with him."

Sergeant Blake nodded his agreement. He noted with interest the gleam in the blue eyes, and his interest was increased when Bony took a pen and wrote on a slip of paper. The writing was pushed towards him, and he read :

"There is someone standing outside the window. Look out and see who he is. Have him in if possible."

Without a sound the Sergeant's chair was raised and lifted back. With catlike tread he moved to the window and then, in swifter action, he thrust his head beyond the sill. The delighted Bony heard him grunt before shouting :

"What the devil are you doing there, Wandin ?"

The answering voice was unmistakably aboriginal.

"Waiting for you, Sargint. Wantum money buy terbaccer."

"Oh, do you ? You come in here, quick."

Blake moved clear of the window, and Bony saw a tall black figure pass it to reach the front door. Followed then the padding of naked feet in the passage. He stood up beside Blake to await the coming of this Wandin, who, he knew, had been leaning against the wall within a foot or so of the wide-open window.

A tall, gaunt, spindle-legged aboriginal entered the office to stand just inside the doorway and gently rub the naked left foot with the toes of the right foot. He was cleanly shaved, and his cotton shirt and dungaree trousers were reasonably clean. He wore no hat. His hair was full and greying. Over his long face was spread a grin as he looked alternately from the Sergeant to Bony. It was a foolish grin deliberately to conceal anxiety, which the black eyes failed to do.

"What were you doing out there ?" Blake asked, sharply.

"Nuthin,' Sargint. Jes' waitin'."

"What for ?"

"Money fer terbaccer, Sargint. No terbaccer. You give me two tree schillin' ?"

Bony now stepped forward to stand close to the blackfellow who was taller than he was.

"You Wandin, eh ?"

"Yes. Too right !"

"You stand outside listening 'cos you want tobacco. Look!"

Wandin bent his head to look at the point of his trousers where a large plug of tobacco was distinctly outlined. When the eyes were again raised to meet the steady blue eyes the unease behind them was stronger still. Yet he continued to smile, foolishly, and said: "Funny, eh? I forgot."

Now Bony was smiling, and swiftly his two hands went upwards to grasp the edges of the open shirt and to draw them farther apart. Wandin stiffened, and from his cicatrized chest Bony's gaze rose again to meet the angry black eyes.

"You plenty beeg blackfeller, eh?" he said softly. "You have plenty magic, eh? You marloo totem feller. Me—I know signs. Now you go out and you go look-see police horse."

The detective turned back to his chair at the desk, and Blake repeated the order to look to the horse in the stable. Without speaking, Wandin left, the soft padding of his feet coming to them from the passage. Through the open window Blake saw him leave the building and round an angle of it before he himself resumed his seat.

"Do you think he was listening to us?" he asked, a frown puckering his eyes.

"He's a most intelligent aboriginal gentleman, Sergeant. I quite think he was listening. Anyway, I hope so. Yes, this case already reveals possibilities of absorbing interest. Is your clock right?"

"Was last night by the wireless signal."

"Good! By the way, in your report you didn't state whether Anderson was wearing a hat the day he vanished. In fact, you haven't mentioned his clothes."

"I took it for granted that he was wearing a hat."

"You mentioned a saddle-bag containing a serviette that had been used to wrap his lunch in, but you did not say whether, also attached to the saddle, there was a quart-pot. Was there?"

"Yes, there was. I saw the saddle later."

"You see, it is necessary to establish what disappeared with Anderson. We know that his stockwhip did. Probably he was wearing a hat, a felt hat. And it is probable that round the horse's neck was a rope, neatly rolled and knotted, with which to secure the animal when Anderson stopped for lunch or was obliged to repair the fences. If that rope was discovered, say, here in your office— You see the point? So it would be with his hat, or any other article associated with him that fatal day. I will go into the matter at Karwir. Would you ring Mr Lacy and ask him if he will put me up? Say Detective-Inspector Bonaparte. He might give Bony room in the men's hut."

Blake grinned and reached for the telephone attached to the wall at his side. When he had called the exchange, and while he was waiting for the connection, Bony said, chuckling:

"The title, added to the illustrious name I bear, often goes far in securing me comfortable quarters. Alas! I love comfort. I am soft, I know, but being soft keeps me back from the bush which to me is ever a great danger."

Blake spoke, addressing Mr Lacy, so that Bony knew not whether father or son was at the other end of the line.

"Mr Lacy will be very pleased to put you up," the Sergeant said, turning back to him. "If you like, he will send his son in the aeroplane for you."

"Thank Mr Lacy. Say I will be glad to accept his offer of modern transport. I am ready to leave Opal Town when the machine arrives here."

"Well, that's that!" Blake said, having replaced the absurd horn contraption on its hook. "You'll like the Lacys."

"Oh yes, of that I have no doubt," concurred Bony. "In fact, I believe I am going to enjoy myself on this investigation. Its basic facts please me immensely—which is why I consented to come."

"Consented to come!" echoed Blake abruptly, very much the policeman.

"That is what I said. You know, Blake, were I not a rebel

against red tape and discipline I should be numbered among the ordinary detectives who go here and go there and do this and that as directed. Team work, they call it. I am never a part of a team. I am always the team. As I told you, I think, once I begin an investigation I stick to it until it is finished. Authority and time mean little to me, the investigation everything. That is the foundation of my successes. Instead of fearing defeat in this case because of the length of time between the day of the disappearance and this day of my arrival, I am confident of ultimate success in establishing what happened to the man Jeffery Anderson. The sands of the bush have buried all the clues. I have not one with which to start. No body, no false teeth, no bloodstained knife or revolver covered with fingerprints. But Sergeant, I have a brain, two eyes, an ability to reason, a contempt for time and red tape and discipline. These things are all I need. Now, please, go out and find what Wandin is doing. Spy on him. Don't let him know you are spying on him if you can help it."

The Sergeant was away for nearly five minutes and when he returned to the office he found Bony once again standing before the wall map.

"You found Wandin, probably in the place he occupies as a camp," Bony said without turning his head. "He was squatted on his heels. His arms were crossed and resting on his knees. He appeared to be asleep. He was, of course, awake, but as you moved quietly he did not know of your approach."

With light tread, Sergeant Blake walked to Bony's side. His grey eyes bored steadily into the beaming blue eyes. For three seconds he stood there, staring, and then he said:

"How did you know that?"

"In a city drawing-room, a city office, on a city street, I am like a nervous child," Bony began his reply, which was no reply to the policeman. "Here in bush townships I am a grown man. Out there in the bush I am an emperor. The bush is me: I am the bush: we are one." And then Bony laughed, softly, to add: "There are moments when I feel a great pride in being the son of an aboriginal woman, because in many things it is the aboriginal who is the highly developed civilized being and the white man who is the savage. Perhaps your association with me on this case will make you believe that."

CHAPTER FOUR

Old Lacy

BONY and Sergeant Blake stood beside the latter's car at the edge of flat country half a mile north of Opal Town, country which had been cleared and levelled by Old Lacy's men to make a landing ground for the Karwir plane. From this point the town was hidden by a range of low sand-dunes through which wound the little-used track.

"This Young Lacy," Bony said, "is he a reliable flier?"

"Most. Holds his 'B' licence. When he failed to enter the Air Force he wanted to join the flying staff of a commercial company, but the old man persuaded him against it. I think the young fellow stays at home only because his father is growing old. The old man has a lot to commend him, you know. I think I can hear the plane coming now."

"Yes, it's coming. I can see it. By the way, give that tracker of yours his marching orders. He is too dangerous a man to have hanging round a police station."

"Dangerous?" Blake echoed. "I've found him willing enough and reliable."

"Perhaps Abie will consent to return," suggested Bony. "Anyway, exchange Wandin for a much younger man. A young man won't know so much about magic and uncomfortable things of that kind. Ah, quite a smart machine!"

The silver-painted aeroplane landed with hardly a bounce, and, with the propeller ticking over, it was expertly taxied to a halt within fifty yards of the car and facing the light wind coming from the west. Young Lacy jumped to the ground, ignoring the step inset in the fuselage immediately behind the near-side wing. Bony watched him striding towards them, noted the red hair when the airman snatched off his helmet, and instantly liked the open cheerful face. Before reaching them, Young Lacy shouted:

"Good day, Sergeant! How's the spotted liver this afternoon? I've been sent to pick up Inspector Bonaparte."

His clear hazel eyes gazed about and beyond Bony on whose face was painted a hint of a smile. It was obvious that Young Lacy was looking for a white man, and Sergeant Blake made a noise from way down in his throat.

"In the departmental records, Mr Lacy, I am listed as Inspector, Criminal Investigation Branch," Bony said gravely. "Actually, of course, I am not a real policeman, but being a family man I have no hesitation in accepting the salary. My name is Napoleon Bonaparte."

During this somewhat grandiose self-introduction Young Lacy's eyes opened wide and the cheerful smile gradually gave place to an expression of bewilderment. Sergeant Blake offered an observation.

"Inspector Bonaparte's reputation is to be envied, Mr Lacy," he said stiffly. "He mayn't be a real policeman, but he's a real detective right enough."

"Oh—ah—yes, of course! Pleased to meet you, Inspector Bonaparte. Boorish of me to be so dense," Young Lacy hastened to say. "I was expecting to see a bull-necked, flat-footed bird with jangling irons in his pocket. The old man will be disappointed."

"Indeed! Why?"

"He's waiting to receive the detective I was expecting to find waiting here. He's dreaming dreams of taking him out into the bush and losing him. Still, I'm glad to meet you and not the other kind."

"And I am most happy to make your acquaintance, Mr Lacy," Bony said warmly. "I mean it more especially after having watched you fly that machine. I'm not air-minded, you see. The last time I went up was several years ago with Captain Loveacre."

"Loveacre! You know Loveacre, eh! I last met him—why, red wine and laughing eyes! I remember Loveacre telling me about you and your Diamantina case. He called you Bony."

"He would, Mr Lacy. Everyone does. I wish you would, too."

"Bony it is, then. I'm Young Lacy to all hands. And now we are friends, what about getting home? The old man will be waiting with all his little sayings ready saved up."

Young Lacy stowed the suitcase, assured himself that the second helmet was securely on Bony's head and Bony himself safely strapped into the rear cockpit.

"So long, Blake!" he called when he had taken his position at the controls. "Don't forget to remember me to Mrs Blake."

The throttle was opened, the engine roared to drown the Sergeant's reply and make him skip back to the car away from the dust. A short even run and the ground was slipping away from under, and into view sprang the township, to fall into the centre of a great green and brown disk. Bony saw the road to "outside" winding away to the eastern horizon, another road curving this way and that far to the north, and a third road lying like a snake's track from the town to where the sun was destined to set. He wrote with a pencil on a spare envelope:

"Kindly follow the road to Karwir. I want to see Pine Hut on Meena. Fly low, please."

He thrust the note over Young Lacy's shoulder. The pilot took it, read it, and, glancing back, nodded. With the stick held between his knees, he also used the envelope to pencil a note:

"Will fly low, but it will be bumpy. Might make you sick."

On seeing Bony shake his head and indicate with a hand his desire to be flown nearer the ground, the pilot sent the ship sharply down to follow the track snaking westward. The earth was painted with a crazy pattern of greens and browns, green scrub and brown sand-dunes. Only the road possessed continuity, now plainly marked by the shadows lying in the deep wheel-ruts on soft sand, now faintly limned by putty-coloured ribbons made by the wheels of motors crossing cement-hard claypans.

A wire fence rushed to meet them and passed under them. Bony knew, by his study of Blake's wall map, that it was the Opal Town Common fence, and that now they were flying over Meena Station. It was quite a nice little property, though not to be compared with the big runs like Karwir. He would have to visit the Gordons, and Nero and his tribe, too. Nero would be sure to interest him, because, of course, by now Nero would have had word of his flying to Karwir.

At the average altitude of six hundred feet, Young Lacy sent the machine over the winding road. Little brown and white dots away to the north represented grazing cattle. The road was behaving erratically, falling away and swinging upward to them as the machine entered air pockets, passed through them, and rose again when propellor and wings bit into the air.

Only a few minutes of this and then the iron roof and the windmill of Pine Hut flashed up above the horizon and slid swiftly towards them. The sun glinted on the revolving fans of the mill, and, striking the water in two iron troughs, made of it bars of gold lying rigidly on a light-brown cloth. As though the mill were the hub of a wheel, four fences radiated from it, their thin straight lines quartering the carpet of earth. The road junction was easily discernible—that to the west connecting Meena homestead with Opal Town, the road to Karwir turning widely to the south to enter a mulga forest extending over the rim of the world.

The sun swung sharply round to Bony's right shoulder when the machine turned to follow the southward road to Karwir. No smoke rose from the chimney of the hut below them. No dogs moved. There were no horses in the yards down there, or human beings to wave at the passing plane.

Fascinated by the speed with which the road unwound to thrust the scrub trees towards and under the machine, Bony was unconscious of time. He saw cattle lying in the shade beside the road. Now and then he saw a running rabbit, and noted how the rodents appeared to be chased by tiny balls of red dust. Sometimes he saw the thin thread of the telephone wire stretched from tree to tree.

Now the trees thinned to terminate in a clearly defined line. The machine began to cross a wide ribbon of grey and barren land bordered on its far side by an irregular line of coolabahs, in which no foot of wood is straight. The coolabahs passed under, and again the machine crossed a wide ribbon of treeless and bare grey ground, to be met with another line of coolabahs. A third grey ribbon of bare ground was crossed before the machine again flew above massed trees bordering the everlasting road. They had passed the Channels stated by Sergeant Blake and shown by the wall map to extend from Meena Lake to Green Swamp.

Two minutes after crossing the Channels, there appeared far along the road a white blob that magically resolved into a painted bar-gate. It was the gate that darted towards them, not they towards the gate. Beyond it stretched a thin, dark line, to cross, in the far distance, a blue-grey crescent rising above the rim of the world. It was the fence crossing the plain to Karwir, the fence separating Green Swamp Paddock from North Paddock. It was rule-straight, but the road skirting its east side continued to curve like the track left on sand by a snake.

What made Bony look to the westward when the machine passed over the boundary fence, instead of to the right to

observe Green Swamp Paddock that seemed to be so important to his investigation, he could not recall. As the gate passed
beneath the plane, he saw the netted and barb-topped barrier
lying like a knife blade along the centre of a rule-straight
brown sheath dwindling to a point some three miles away.

For only a half-second did he see this cut line and the fence,
but, during that fraction of time, he saw, about three-quarters
of a mile westward of the gate, a white horse standing in the
shade of a tree on the Karwir side of the barrier. Opposite
this horse, on the Meena side of the barrier, stood a brown
horse, also in the shade cast by a tree. Both animals were
saddled, and appeared to be neck-roped to their respective
trees. Stockmen chance-met and enjoying a gossip, Bony surmised.

The machine now was flying along the seemingly endless
fence towards the homestead beyond the plain already sliding
to pass beneath them. It appeared like strands of black cotton
knotted at regular intervals, the knots being the posts. The
plain folded away mile after mile to the clean-cut horizon
west and south and east. Behind them, the mulga forest was
drawn over the swelling curve of the world.

The miles were being devoured at the rate of two a minute.
Down there on that road loaded wagons drawn by bullocks
once moved at two miles to the hour.

The horizon to the south grew dark, darker still, to become
saw-edged with tops of tall trees, the blood-wood-trees bordering the creek against which stood the Karwir homestead. Tall
and taller grew the trees like a row of Jack's beanstalks, and
at their feet straight-edged silver panels resolved into the iron
roofs and walls of buildings. The fans of three windmills
caught and sent to the oncoming plane the rays of the sun.
Dust rose from toy yards constructed of match sticks, yards
containing brown and black ants and two queer things that
were men.

With interest Bony gazed down upon the big red roof of the

The Bone is Pointed

homestead itself, noting the orange-trees almost surrounding
the building, the trees themselves surrounded by what
appeared to be a canegrass fence. They passed over a narrow
sheet of water, another line of bloodwoods, and now a little to
the left stood the corrugated iron hangar beyond which was
the spacious landing ground. A few seconds later they were
on the ground, once more earth-bound. The yawning front of
the hangar opened wide and wider to receive its own as
Young Lacy taxied the machine into it. Then came abruptly
an astounding silence in which lived a very small voice.

"There you are, Bony. We have arrived," announced
Young Lacy.

"And to think that twenty years ago one would have had
to travel that road on a horse or in a buckboard," Bony said,
smiling down at Young Lacy who first reached the ground.
The cheerful young man accepted the proffered suitcase and
waited for Bony to join him.

"I'll come back to put the crate to bed," he said. "Come
on! The old man will be waiting to meet you. Be prepared to
meet a lion. The dad's got a lot of excellent points, but
strangers find him a bit difficult. The best way to manage him
is to refuse to be shouted down. To begin well with him is to
continue well."

Bony laughed softly, saying:

"Thank you for the advice. In the art of taming lions I
have had long and constant practice. It seems that your father
conforms to a type to which belongs my respected chief,
Colonel Spendor."

Young Lacy conducted the detective across a bridge spanning the creek, thence to a narrow gate in the cane-grass fence
enclosing the big house. Within, he was met with the cool
fragrance of gleaming orange-trees, and the scent of flowers
in beds fronting the entire length of the fly-proofed veranda
along the south side of the house. He followed Young Lacy
up two steps, and stepped on to the veranda, linoleum covered

50

and furnished plainly but with studied comfort. Standing before one of several leather-upholstered chairs was Old Lacy—a patriarch of the bush, with a pipe in one hand and a stock journal in the other. His feet were slippered. Gabardine trousers reached to a tweed waistcoat open all the way. His plain white shirt was of good quality, but he wore no collar and no coat. His hair was thin and as white as snow. His beard was thin and as white as his hair. There was power in the grey eyes, and character in the long Roman nose. No smile welcomed the detective.

"This is Detective-Inspector Bonaparte," Young Lacy announced.

"Eh?" exclaimed Old Lacy, like a man who is deaf. Young Lacy did not repeat the introduction. Bony waited. To have spoken would have indicated weakness. "A detective-inspector, eh? You? 'Bout time, anyway, that that fool of a Police Commissioner sent someone to look into this murder business. Well, the lad will show you to your bunk."

"Mr Bonaparte," Young Lacy said with slight emphasis on the title, "can remain here with you, dad. No arrangements will have been made for Mr Bonaparte because Diana went out before I left for Opal Town, and I forgot to tell Mabel to prepare a room. I'll get her to make a pot of tea, and then fix one of the rooms."

"Humph! All right!" Old Lacy seated himself in the chair he had but recently vacated, and he pointed to another opposite. "Sit down there, Bonaparte. What are you, Indian or Australian?"

"Thank you." Bony sat down, quite happily. "I am Australian, at least on my mother's side. It is better to be half-Australian than not Australian at all."

"How the devil did you rise to be a detective-inspector? Tell me that," the old man demanded with raised voice.

With effort Bony restrained the laughter in his eyes, for he clearly understood that this baiting was a real man's method

51

of testing a stranger. Before him sat a man who, having conquered life by fighting all comers, detested weakness; one who, having fought all comers, continued to do so by habit. Calmly, Bony said:

"My career as a detective, following my graduation from the university at Brisbane, would take a long time to describe in detail. In this country colour is no bar to a keen man's progress providing that he has twice the ability of his rivals. I have devoted my gifts to the detection of crime, believing that when justice is sure the community is less troubled by the criminal. That I stand midway between the black man, who makes fire with a stick, and the white man, who kills women and babes with bombs and machine guns, should not be accounted against me. I have been satisfied with the employment of my mental and inherited gifts. Others, of course, have employed their gifts in amassing money, inventing bombs and guns and gases, even in picking winners on a racecourse. Money, and the ownership of a huge leasehold property, does not make a man superior to another who happens to have been born a half-caste, and who has devoted his life to the detection of crime so that normal people should be safe from the abnormal and the subnormal individual."

Into the grey eyes slowly had crept a gleam. When Old Lacy again spoke his voice was less, much less, loud.

"Damned if I don't think you're right," he said. "I've known lots of fine blackfellers and more'n one extra good half-caste. I've known many white men who've made a pile and think themselves king-pins. And as for those swine dropping bombs on women and children, well, they're less than animals, for even dingoes don't kill their females and the little pups. Don't mind me. I'm a rough old bushy in my ways and talk. I'm glad you came. I want to see justice done for what I think happened to Jeffery Anderson. You'll be a welcome guest at Karwir, and you can expect all the help we can give. You'll want that, after these months following Jeff's disappearance."

"Of that I am sure, Mr Lacy," Bony asserted, conscious of the warm glow within him created by yet one more victory over the accident of his birth. "The lapse of time since Anderson was last seen will, of course, make my investigation both difficult and prolonged. I may be quartered on you for a month, possibly six months. I shall not give up, or return to Brisbane, until I have established Anderson's fate and those responsible for it."

"Ah—I like to hear a man talk like that. It's the way I talk myself, although not so well schooled. Ah—put it down here, Mabel."

The uniformed maid placed the tea tray on a table between the two men, then vanished through one of the house doors. Bony rose to say:

"Milk and sugar, Mr Lacy?"

"No sugar, thanks. Can't afford it at my time of life. In fact, I never could."

"Sugar is expensive, I know," murmured Bony, taking two spoonfuls. "Still, aeroplanes and things are expensive, too."

The old man chuckled.

"I think I am going to like you, Inspector," he said.

Old Lacy's Daughter

"Now, Mr Lacy, let us go back to the vital day, the eighteenth of April," request Bony. "What was the weather like that morning?"

"Dull," instantly replied Lacy, in whose life weather conditions were of the greatest interest. "A warm, moist wind was blowing from the north, and from the same quarter was drifting a high cloud belt with never a break in it. We did not expect rain; otherwise I wouldn't have sent Anderson to ride the fences of Green Swamp Paddock."

"Kindly describe the subsequent weather that day."

"About eleven the sky to the north cleared, and the last of the cloud mass passed over us about twelve o'clock. At this hour another mass of cloud appeared, coming from the northwest, and the front edge of this mass passed over a little after one. It began to rain shortly after two o'clock, beginning light and gradually becoming steady. When I went out to the rain gauge at four o'clock, fifteen points had fallen. The rain kept on steadily for the remainder of the day, and stopped only some time early the next morning."

"How often has rain fallen since, and how much?"

"No rain has fallen excepting a very light shower on the seventh of August. The water didn't run in the sand-gutters."

Not yet was Old Lacy able to make up his mind that Bony

was master of his particular job. The questions that followed helped him to do so.

"Did you give Anderson his orders that morning?"

"Yes. After I had dealt with the men, I spoke to him. Not only was he to ride the fences, he was to take a look at Green Swamp itself and report on the water remaining in it. When the water is low the swamp is boggy; then it has to be fenced off and and the well out there brought into service."

"Can you recall the time that he left the homestead that day?"

"We had breakfast here at eight," replied the squatter. "Anderson occupied a room in the office building, but he ate his meals with us and sat with us in the evenings when he felt inclined. I didn't see him actually leave that morning, but it would have been about twenty minutes to nine."

"Thank you. Now this is important. Did you instruct him which way to ride the fences—clockwise or anti-clockwise?"

"He rode opposite the clock. That is, when he left here he turned east along the south fence."

"How do you know that?" persisted Bony.

"Know it? The groom saw him ride that way."

"Ah, yes, the groom. I'll come to him in a minute. Now where, do you estimate, would Anderson have been at noon that day?"

"Well, he rode a flash horse called The Black Emperor. The mileage of the south fence is eight miles. Assuming that he had no work to do along that section, and I don't think he would have had any, he should have reached the first corner of the paddock at about eleven o'clock. He'd then ride northward along the east fence for almost eight miles, when he'd reach the sand-dunes back of Green Swamp, arriving there, say, at one o'clock or a little before. From this point he'd leave the fence and strike across country westward for half a mile to reach the hut beside the Green Swamp well. At the hut he would boil his quart-pot for lunch."

"But," objected Bony, "the following day when the searchers examined the hut there was no sign that Anderson had boiled his quart-pot."

"That's so," agreed Old Lacy. "I'm not saying that he did spend his lunch hour at the hut. He might have camped for lunch when he reached the edge of the sand-dunes. He could have filled his quart-pot from the horse's neck-bag."

"So the horse carried a water-bag? There was no mention of a water-bag in Blake's report. Was the bag on the horse when it was found the next morning, by the groom, standing outside the gate?"

"Yes. It was there all right."

Bony smiled at his host, saying:

"We are progressing, if slowly. Let us assume that Anderson did not eat his lunch at the hut, that he halted for lunch beside the fence where it meets the sand-dunes. According to your observations, when Anderson reached the sand-dunes that second cloud mass was approaching. Being a man like yourself, having had long experience of weather portents, would he think that that second cloud mass would bring rain?"

"By heck, he would!" agreed the old man.

"Very well. You say that it began to rain shortly after two o'clock. Supposing that Anderson found work to do that morning, and that he didn't arrive at the sandhills till some time after one o'clock, and that it began to rain while he was eating his lunch, would he think it necessary to leave the fence to visit the swamp?"

Answering this question Old Lacy almost shouted.

"No, he wouldn't. The purpose of visiting the swamp was to see how much water was left in it, and so to establish the degree of danger to stock. If it rained the danger would be non-existent. I see your drift, Inspector. Assuming that it rained before Anderson left his lunch camp, he'd most likely continue riding the fence northward to the next corner, there turn westward and leave the fence somewhere north of the swamp to examine it if by then the rain had stopped."

Bony's eyes were now shining. He said :

"We can now understand why he did not visit the swamp and the hut. The rain coming when it did, when Anderson was where he probably was, relieved him of the duty. I have, of course, to prove that he rode as far north as those sanddunes. By the way, it has not yet been established by anyone that, on this day in question, Anderson's horse carried its neckrope as was usual. What is your opinion about it?"

"No one can speak of the neck-rope with certainty, but I'm sure the horse carried a rope. The man wouldn't go without it."

Bony rolled and lit a cigarette, and now leaned back in his comfortable chair and permitted his mind to relax. He was experiencing satisfaction that he had impressed this hard old man with his mental ability.

"You will, I know, recognize the difficulties confronting me," he said. "This case interests me. It is one worthy of my attention. My investigation may occupy me for a considerable time, so I dare to hope that you will not become bored with me if I am quartered on you for several weeks, even months."

"I don't mind how long you are with us, Inspector," Old Lacy said with emphasis. "Anderson was a good station man, but he had a bad temper. No doubt you've heard about him putting Bill the Better in hospital, and thrashing a black named Inky Boy. I made him square up over that, and one or two other matters, but when he had the damned cheek to ask me to persuade my gal to marry him, he reached the limit. You haven't met my gal yet. She's out riding this afternoon. You'll see her later."

"A good horsewoman?" inquired Bony.

"There's no woman in these parts can beat her. When she's riding Sally, a pure white mare, she looks a picture."

"Indeed! Is she out on Sally this afternoon?"

"Yes."

Bony was seeing now a different picture, a picture seen in a
flash of time—the white horse neck-roped to a tree a few
yards back from the Karwir boundary fence, and the brown
horse neck-roped to another tree on the Meena side of the
barrier.

"Miss Lacy was not in love with Anderson?" Bony mildly
prompted.

"In love with him! Of course not. She's only twenty now,
and he wanted to marry her a full year back. Hell! What he
said to me after what I told him, wasn't worth saying. Him
my son-in-law!"

"You didn't sack him—evidently."

"Sack him!" again echoed Old Lacy, but now his eyes were
twinkling. "Not me. Why, the place would have been dead
without him. It's been mighty quiet here since he disappeared.
Anderson was never a good boss's man, and he wasn't any
man's boss. If I'd made him overseer that time my last one
left, I'd have been always writing pay cheques and looking
for new hands. Him my son-in-law! I'm getting old, but I'm
not that old. Anyway, my gal had no time for him."

Bony laughingly said:

"I suppose she is still heart-whole?"

"Yes, she is that. Never had a love affair yet, to my knowing, and she would have told me if she had."

Still thinking of the meeting of the riders of a brown and
a white horse that was undoubtedly Sally, Bony was not as
certain as was his host on this point. A possibility occupied his
mind for two seconds, and then he asked:

"A violent man like Anderson would almost surely have
enemies. The blacks would not be friendly towards him. What
about the groom whom Anderson beat up and sent to
hospital?"

"A weed of a man. Like a rabbit. He was paid good compensation. You can leave him out. The blacks make a differ-

ent matter of it, though. I have always thought they caught
Anderson and fixed him in revenge for what he did to Inky
Boy, as well as for a nasty business with a young gin em-
ployed here in my wife's time."

Bony made a mental note of the seeming fact that his host's
sympathies were not with the victims of the missing man's
violent temper. It was strange that Old Lacy appeared still to
have some regard for a man with whom his association had
not been cordial. When Bony spoke again he did so with
unusual slowness.

"We must not lose sight of a possibility," he said. "I expect
that, like me, you have known of men being lost in the bush
and, despite extensive searches, their bodies not being found
till years afterwards, if ever. Anderson may have been thrown
from his horse in Green Swamp Paddock and killed by the
fall. That the paddock was thoroughly searched does not pre-
clude the possibility. He may have received concussion, besides
other injuries, and then have wandered right out of Green
Swamp Paddock to die somewhere in adjoining country."

"All the country adjoining Green Swamp Paddock was
carefully examined, because we recognized that possibility,"
countered Old Lacy. "If he did that, what became of his hat,
his stockwhip, and the horse's neck-rope that I'm sure it had
that day?"

"I grant you that the absence of the neck-rope provides a
strong counter-point to the thrown and injured supposition,"
Bony conceded. "I would like to examine his horse, The
Black Emperor. Could he be brought to the yards to-morrow
morning?"

"He could, but he's over in the yards now with a mob of
horses containing a couple of young uns the breaker's working
on. We'll go across and look him over if you like."

They rose together, and Old Lacy led the way to the
veranda door. He extolled the virtues of the great horse, but

59

did not allude to its vices, while he conducted the detective
through the garden and across the open space to the yards.

In the same yard with The Black Emperor were a dozen
other horses that gave him half the yard to himself. Bony's
eyes glistened when they saw this beast, and the soul of him
thrilled to its jet-black beauty. A king of horses. Indeed, an
emperor's mount.

"He's six years old," the squatter said, faint regret in his
strong voice. "He's the finest horse in Queensland to-day, but
he's no damned good. He'd throw a man and then kick him
to death. Anderson and he were a good pair in more than in
looks."

"I'll ride him to-morrow if you will permit," Bony said, a
lilt in his voice. "What a beauty! Was he never shod?"

"No."

"His feet want trimming."

"If you're game to ride him, Sam, there, the breaker, and
Bill the Better can put him into the crush and do his hoofs."

"Very well. They want doing. But I will cut the hoofs."

The Black Emperor snorted and laid back his velvety ears
when Sam, a lank, seemingly indolent man, approached him
with the bridle. But the horse was not to be caught so easily
and eventually had to be roped, the old man continually
shouting unnecessary directions. When The Black Emperor
was in the crush, Bony trimmed the hoofs with the long chisel
and mallet, expertly removing growth so that they became as
nearly as possible the shape they were when the animal was
last ridden by Anderson. He then led the horse from the
crush back into the main yard, and Old Lacy and Sam and
Bill the Better, sitting on the top rail, watched him subdue
the brute's temper until The Black Emperor stood quiet and
apparently docile. Even when the bridle was removed the
horse did not attempt to break away but permitted Bony to
fondle his glossy black neck.

"I would like to ride him to-morrow morning," Bony said

when he joined the others on the top rail of the yard. "He will be too unreliable for ordinary work, worse luck."

"Well, you bring him in with the horses in the morning, Bill," instructed Old Lacy.

Bill the Better was sitting beside Bony, and he said:

"Bet you a coupler quid The Black Emperor will throw you."

"You would lose your money," Bony replied, with a laugh.

No one of the four noticed the girl on the white horse reach the gate spanning the road to Opal Town, nor did they notice her until she had led her horse to a position immediately below their high perch. Bony saw her first, and at once jumped to the ground. The old man said more loudly than was warranted:

"Hullo, me gal! You home?"

With remarkable agility considering his years, he lowered himself to the ground, to be followed by Sam who went back to his work and Bill the Better who took away the white mare.

"Meet Inspector Bonaparte," Old Lacy said. "Inspector, this is my daughter, Diana."

"Inspector—of what?" inquired the girl, her voice clear and her eyes critical.

"Why, an Inspector of—" began Old Lacy, when Bony cut in.

"Of nothing, Miss Lacy," he said, bowing. "I am made happy by meeting you. I am supposed to be a policeman, but really I'm not, as Colonel Spendor would be ever ready to agree. My name is Napoleon Bonaparte, and I am an officer of the Criminal Investigation Branch."

Diana Lacy was *petite* and dark. She stood now regarding the dark handsome face of this stranger with whom her father had become quickly familiar, in itself a remarkable thing. The light switch tapped softly the leg of her jodhpurs, and her blue eyes were wide open despite the glare of the sunlight.

Bony was swift to see the forceful personality behind the

eyes of this Karwir woman who was still a girl. She was more like Old Lacy than was Eric her brother. Now debonair, his manner a trifle too polite, he was yet quick to see the flash of alarm in her eyes before it was replaced with an expression of faintly amused interest. She looked as though she had stepped from the pages of a society paper.

"Inspector Bonaparte has come to solve for us the mystery of Jeff's disappearance," boomed Old Lacy. If the girl heard this she gave no indication of it. Her mind was working fast —and Bony knew it. She had perfect control over her features, but she had not thought of her hands—until she saw Bony glance at them. Then she knew that her hands were slowly clenching and unclenching, and casually she thrust them into the pockets of the jodhpurs.

"It has been a great day for a gallop, Miss Lacy," Bony remarked pleasantly. "And fine country to gallop over, too. I shall enjoy taking The Black Emperor out to-morrow."

"You should, Inspector," agreed Old Lacy.

The tension had ended and the girl turned to gaze between the yard rails at The Black Emperor.

"You will want to be careful, Inspector Bonaparte," she said without looking at him or her father. "Mr Anderson often said he had never ridden a horse having an easier action." She turned towards them, glanced at the sun, and suggested crossing to the house for afternoon tea.

"How did you come?" she inquired of Bony.

"Your brother brought me from Opal Town in his aeroplane."

To her father Diana said:

"Has anything been done for Mr Bonaparte's accommodation?"

"Yes. The lad got Mabel to fix a room. We've already had a drink of tea, but another won't come amiss."

"I promise not to make more trouble than I can help, Miss Lacy," Bony said when they were crossing to the garden gate. He was wondering a little at her coldness, and thought he could guess the reason of her unease immediately after he was presented to her. "Unfortunately for Karwir, I may be here some time. You see, beginning an investigation so long after the paramount events means great difficulties to be overcome."

If he successfully impressed her she did not let him know. She appeared to take him as she doubtless would take a fence —for granted. After a little silence she spoke, and now he decided that she was going to be one of the difficulties he mentioned.

"Your stay here will not put us out, Mr Bonaparte," she said, with disapproval but thinly veiled. "We can, of course, understand your difficulties, but you have come rather too late to do any good, don't you think?"

"Forgive me for disagreeing, Miss Lacy," Bony assured her with undaunted cheerfulness. "You know, if I failed to solve this mystery I should be truly astonished."

They were now arrived at the gate which Bony held open for Old Lacy, who was chuckling, to pass first into the garden. He smiled at her whilst she stood waiting for her father, noted her trim small figure, her haughty face, the cold blue eyes with their violet irises. Then she was passing him, to flash at him a sidewise glance and to say softly, as though for his sole benefit:

"It's quite likely that you *will* be astonished."

63

Beside a Little Fire

IT had not rained over Meena since that night of Mary Gordon's suspense, and the pastoral prospects were very dark for vast areas of inland Australia. Hope, engendered by the April rain, slowly evaporated as the spring sunshine evaporated the moisture that had given a short impetus to plant life.

Riding northward in the late afternoon of the day that Napoleon Bonaparte arrived at Karwir, John Gordon was feeling depressed, a condition of mind caused not by the imminence of a worrying summer so much as by the seemingly inevitable see-saw of life. At the beginning of the winter Meena Station had stood financially upon a sound foundation, but now at the beginning of the summer the foundation would have to be strengthened by the materials of economy and greater care for the stock.

There was still an abundance of feed in the paddocks, but there was little prospect of this being replenished before the hot winds of summer wiped it off the face of the burning earth. Fortunately, thanks to the forethought of the second John Gordon who had put down many bores and wells, there was no water shortage on Meena even when the lake occasionally became dry.

John Gordon the Third had spent all day in the Meena South Paddock, riding over the plain-stubble of ripened tussock grass, through the mulga-belts, and across the wide, barren depressions named the Channels. Often he had ridden by small communities of rabbits, isolated and with no young ones to prove that this was a normal summer.

He approached Meena Lake from the south-west, his horse carrying him over a grassy plain and up an imperceptible gradient. The top of the gradient was reached without warning, and quite abruptly John Gordon came to look down and over the great bed of the lake. Save at three points, the lake was surrounded by sand-dunes backed by box-trees. One point was where the Meena Creek fed the lake with water from the distant hills to the north-west; another was the high plateau to the east whereon stood the red-roofed and white-walled buildings comprising the homestead; the third was the outlet creek which carried the overflow for two miles to spread it into the various channels.

Although the water was gone, the blue jewel itself, the brilliant setting still remained. Outward from the lake's bed, roughly circular and some two miles across, lay a wide ribbon of pure white claypan, edged by the reddish sand-dunes that in turn were bordered by the green of the trees. Ah, what a place when the jewel itself was there!

And now when Gordon rode down the slope to the trees he came upon not isolated rabbit communities but the camp of a mighty host that entirely encircled the lake that was swiftly devastating the land that had given it birth.

Evening was come and life that drowsed all the warm day was bestirring itself to fill a gigantic stomach. Along the ground slope outside the tree-belt rabbits sat cleaning themselves like cats, or gambolled about like kittens, before the entrances to countless burrows. Within the tree-belt itself untold numbers were eating the windfalls of the day—the leaves—and were nibbling at the bark of the surface roots. Gordon saw several of them high in the trees beneath which he passed; they had climbed a sloping trunk to get at the tender bark of young branches.

Eagles, the great golden kings and the wedge-tails, planed low over the land or sailed with never a wing-flap high against the burnished sky. The crows were following the eagles, or cawing among the trees, or strutting over the earth like moving blots of ink. It was too early for the foxes, but they were there waiting to take their nightly toll of the rodents.

The horse, now eager to be home, carried Gordon through the tree-belt and across the sand-dunes that now were wearing a garment of fur. Then onward down to the claypan belt where the going was easy. Here the man pressed his right knee hard against the horse's side and the intelligent beast turned sharply to follow the white ribbon that would take them round to the homestead.

Still a little of the herbal rubbish remained in the very centre of the lake, and the vanguard of the rabbit army was already on the move to feed upon it. Both before and behind John Gordon they were leaving the dunes to run across the bare grey rubble between claypan and herbage. Now and then an eagle would swoop, fly low above the ground, scatter rabbits right and left, and land at the instant its iron talons sank into the body of a screaming victim.

For three years now had the rodents taken command of Meena Lake, breeding steadily and without halt until late the preceding summer when the water had vanished and there had been no green feed left on the surrounding uplands. The April rain had given the host another lease of reproductive life, and throughout the gentle winter endless relays of young rabbits had appeared, to grow to maturity in nine weeks, when the does began to vie with their mothers. Then, in early September, an unknown intelligence, foreseeing the drought, commanded the breeding to cease that the host might be strong to wage the battle with advancing Death.

Familiarity, it is said, breeds contempt—or indifference— and Gordon failed to appreciate the glowing colours of the red and white homestead buildings set upon a red base and backed by a blue-green canopy. The horse carried him upward among the dunes to reach the edge of the plateau and thus to pass the main building and halt outside the harness shed.

The man patted the animal before removing the bridle and allowing it to walk, shaking its hide, to drink at the trough. Two barking dogs claimed his attention. He freed them from their chains, and they raced madly about him as he walked across to the men's quarters.

All this belonged to him, and the three hundred thousand acres of excellent country surrounding it. In comparison with Karwir, and other great stations, Meena was almost a selection, but it provided the Gordons with a living as the lake had provided the Kalchut tribe with sustenance for countless years. Upon his shoulders rested responsibility inherited from the first and the second Gordons; for, besides his mother, there were the blacks under Nero who looked upon him as someone infinitely more powerful than their own chief. He could hear the cries of their children from along the lake's shore, and as he drew near the men's quarters he heard, too, the strains of an accordion being played with no little skill. John Gordon, unlike Eric Lacy, was years older than his age.

Entering the men's quarters he was met by a smiling Jimmy Partner who, softening his music, said:

"Hullo, Johnny Boss! You lookin' for a wrestle?"

"Wrestle, my foot!" Gordon exclaimed somewhat impatiently. "Wrestling is all you think about. If I could only beat you now and then we'd hear less of it." Then, as though to atone for the impatience, he laughed, saying: "Why, you big boob, if you couldn't wrestle so well I could box you for the count any day."

White teeth flashed.

"Too right you could, Johnny Boss. Good job I can wrestle, else you'd be walkin' round with your head and your feet about a yard behind your tummy."

Jimmy Partner laughed at his own witticism, a deep-throated, musical laugh, and now he set the accordion upon the heat-blistered mantelshelf and stood up to fall into the true wrestler's pose. Home before his tribal brother, he had already washed all over and was now wearing clean mole-skin trousers and a white tennis shirt. His hair was brushed and parted down the centre, and his dark-brown face was shining. Not excessively big but beautifully proportioned and in the prime of his life, he began to advance on John Gordon, moving on the balls of his feet and with his arms held out invitingly.

Gordon backed swiftly out of the doorway and seized the wash-basin on the case standing near the door. It was still nearly full with Jimmy Partner's recent suds.

"Come on!" cried Gordon. "It's here waiting for you, my Salvoldi."

Jimmy Partner did not emerge. From within he laughed again and shouted:

"No, no, Johnny Boss! I've just put on a clean shirt. It's the only clean one I've got, and the other's drying."

"Very well, then. No nonsense, or you'll get it," Gordon told him laughingly, and, carrying the basin, he entered to see Jimmy Partner again seated and fondling his instrument. Setting the basin down on the table within easy reach, he sat himself beside it. The lighter mood subsided, and he became serious.

"How were the traps?" he asked.

"I seen 'em all," Jimmy answered. "Two were sprung. There was a dingo in that one we set over near Black Gate."

"Good! Pure bred?"

"Not quite. Things is getting dry, Johnny Boss."

"Yes, they are, and it looks as though they'll be pretty bad everywhere before the summer has gone. By that time you and the blacks will be richer than me."

"No fear," instantly argued Jimmy Partner. "You want

cash, you take it outer my bank. You can take the tribe's money, too, when you want it. What's money, anyhow?"

"Ha-um! It won't come to that, Jimmy. Do you know how much you've got in the bank?"

" 'Bout a hundred."

"A hundred and eighty-two pounds ten shillings."

"You can have it, Johnny Boss. All I want is another shirt."

"But mum got you shirts only last week. Where are they?"

"Nero wanted a couple."

Gordon frowned, saying:

"You keep your own, Jimmy. The tribe's account is more than enough to keep them all going. Why, when I bank the dog-scalp money there will be close on seven hundred pounds behind them. What with the rabbit skins and fox skins got last month, the Kalchut will weather any drought."

"It weathered droughts before Grandfer Gordon came, and it didn't have no money and no bank then."

"Rot! Times are not what they were, Jimmy."

For seven years, since he had reached his twentieth year, Jimmy Partner had drawn station hand's wages from Meena. It had been no easy task to make him save a little of the money earned, but once the pounds and the shillings were in the bank there was no getting it out, since it was controlled jointly by Mrs Gordon and her son.

They controlled, too, an account for the Kalchut tribe, paying into it all money earned by the tribe by the sale of rabbit and fox skins, drawing from it money to buy the meagre clothes necessary for winter wear. The Kalchuts were no mendicants, and never had been, and during these last few years they had reaped a harvest of fur around Meena Lake. The supply to them of the white man's rations had always been kept down to a minimum and the accounts accurately kept.

"Anyhow, you seen Nero?" inquired Jimmy Partner.

"No, why?"

"He come along half-hour ago to say that big feller black-feller p'liceman come to Opal Town."

Gordon's easy attitude at once became stiff, and into the hazel eyes flashed unease.

"What for? Did Nero say?"

"No," answered Jimmy Partner indifferently.

"What else did Nero say?"

"Nothin'. Only to tell you when you came home. Wandin sent him the mulga wire, I suppose."

"Is that so? Well, I don't quite understand it, and dinner must be ready. See you later."

Gordon was walking towards the gate in the wicket fence surrounding the house when his mother beat a triangle with an iron bar, announcing that dinner was ready. Seeing her son coming, Mary stood at the edge of the veranda, her tall, spare figure encased in blue striped linen that had the effect of reducing her age and the number of lines about her smiling eyes.

"There's a cheque come from the skin agents for seventy-two pounds odd for the rabbit skins the blacks consigned last month," she said brightly.

"They may want it if this dry spell keeps up," John said, smiling at her. "Anything else?"

"Only receipts and a letter from the windmill people. How did you find South Paddock?"

"Still in good nick, but the cattle are falling off a little."

She turned away to the living-room-kitchen and he to the bathroom detached from the main building. Fifteen minutes later this household sat down to dinner as it had done for years: John occupying his father's place at the head of the table, his mother at his right, Jimmy Partner at the other table end. They spoke of the skin cheque, the rabbits, the season and the stock, the cricket and the chaos of Europe and Asia.

The John and Mary Gordons are not rare in the inland,

but the presence of an aboriginal at their table is so. Jimmy Partner was a splendid product of "beginning on them young." He was a living example, showing to what degree of civilization an Australian aboriginal can reach if given the opportunity. He sat before this table upright and mentally alert. He ate with no less politeness than did the woman who had reared him that he might be a companion to her own child when it was evident he would have no brother. He spoke better than many a white hand, and his voice was entirely free of the harsh accent to be heard in the voices of many university professors, and other literate Australians. He could and did discuss well the topics found in the weekly journals that he read. His personal habits were above reproach. He was the crown of achievement set upon the heads of Mary Gordon and her dead husband.

At the close of the meal John Gordon reached for tobacco and papers and matches, but Jimmy Partner began his customary after-dinner service of washing the dishes whilst the "missus" attended to her bread batter. John crossed to the hen house to lock the fowls safely in from the foxes, and then in the dusk of advancing evening he passed through the gate in the wire fence and so trod the winding path taken by his mother that night of rain in April.

At the camp the tired children were playing as far distant from the communal fires as fear of the dreaded Mindye, that bush spirit ever on the watch to take black-fellows who wandered at night, would permit. The lubras were gossiping in a group near one of the bag and iron humpies and the men were talking gravely whilst crouched about another fire. All the children ran to "Johnny Boss" to escort him into the camp, a toddler clinging to each hand. The lubras ceased their chatter and, unabashed, smiled at him. The men saluted him with:

"Good night, Johnny Boss!"

Observing Nero squatted over a little fire a hundred odd

yards distant from the camp, Gordon replied to their saluta-
tions, patted the toddlers on their black heads, and walked
on to join the chief, his pace unhurried, his face lit by the
lamp of prideful affection for all these sixty odd members of
the Kalchut tribe.

Old Nero squatting on his naked heels before his little fire
was not unlike an ant standing at bay before an enemy,
when its body is upright and almost touching the ground. His
little fire was being fed with four sticks that now and then
were pushed farther into the glowing mound of red embers.
John squatted likewise on his heels opposite the chief, so that
the little fire was between them and the tiny flames made
dark-blue the spiral of smoke rising like a fluted column between their heads.

"Good night, Johnny Boss," Nero said softly, his black eyes
regarding the white man casually but benignly.

When he spoke Gordon used a different language from
that in which he conversed with his mother and Jimmy Partner. Nero, like others of the tribe, had been saved from becoming de-tribalized.

"Jimmy Partner he say you tellum big feller black p'liceman come to Opal Town," he said, interrogatively.

"Too right, Johnny Boss. Wandin he bin tellit me mulga
wire."

"What Wandin mean beeg feller blackfeller p'liceman?"
Nero shook his whitened head.

"No tellum," he replied.

"What he come for? Find Jeff Anderson, eh?"

"P'haps. He not say properly. He not make smoke signals.
Nero not ready."

Gordon fell to staring downward at the tiny glowing fire
whose light reddened the fat old face so close to his own.
A pair of old dungaree trousers covered Nero from the waist
down, and the firelight revealed the flint cuts crossing his
torso. Neither man rose to stand beside this aboriginal fire for

relief of leg muscles. Neither found it necessary to obtain any relief from a posture so foreign to people less "primitive" than the race to which Nero belonged.

The fact that Nero had made this little fire held significance for John Gordon. Urgent affairs of state demanded that Nero, being the tribe's head man, should commune with the spirits, and Gordon knew very well that the matter of importance now being considered was the purport of the message sent by Wandin in Opal Town without the aid of wires or a wireless transmission set.

"What time Wandin tellum you about beeg feller blackfeller p'liceman?" he asked.

Nero carefully rearranged the tips of the burning sticks to give additional light, and then he drew with a finger point on the ground, a perpendicular mark from the base of a horizontal mark, the horizontal mark representing the shadow cast by the perpendicular one about two o'clock.

"You been trying hearim Wandin again?"

Nero nodded, saying:

"Wandin, he no talk."

They fell silent again, and over Nero's shoulders Gordon saw the children gradually close in about the communal fires, and disappear one after the other to the humpies. The lubras began to do likewise until only the men remained in his sight. Usually a little boisterous, this night their spirits appeared to be repressed by the conference at the little fire.

Gordon was about to rise preparatory to returning to the house when several of the dogs began to bark. Those at the communal fire shouted at them, and from barking they fell to whimpering. Then from out the encircling blackness beyond the near box-trees, Gordon saw emerge the tall and gaunt figure of Wandin.

"Wandin come," he said to Nero whose back was towards the traveller from Opal Town.

Wandin passed first to those about the communal fire, and

73

one of the young men rose and brought him water in an old billycan. Wandin drank long and deeply, then, giving the billy back to the same young man, he crossed to the little fire and without greeting squatted between Nero and Gordon. Not until he had bitten a chunk of tobacco from a plug did he say, his voice low and guttural :

"Sargint pay me. Tellum git to hell outer it."

Gordon offered no remark and Nero remained silent. At the expiration of a full minute's chewing, Wandin went on :

"White blackfeller p'liceman come on mail car. He eat tucker along Sargint and missus. Then he have wongie along Sargint in office feller. White blackfeller wantum know 'bout old Sarah, an' Sargint he tellum she goodoh. White blackfeller him wantum know what time Abie he come go to Deep Well that time we go walkabout an' sit down Painted Hills."

A course of tobacco chewing interrupted the tale, Then :

"I sit down close office feller window. I hear beeg feller white blackfellow tellit Sargint he find out 'bout Jeff Anderson. The Sargint he look-see outer window and see me, an' he tellit me go into office feller. In office feller I see white blackfeller. All flash like Johnny Boss when he go Opal Town. White blackfellow he wantum know totem feller all belong me. Then he do this——" Wandin pulled apart the throat of his shirt. "Then he say ah you big feller blackfeller, eh? You know plenty magic, eh, all too right. He laugh. Him plenty beeg p'liceman all right."

Again Wandin fell to chewing, and Gordon knew full well that to reveal impatience would be to commit error. Then Wandin went on :

"Sargint him bin tellit me got to 'ell outer it. So I go sitdown and send message. Long time I send message. I say one beeg feller blackfeller p'liceman 'cos I no gabbit half-caste p'liceman. Bimeby him and Sargint go out to motor and go way out to landing feller belonga plane. I go, too. Bimeby plane him come and I look-see Young Lacy get out and bimeby him and half-caste p'liceman go in plane feller and fly away Karwir."

Again Wandin became silent. Nero grunted but did not speak, waiting for Johnny Boss to answer the riddle.

"What name half-caste p'liceman?" questioned Gordon.

"When him and Sargint go in motor, Sargint him bin call 'im Bony."

"Bony!" echoed Gordon. "Oh! I've heard of him. You sure Sergeant call him Bony?"

"Too right! Then Sargint him come back and tellit me get to 'ell outer it and he pay me—three quid."

"You give it money Johnny Boss," ordered Nero, and Gordon pocketed the three pound notes later to be banked for the Kalchut.

The following silence was much prolonged. Nero sometimes emitted a soft grunt. Gordon smoked a couple of cigarettes. Wandin chewed vigorously, evidently still perturbed by the suddenness of the official dismissal. Then, when Gordon rose to his feet, the two aborigines rose with him.

"I'll get along and tell Jimmy Partner to go out after the working horses," he announced. "You tellum Inky Boy and Abie come along to horse yards. That Bony feller he no good. Young Lacy tellit me 'bout him. He clever feller all right. Malluc and his lubra can come along us, too. They all bring blankets. Make camp along boundary fence."

Wandin and Nero grunted acceptance of these instructions, and John Gordon walked swiftly away into the darkness to take the path leading to the homestead.

The Hunt Begins

THE following morning Bony began the practical part of his
investigation at Karwir. Bill the Better had found the wo.
ing horses early and had them at the yards when Bony arrived
at seven o'clock.

The Black Emperor was among them, but this morning it
took Bony ten minutes to catch, bridle and saddle him; then
he walked him across to the gate giving entry to Green Swamp
Paddock and the road to Opal Town. The keenly interested
groom, who had followed to the gate, even forgot to bet with
himself that Bony would be tossed within sixty seconds. But
the horseman in him made him want to cheer at the half-
caste's quick mastery of a horse that had long since forgotten
how to buck. After a turn of pig-rooting, the animal was
given his head and the steam was taken out of him by a long
gallop. He was now amenable to reason and was ridden along
a hundred-yards beat—first at the gallop, then at a canter,
and finally at a walking pace, before being returned to the
yards and unsaddled.

Bony was examining the tracks along the beat when the
Lacys, father and son, joined him, Old Lacy demanding to
know what was the "idea."

"I have to memorize The Black Emperor's tracks," Bony
replied. "The shapes of his hoofs will not be like they were
five months ago, but he hasn't altered the manner in which

he places his feet on the ground. A book could be written on how individual horses walk and canter and gallop. To the expert no two horses do these things alike. I forgot to ask—— Has The Black Emperor been ridden, or run free, in this paddock since Anderson disappeared?"

"No," replied Old Lacy. "He's been running with the unwanted hacks in another paddock."

"Ah! Then my task of finding his tracks made five months ago will be comparatively easy."

"But, hang it, Bony, we all rode over this paddock hunting for the horse's tracks immediately after Anderson disappeared!" objected Young Lacy, and Bony was about to make reply when the old man roared:

"Since when have you dared to be so familiar with the Inspector, lad?"

"Since yesterday," Bony got in. "You see, all my friends call me Bony. Eric is accounted one of them. What about you?"

"Do me," assented Old Lacy succinctly. "Curse the misters and the inspectors and things. Come on! We'd better go in for breakfast."

Breakfast over, Old Lacy and Bony returned to the yards, the old man carrying a seasoned water-bag, Bony carrying his lunch and quart-pot. The few personal necessities required at Green Swamp hut were to be taken there later in the morning with the rations, bedding and horse feed.

"You can expect me only when I arrive," Bony told Old Lacy. "I may be out there for days, perhaps weeks. I've got to go bush, to be one with the bush, to re-create the scene and imagine the conditions out there that day Anderson last rode away."

"Well, remember that your room will always be ready for you, and that we'll be glad to see you any time," said the old man. "We're plain folk, but we never have too many visitors. Anything you want out there, anything we can do, just ask in the ordinary way."

"You are very kind," Bony murmured.

"Not a bit, lad—er—I mean, Bony. I'm wanting to know what happened to Jeff. Y'see I didn't treat him right, meaning that I could have treated him better, you understand. I suppose no man will ever act so's he won't do things he'll some time regret. You takin' The Black Emperor?"

"No, much as I'd like to. He wants riding and I haven't the time to ride him." Bony laughed and went on. "You know, if I were a squatter, I wouldn't have a flash horse on the place, except perhaps for pleasure riding. I'd reason thus: I pay men to boundary-ride the fences and to carry out stock work, not to ride a flash horse that interrupts the performance of such work."

"By heck, there's a lot in that, Bony."

"There is. From now on I have to employ my mind searching for five-months-old tracks and clues hidden by the rain and the dust. How can I do that if I have constantly to keep looking to my horse, forcing it to go where I want it to go, guarding against being bucked off, crashed against a tree trunk, swept off its back by a tree branch? That kind of horse is of no use to me."

So it was that Bony selected a mare of the famous Yandama breed, a chestnut with white hocks and a white forehead blaze, old enough not to play the goat and quiet enough for a child to clamber between its legs.

It was a calm, warm day when at nine o'clock Bony entered Green Swamp Paddock to ride eastward along its southern fence. Yet he was not happy. He felt that Diana Lacy was prejudiced against him because he was a half-caste, and that her prejudice was largely due to shortcomings in himself at the moment of their meeting at the yards. In any other man such a matter would have been quickly pushed aside as of no moment; but in Napoleon Bonaparte failure to win the approval of this girl of Karwir was emphasized by that torturing imp named inferiority, ever so alive in his soul.

Karwir hospitality was admirable. The dinner of the preceding evening and the breakfast that morning had been good and well served. But during the dinner Diana had rarely spoken, and when she did speak, her frigid politeness revealed the full sting of her contempt. He had not seen her since, but he recalled how, during that meal, her blue eyes had regarded him with a coldly impersonal stare.

However, the sunlight and the soft breeze from the east, the movement of the fast walking mare, named Kate, and the quickly changed scene when they entered the mulga forest overlapping into this paddock from the southern country, quickly lifted the depression that was alien to Bony's sunny nature. As a further anodyne, he listed the difficulties he had to surmount.

Into this paddock five months ago a man had ridden The Black Emperor a few hours before a heavy fall of rain. To ride round its boundary fences meant a journey of thirty-six miles. Most fortunately it was a small paddock, comprising only eighty square miles of plain, mulga and other scrub-belts, water channels and sand-dunes. He knew the shape of this paddock, the taking in of Green Swamp from Meena having produced an angled bite in its north-west corner.

Considering the lapse of time since Anderson rode out never to be seen again, the task of solving the mystery of his disappearance might well have seemed hopeless to a lesser man. Bony had no starting point such as the body of a murdered man, nor any clue to provide a basis for theory from which fact might emerge. What had happened to Anderson, to his hat, to his stockwhip, to the horse's neck-rope? Where now were these three articles and the man? For days and weeks stockmen and the aborigines had hunted and found nothing. It was as though the falling rain were acid that dissolved solids and washed them into the thirsty earth.

Such handicaps, however, to a man of Bony's inherited tenacity and patience were but a spur to sustained effort and the determination to succeed. The disappearance of the neckrope, which was almost certain to have been attached to the animal, seemed to support the supposition that Anderson had been killed and his body carefully hidden. Had he merely been thrown the chances of his not being found were indeed small. Had he deliberately vanished, as so many men do every year in every city, without doubt he would have taken his hat, and, because he was such an expert with a stockwhip, he would have taken his precious whip. But why, supposing this were the case, should he have taken his horse's neck-rope, but not the water-bag which, it was reasonable to expect, would have been indispensable to him?

Bony's spirits rose high as he considered these difficulties. He smiled when recalling the sternly given verbal order that on no account was he to spend longer than two weeks on this case, for he had been sent only to quieten a boisterous letter writer. If in the time assigned him he discovered a lead hinting at foul play, then he could return to Karwir at a later date more convenient for the department overloaded with work.

As though he, Napoleon Bonaparte, cared twopence for orders once he began an investigation, and such an investigation as this promised to be! As though he were a mere policeman to walk this beat or that according to the orders of a superior! Bah!

Shortly after leaving the homestead gate the fence led him into the mulga where the ground was sandy and easily windblown, where grew buckbush and speargrass and rolypoly. The stockmen riding the fence over the years had left a plainly discernible horse pad, and this pad was followed by Bony's horse. Here was a country into which the light wind failed to penetrate, a reddish-brown world pillared by short dark-green tree trunks, and canopied by a brilliant azure sky. At twelve o'clock Bony reached the first corner, eight miles due east of the homestead.

Here he camped for an hour, boiling his quart-pot for tea and eating the lunch daintily prepared and enclosed in a serviette. So far, the country he had traversed could not possibly offer a clue to Anderson's passing. The ground was too soft and sandy to have left unburied any clue.

From this first corner post the fence took a northward direction, and, after a further mile of the mulga forest, Bony emerged on to the plain that composed the southern half of the paddock. Now the sunlight was brighter and the wind could be felt. The horizon fled away for miles, cut here and there by cleanly ridged solitary sand-dunes and the tops of groves of trees raised into spires by the mirage. Five miles from the corner Bony came to an area of claypans across which his horse had to pass—and across which The Black Emperor must have passed when he carried Jeffery Anderson.

At these claypans Bony dismounted and led the horse with the reins resting in the crook of an arm. Now he walked in giant curves and smaller circles. Now he crouched to look across a claypan at an oblique angle. Four times he lay flat on his chest in order to bring the cement-like surface to within an inch of his eyes.

His examination of The Black Emperor's tracks that morning had revealed to the half-caste that the gelding pressed harder with the tip of his off-side fore hoof than with that of the near-side fore hoof, and, to make a balance, harder with the near-side hind hoof than with the off-side hind hoof. When he had cut the animal's hoofs in the yards the evening before, he had been careful to note the faint colouration of the growth since April, when Anderson had last cut them, and he had cut them as closely as possible to their former shape.

After five months it would have been stupid to expect to find The Black Emperor's tracks on sandy ground, on loose surfaces such as composed most of the plain, or on surfaces scoured by the rainwater that followed Anderson's disappearance. The claypans, however, always gave promise, for they could retain imprints for years, even if the imprints required the magnifying eyes of a Napoleon Bonaparte to see them. And, at irregular spaces across these claypans, Bony thought he could discern the faintest of indentations that could have been made by a horse before the last rain fell. He thought it, but he could not be sure.

For nearly eight miles Bony rode northward, again to dismount at the edge of the maze of sand-dunes stretching away into Mount Lester Station from Green Swamp. Here, where the fence rose from the comparatively level plain to surmount the dunes like a switchback railway, Bony and Lacy surmised Anderson to have stopped for lunch. A little way back from the fence grew a solitary leopardwood-tree, to which The Black Emperor could have been conveniently roped for the lunch hour.

Bony was now thrilling as might a bloodhound when in sight of the fugitive. He walked his horse to a tree distant from the leopardwood, neck-roped her to it, then returned to the leopardwood and began a careful examination of its trunk at about the height of the black gelding.

Now the bark of this tree is soft and spotted and green-grey, and Bony hoped to find on it the mark made by rope friction caused by an impatient horse. He found no mark. The tree grew above ground covered with fine sand, and those of its roots exposed he examined inch by inch for signs of injury from contact with an impatient horse's stamping hoof. He found no such injury. With the point of a stick he dug and prodded the soft surface, hoping to uncover spoor buried by wind-driven sand. He found no spoor, but he unearthed a layer of white ash, caked by the rain and covered by dry sand blown over it after the rain. Here Anderson had made his lunch fire.

His blue eyes gleaming, Bony stood up and smiled as he made a cigarette and smoked it like a man knowing he deserved the luxury. Leaning against the smooth trunk of the tree, he faced to the east. To his right began the plain, to his left the sand-dunes, before him, some twenty yards distant, was the plain wire fence separating Karwir from Mount Lester Station.

Here Anderson had stood or sat while he ate his lunch. He had observed the rain clouds approaching. Possibly it already had begun to rain. He had decided that to visit the swamp and the hut would be unnecessary. What had he done then? Had he mounted his horse and continued northward along the fence? Had he climbed over the fence into Mount Lester Station for any reason, any possible reason? Far away to the south-east Bony could see the revolving fans of a windmill and what might be an iron hut at its foot. It was two miles off the fence. Had Anderson walked over there, even strapped the wires together and induced The Black Emperor to step over the fence that he might ride there? It was a possibility that might yet have to be accepted and investigated.

There were claypans all along the foot of the sand-dune country, but Bony did not stay to examine those near by, for Anderson would have crossed them before the rain fell and they would have provided him with a clue no more definite than those others had given him. Then, too, he was satisfied by the remains of the small fire that the man really had camped at this place for his lunch.

Again mounted, he followed the fence into the sand-dunes, into a world of fantastically shaped monsters, gigantic curling waves, roofs of sand that smoked when the wind blew, cores of sand tightened with clay particles to be fashioned by the wind into pillars and roughly inverted pyramids, nightmarish figures and slim Grecian vases.

For two miles Bony continued to ride over these dunes till he arrived at the second corner of the paddock. Here the

plain wire fence joined a netted and barbed barrier, the
northern fence of Green Swamp Paddock and the boundary
fence of Karwir and Meena stations from this point to westward. To the eastward lay Meena and Mount Lester
stations.

From here Bony's course lay to the west, continuing over
the dunes to their westward edge and for another mile before the third corner was reached; the fence then sent Bony
southward to cross the wide and shallow depressions separated by the narrow ridges of sand on which grew only the
coolabahs. Over these depressions the netted barrier was in
bad condition, the netting having rotted at ground level since
the depressions had last carried water. Now the netting was
curled upward from the ground and an army of rabbits would
have found it no barrier at all.

Where the fence again angled to the west to reach its fifth
corner just westward of the gate spanning the road to Opal
Town, lay the southernmost of the depressions. The corner
was almost dead centre of this depression, and from it could
be seen the track from the main road to the hut at Green
Swamp.

Here Bony left the fence and rode eastward till he reached
the road which took him into a wide belt of shady box-trees
growing about the swamp. The hut was situated on the south
side, erected on higher ground to be above possible flood
level. For this reason, too, the well had been sunk and the
mill erected over it. The place was well named Green Swamp,
for a wall of green trees shut away the sand-dunes behind
them.

As the sun was pushing the tip of its orb above these trees
the next morning, Bony was riding towards the corner of the
fence he had left the evening before, and he was no little
astonished to see how badly the netted barrier needed repairs
along this further section of it.

He had proceeded about a third of the distance to the main

road gate when he saw ahead several men working on the fence. Then he saw the smoke of the campfire among the scrub trees and the tent twenty or thirty yards in Meena country. Approaching nearer the working party he saw that it consisted of three aboriginals. He passed the tent before reaching them, to observe the empty food tins littering the camp, indicating that it had been there several days. Coming to the workers, he cried:

"Good day-ee!"

"Good day-ee!" two of them replied to his greeting, the third continuing at work. They were footing the fence with new netting: digging out the old, attaching the new to the bottom of the main, above-ground wire and burying it, thus making it as proof against rabbits as when the barrier was first erected.

"The fence here is in bad condition," remarked Bony, taking the opportunity of the halt to make a cigarette.

"That's so," agreed the man who had not replied to the greeting. From Sergeant Blake's description, Bony recognized him.

His clear voice and reasonably good English, his powerful body and legs, tallied with Blake's word picture of Jimmy Partner. He seemed to be a pleasant enough fellow and was obviously in charge of the party. Of the others, who appeared younger, one was shifty-eyed and spindle-legged, and the second, although more robust, had his face set in a stupid, uncomprehending grin.

"Have you been working here long?" asked Bony.

"Three days," replied Jimmy Partner who, having leaned his long-handled shovel against the fence, drew nearer to Bony the better to examine him while he rolled a cigarette. "Haven't seen you about before. You working for Karwir?"

"Well, not exactly for Karwir. I am Detective-Inspector Bonaparte, and I'm looking into the disappearance of Jeffery

85

Anderson. Was the condition of this fence then like it is now?"

"No. It was bad, of course, but the April rain made it like this. Looking for Anderson, eh? I don't like your chances. He was looked for good and proper five months back, and the wind has done a lot of work since then."

"Oh, I fancy my chances are good," countered Bony airily. "All I want is time, and I have plenty of that. What's your name?"

The question was put sharply to the spindle-legged fellow and he goggled.

"Me! I'm Abie."

"And what's your name?"

The grin on the face of the other had become a fixture, and Abie answered for him.

"He's Inky Boy," he said.

Bony's brows rose a fraction.

"Ah! You're Inky Boy, eh! Sergeant Blake told me about you. You're the feller that Anderson beat with his whip for letting the rams perish."

Inky Boy's grin vanished, to be replaced with an expression of furious hate. Jimmy Partner cut in with:

"An ordinary belting would have been enough. It wasn't cause enough to thrash Inky Boy till he took the count. Still," and he tossed his big head and laughed, "Inky Boy won't never go to sleep and let any more rams perish."

"I don't suppose he will," agreed Bony who did not fail to detect the absence of humour in Jimmy Partner's eyes. "Well, I must get along. I may see you all again soon. Hooroo!"

He clicked his tongue, and Kate woke up and began to walk on. Jimmy Partner fired a last shot.

"You won't find Anderson anywhere in Green Swamp Paddock," he shouted. "If you do I'll eat a rabbit, fur and all."

Bony reined his horse round and rode back to them.

"Suppose I find him within ten miles of Green Swamp Paddock, what then?"

"I'll eat three rabbits, fur and all. You won't find him 'cos he's not here. We all made sure of that when he disappeared. No, he bolted clear away. Sick of Old Lacy and Karwir. Anyway, what with things he done the country was gettin' sick of him."

"Well, well! It all has to be settled one way or the other, Jimmy, and I'm here to settle it. So long!"

Now as he rode away towards the boundary gate, Bony examined the new earth piled against the new footing. The extremely faint difference of the colouring of the newly-moved earth plainly informed him that this party of aboriginals had not begun work here three days back but only the morning of the day before, the morning he had left the Karwir homestead. He was aware, of course, that time is rarely accurately measured by an aboriginal, but it had been Jimmy Partner who had stated the period, and he was too intelligent, too well educated, inadvertently to have made such a mistake.

Bony came to the gate spanning the road to Opal Town, and saw the west fence of Green Swamp Paddock coming from the south to join the netted barrier beyond the gate. In it, too, there was a gate, a roughly made wire gate. Beyond it ran back the cleared line cut through the mulga forest along which was erected the boundary netted fence, and Bony instantly understood that no one standing on this road, or riding in a car, could have seen the white horse tethered to a tree on the Karwir side and a brown horse similarly secured on the other side.

To read the page of the Book of the Bush on which that meeting of Diana Lacy with an unknown had been printed, Bony opened the gate in the plain wire division fence, mounted again on its far side, and so rode the boundary fence in the Karwir North Paddock.

From the plane he had estimated that the meeting place was a full half mile from the gate and the road, hidden from any passer-by on the road by a ground swell. He rode a full mile before turning back over his horse's tracks, for he must have passed the meeting place. He spent a full hour looking for the tracks of horse and humans. He failed utterly to discover them.

CHAPTER EIGHT

The Trysting Place

THE frown drawing Bony's narrow brows almost together was chased away by a quick smile. Then he frowned again, squinted rapidly at the sun, flashed a glance at his own shadow, thus judging the time to be a quarter after ten o'clock, and decided to boil water in his quart-pot for tea.

"Delightful!" he cried softly as he neck-roped the mare to a shady cabbage-tree, then made a fire and set the filled quart-pot against the flame. "I believe I can guess correctly what has been done to bluff poor old Bony, as though poor old Bony, *alias* Detective-Inspector Napeon Bonaparte, could be bluffed. What a beautiful tree is that bloodwood! What a striking feature it makes in this most limited locality! How shady, how ideally situated amid this low scrub, to be a trysting place easy to remember. When I was young, and the world was young, and the girl I loved with me! Dear me, I must be careful."

It was almost a freak of nature, this tree growing away from a creek or billabong. Its foliage was brilliant and full, its wood beneath the bark as red as blood. In its symmetry, in its virile life, the bloodwood is the very king of all the gums.

This tree was not difficult to climb, and Bony climbed it till he could climb no higher. Now the fence was dwarfed, and he could see along its cut line the white gate spanning the road, and far away over the tops of the lesser scrub. And there, a mile or two to the east, was rising, in interrupted lengths, a column of brown smoke that swelled into a mushroom-shaped cloud five thousand feet above the world. And Bony's eyes blazed and his nostrils twitched with the excitement growing in his mind.

It was a perfect day for this ancient method of conveying a signal, and the mind of Napoleon Bonaparte laboured to solve the meaning of this one. That it was merely a signal conveying an idea and not a message, Bony came to be confident. The spacing of the smoke bars was too ragged for the sending of a message which through naturally imposed limits had to be nothing more than a generality. And what the blacks working on the fence would have to tell their own people would be much more involved than a generality such as: "I'm coming home," or, "You come over here."

So quiet the day amid these drowsing trees that, when the water in the quart-pot boiled over the rim, Bony heard the hiss of its sputtering on the hot embers of the small and smokeless fire. A crow came from the south, circled about the bloodwood, cawed thrice and alighted in a mulga-tree just beyond the fence, there to watch with its head cocked to one side this strangely behaving animal that could kill with a noise, and throw stones and sticks.

For a little while longer Bony remained on his high bough, alternately gazing eastward along the fence towards the gate and the black fencers' camp, and away to the north-west where were situated Meena Lake and Meena homestead. He hoped to see a smoke signal rise in that quarter, and when none did he was still more confident of the purpose of the signal made by Jimmy Partner and his friends.

"Drama and a little comedy mixed with the spoon of tranquillity give the cake of life," he said to the watching crow. "Drama without comedy or comedy without drama produces the soddy dough of phantasmagoria. First the wager of eating rabbits, fur and all, and now the broadcasting of news by a method forgotten by the world save among the allegedly primitive peoples."

On reaching the ground he made tea with the water remaining in the quart-pot, and carrying the brew to the shade of a thriving currant bush he reclined on the soft warm earth to sip the black liquid and to smoke a chain of cigarettes. The crow cawed once because the bloodwood hid the man from it, then flew cawing in a giant circle before perching in a tree from which it could watch with only its black head and one beady eye to be seen.

"My dear undertaker, I'm not yet dead," Bony blithely remarked to it. "In fact, I am more alive than I have been for a long time. This case is beginning to unfold before me as a flower unfolds to be kissed by the new-risen sun. You didn't know I was a poet, did you? I mayn't look like one, but then I don't look like a detective-inspector.

"For the first time, no, the second, in my career I am apparently opposed by aborigines, worthy opponents, opponents who never make the stupid mistakes fatally made by the so clever, so highly civilized white man. I wonder how! Did those blacks signal my passing their camp in a code arranged just to fit the news, or did they signal the announcement that one of them was about to begin a broadcast? And having begun the broadcast, which of them is now seated on the ground with his arms resting on his raised knees and his forehead resting on his arms while he transfers to the mind of another at Meena thought pictures of my arrival at the camp, my statement concerning the discovery of Anderson, my passing on to the road, and possibly my being camped just here?

"Everyone of them was a young man, and therefore the probability is that the signal merely announced that I have arrived on the job."

The crow cawed, and then realistically gurgled like a man being strangled.

"Be quiet," Bony said to it. "Now let me go back to that

instant when I saw a cut line through the scrub, a line of netted fence along the centre of the cut line, and a white horse and a brown one tethered to a tree either side of the barrier. Those horses were standing not far from this place."

Bony closed his eyes, and found that before he could concentrate he had first to subdue the excitement created by the smoke signals. Presently he became tranquil, his mind amenable to control. He imagined the roar of the aeroplane engine. Imagination lifted the curtain to show not the last act but the prologue. He saw again the white gate spanning the Karwir track growing larger and larger till it vanished below the machine at the instant he turned his head to gaze along this same cut line. Again he saw the two horses standing motionless in the shade cast by trees. And now he saw beyond and above the white horse the tall, vivid green bloodwood-tree. The white horse was standing in the shade cast by a tree growing nearer to the gate than was the bloodwood.

Bony sighed his satisfaction. He was now sure that he knew the site of the trysting place.

"Great is the mind, my undertaking friend," he told the crow. "A wonderful servant but a tricky master. Now to establish if my mind has served or tricked me."

He walked direct to a mulga-tree growing several yards beyond the bloodwood and nearer the road gate. The ground about the base of this tree was smooth and empty of tracks. A centipede would have left its writing on this page of the Book of the Bush. Bony searched the ground about the tree next in the same direction. Here, too, the ground was smooth, but on it lay several long, needle-pointed, curled and dead mulga leaves. There were tracks made by a small bird and a medium sized scorpion. Back again at the first tree, Bony again searched the ground, his eyes pin points of blue as they contracted the better to magnify. No page in the Book of the Bush is entirely devoid of writing. This page had been cleaned, and cleaned within forty-eight hours.

A blowfly buzzed and Bony spun about to search for it. He did not see it in flight, but he saw it when it alighted on the ground some ten or twelve feet out from the tree trunk. The half-caste stepped to the place, went to ground and sniffed. He smelled horse. The white horse ridden by Diana Lacy had stood here in the shade cast by this tree. No evidence of its stand here remained. The ground was smooth—too smooth.

With those all-seeing eyes of his he examined the surrounding scrub. Only along the fence line could he see for any appreciable distance. Either side of the fence line the trees crowded upon him, presenting a mass formation that could be penetrated only for a hundred yards at most. He could not be sure that he was unobserved. He could be watched by a thousand unseen spies.

On the far side of the fence, he established to his entire satisfaction that the brownish bruise on a tree trunk had been produced by the rubbing of a rope—a horse's neckrope. About this tree, too, the ground was smooth and empty of tracks when surrounding ground was littered with the scrub's debris and imprinted by the scrub's life. He could smell no horse at this place, nor could he find any foreign material caught by the barbs of the fence wire. He spent a full hour trotting on his toes around and wide of the bloodwood, and although he found small areas where the ground was too smooth and too clean, he saw not a fractional part of one track left by hoof or boot, or naked foot.

An object of peculiar and significant interest was a small grey feather with a dark-red stain along one edge.

Throughout his examination of this locality the crow had been an interested and a constant spectator. Now and then it cawed with rude defiance, sometimes with puzzled annoyance. Bony's lack of interest in the bird was only apparent. While he worked he was ever conscious of its proximity and, from its behaviour, he concluded that he was not spied upon.

A spy, black, white or yellow, would not have remained concealed from that crow.

The half-caste hummed a lilting tune as he walked to the now cold fire and made another with which to boil the quart-pot for tea with lunch. He was experiencing mental exhilaration, based not on achievements but on crowding difficulties. The greater the number of "whys" that rushed at him to demand answers the happier he became. He now was living when normally he existed. The blood was tingling his scalp and the balls of his fingers and toes.

Why! Why! Why!

Ah well! Let him attend to these pestering whys.

Why had Diana Lacy ridden to this place, dismounted from her white horse and neck-roped it to a mulga-tree growing only a few yards from Meena country? Why had a person—sex not proved—ridden over Meena country to dismount on the far side of the fence and there to neck-rope his horse to a mulga-tree? Had that meeting taken place through design or accident? Why had someone come to this place after Diana had left it, and probably after the other person had also left, for the express purpose of efficiently wiping away all traces of it? The wind had not accomplished the effacement. There had been no wind of sufficient velocity to have wiped out the marks left by a naked foot, let alone by the hoofs of a horse. And if the wind had accomplished so much it would not have left small areas of ground unlittered by the scrub debris.

The human eraser of the tracks first bathed his naked feet in blood and then dipped them into bird's feathers until the blood dried and stuck fast the feathers to the feet, aware that feet so treated leave no faintest mark on the ground. That an aboriginal had carried out this effacement was reasonably certain. A lubra would have scattered leaves over the ground after she had smoothed it. However, the methods used by the person doing the effacement, as well as the actual effacement itself, were of less importance at the moment than the why behind it all.

No one knew when he, Bony, was to arrive at Opal Town, and, when Sergeant Blake had arranged with Old Lacy for his transportation to the Karwir homestead, Diana Lacy had been out riding her white mare. Unless Young Lacy flew over her and dropped a note stating the reason for his flight to Opal Town, she could have known nothing of his arrival.

The person whom she met had evidently come from Meena, and he—assuming it had been a man—would not know of Bony's arrival at Opal Town and his subsequent flight to Karwir. It was, of course, possible that she had informed him of it, having herself been informed by Young Lacy, but it was not probable because Young Lacy would fly direct to the township, passing over Green Swamp several miles to the east of the main road from Karwir. It was a point demanding proof.

What most likely had happened was that the person who had met Diana Lacy knew nothing of Bony's arrival until informed of it by Wandin late that day Sergeant Blake had dismissed him.

Anyway, it was of less importance—how this person had been informed and by whom—than the reason behind his decision to prevent an investigating detective officer coming to know of his meeting with Diana Lacy. Why was it considered so essential that he, Bony, should not know of it? Neither the girl nor the person she met was to know that he had seen their horses at the trysting place, but he—still assuming it was a man—had sufficient imagination to know that traces of the meeting would be found and read, if not obliterated.

Yes, there were plenty of whys, and yet another came to demand answer. Was the meeting in any manner connected with the disappearance of Jeffery Anderson? Hardly, after the lapse of five months. Was it a chance meeting, resulting in a period of harmless gossip? No, because the traces of such a chance meeting would not have demanded effacement. What appeared to be most likely was that Diana Lacy had met beneath the bloodwood-tree a man who was her lover, and because he came from Meena it was more than probable that he was John Gordon. And Gordon being comparatively poor, and Old Lacy ambitious for his daughter, and Diana not yet being of age, the lovers feared that their secret would be revealed. That must be the reason for the meeting and for its effacement.

A smile flitted across Bony's clean-cut features and lit his eyes. Lovers had nothing to fear from him, he who was at heart a romantic sentimentalist.

However, the whys were not quite so easily appeased.

The many whys raised significant possibilities and probabilities between which there was a gulf. There was no proof that this bloodwood-tree had shyly witnessed a meeting of lovers. It might have been a meeting of confederates. Nothing could be taken for granted until proved—and the effacement of all traces of the meeting by a person or persons whose naked feet were covered with blood and feathers gave that meeting a sinister air.

Then there was the matter of that smoke signal made so soon after Bony's appearance in Green Swamp Paddock. That more than hinted at urgency. It strongly pointed to an interest in him much deeper than casual curiosity, and the fact that the fence work had certainly not been begun until the morning following his arrival at Karwir seemed to harden the supposition that the person who had met Diana Lacy had, when informed of his (Bony's) arrival, instructed the blacks immediately to undertake the fence work in order to be near the investigator and at once to report on his work.

"If Bill the Better were here I'd bet him a level fiver that that's how it is," Bony remarked to his horse as he untied her neck-rope from about the tree and proceeded neatly to knot it under her throat. He mounted easily, and then, removing his hat, he bowed mockingly at the crow, which cawed derisively. Turning the horse's head towards the road, he said to her:

"This is going to be a most interesting case, Katie dear. As the fortune teller says: there is a dark man, in fact many dark men in your life, Mr Detective-Inspector Napoleon Bonaparte. There is at least as much black as white in this disappearance case. And such a case! It is almost made for me. Five months have gone since the man vanished in a paddock eighty square miles in area. There's no body to give me a start, no pistol, no false wig, no finger-prints, no informers without whom my esteemed colleagues are almost helpless. I shall have to dig from the Field of Time five solid months, and turn them over to see what lies beneath them in this world of sand and mulgas, plain and sand-dune, water-gutter and claypan."

They had almost reached the gate in the plain wire fence when the half-caste said to his horse—and she turned round her ears the better to hear him—in excellent imitation of the irate Chief Commissioner:

" 'Damn and blast you, Bony! As I've told you a hundred times, you're not a cursed policeman's shadow. . . .' Too true, my dear Colonel, too true. But I'm going to prove once again that I'm a cursed good detective."

CHAPTER NINE

Progress

THOSE at Karwir did not see Napoleon Bonaparte again until the afternoon of the seventh of October. The weather was clear and warm, but the first heat wave of the summer had not yet come.

Old Lacy, working at his table in the office, saw Bony arrive at the stockyards, and ceased his labours to watch the half-caste unsaddle the horse, take her to the night paddock and there free her. His mind occupied by speculation on what this remarkable man had achieved, the squatter of Karwir found himself mentally unable to continue his work after Bony had disappeared beyond the garden gate. For an hour Bony remained beyond that gate, and when he reappeared he was shaved, showered and arrayed in a light-grey suit. The old man watched him crossing to the office, and wondered. Bony's sartorial taste was as impeccable as that of a fashionable white man.

"I am glad to find you here, Mr Lacy," the detective said on entering the office. "I hope, however, I am not interrupting important work."

Like many poorly educated men, Old Lacy found pleasure in a well-spoken man provided that person attempted to take no advantage—should he attempt it Old Lacy quickly proved that education was nothing.

"Not at all, Bony," he said with hearty assurance. "I'm

finishing up, and what I leave the lad can fix. Can't get along without him, y'unnerstand. Takes after his mother. Neat and particular." A rumbling chuckle issued from the lips framed with white hair. "He takes down my letters in shorthand and then types 'em out in his own language. I say: 'Sir—Why the devil haven't you sent me that windmill part as ordered a month ago?' The lad writes: 'Dear Sir—We regret to have to inform you that at date the windmill part ordered on the 20th is not yet to hand.'

"Only this morning I'm sitting here and the telephone bell goes off. The lad answers it. The call's from Phil Whiting, the storekeeper and postmaster at Opal Town, and from what I can make out the fool is explaining to the lad why our mail-bag was put on the Birdsville mail car by mistake. The lad hums and haws and says the mistake is to be regretted, and that it has caused us great inconvenience. So I grabs the telephone and I says: 'That you, Whiting? Good! What the so-so do you mean making that mistake with our mail-bag? Sorry? What the so-so's the use of being sorry? If you do it again you'll lose the Karwir custom for a year, and that's flat.' Now, which is the best way to deal with 'em?"

"Your way, of course," instantly replied Bony smiling. "You know, if all the polite phrasing were to be cut out of business and official letters some two or three million light years would be saved. Colonel Spendor says often: 'Give me the guts not the trimmings.' The idea may be vulgarly expressed but it is sound."

"Ah, I'll remember that," chortled the old man, and from a drawer he produced a bundle of letters. "These came for you yesterday. Should have been here days ago. Hullo! That's the afternoon tucker gong. Come on! Diana's a stickler for being prompt on the job. How's the investigation going?"

Bony followed Old Lacy outside the building before answering.

"Not fast, but it has progressed."

The Bone is Pointed

Now as they crossed to the garden gate the old man kept half a pace ahead of the detective, walking firmly, his body carried straight, his white-crowned head held high, his hands white in places that once had been scarred with hard work.

"You married?" he asked.

"Yes. I have been married a little more than twenty years," Bony replied. "I have a son attending the university and the youngest is going to the State School at Banyo where I live with my wife and children—sometimes."

"Humph!" grunted Old Lacy, slightly increasing the pace. "This flash education has its points, I admit, but I don't know that it makes people any more content with life. Young people of to-day stand four-square, but I much doubt that they are any better than the young people of my day. That they are not worse is a blessing."

They discovered Diana standing beside the tea table set on the cool south veranda. She smiled at her advancing father, and to Bony she gave the slightest of cool nods. That she was thoroughly interested in him he suspected, and that she now experienced slight astonishment at his taste in dress she admitted afterwards to her father. But she kept herself at a distance from Bony, and he knew it. Yet, undaunted, he said to her:

"Coming to a homestead cannot be unlike coming to an oasis in the Arabian desert. Outside the house the birds are ever numerous, and inside almost invariably are to be found wickedly luxurious lounge chairs."

Diana inclined her head towards a wonderful wicker-work affair.

"Let me recommend you to that super-wicked luxury chair," she said, still unsmiling.

"Thank you." Bony sighed after he had taken the chair, which was not until the girl had sat down to pour out the tea. He wasn't to be tricked too easily into making a social mis-

100

take. "Why cannot some inventive genius evolve a saddle to give the standard comfort set by even an ordinary chair?"

"Look funny, wouldn't it, to see a chair like the one you're sitting in lashed to the back of a horse?" remarked Young Lacy as he approached them.

"They fix luxurious seats in motor-cars these days," persisted Bony.

"And comfortable seats in aeroplanes," Diana added. "The passenger's seat in your ship, Eric, is the acme of comfort."

"My contention," asserted Bony. "Twenty years of air and motor travel have evolved comfortable seats. Saddles to-day are not more comfortable, or rather, not less uncomfortable, than they were hundreds of years ago."

"Comfort! Luxury! Softness!" exploded Old Lacy, settling himself into a leather affair with foot-wide arm rests and a velvety soft bulge to take the neck. "In my young days there was no softness, no luxury chairs."

"Which was your great misfortune, father," countered Diana. "Now take this cup made in England by Grafton, and please don't say you would prefer to drink tea out of a tin pannikin."

"Hur! Thanks, my gal. In your hearts you young people think you're a sight smarter than the old people, but the old people don't think, they know they're smarter than the young folk. And now, as we seem to have settled the family argument, perhaps we can persuade Inspector Bonaparte to tell us something of what he's been doing."

"A real policeman never tells anything to anyone," Bony said sadly, and the Lacys regarded him sharply for the sudden change of mood. "Of course, I'm not a real policeman, as I have told you, but you make me feel like one when you call me Inspector."

"Good for you, Bony! I forgot," almost shouted Old Lacy.

"Ah—that's better. Now I feel more like myself," Bony said with a quick smile. "Progress has been slow, but I am not disappointed because I expected it to be slow. However, the case is proving to be of great interest, and if you, Miss Lacy, will permit me to talk shop——?"

Diana inclined her head. She refused to be drawn, but Bony's penetrating eyes detected her eagerness to hear what he had accomplished.

"Well, then. I have discovered clues which satisfy me that Jeffery Anderson parted from his horse somewhere in the northern half of Green Swamp Paddock. I know that he camped for lunch, that day he left here, at the foot of the sand-dunes where the paddock's east fence rises from the plain country. You see, Mr Lacy, we were right in our reasoning. He camped for the lunch hour at the foot of the sand-dunes, and before he left it began to rain, and he decided it was not necessary to ride over to the swamp and the hut.

"From this point I cannot definitely establish Anderson's movements, but I incline to the supposition that he continued to ride northward along the east fence as far as its junction with the netted boundary fence. There, he turned westward along the boundary fence, which forms the north fence of Green Swamp, and so eventually rode down from the sand-dunes on to flat country bordering the Channels.

"I say that I incline to that supposition. Anderson, when the rain began, might well have decided to take a short cut home by striking due westward from his lunch camp and so come to that corner post on the southernmost depression and continue along the fence to the road gate.

"Let us draw an imaginary line from his lunch camp to that corner post on the depression. We see then that north of the line lies Green Swamp, the sand-dunes east and north of it, and the Channels. At the lunch camp, remember, I discovered proof that Anderson had boiled his quart-pot there. And, south of the line and south of the corner post on the depression, I found tracks made by The Black Emperor not before it rained or after it had stopped raining, but while it was raining, when it had rained about half an inch.

"Now, Mr Lacy, you said that at four o'clock that afternoon you went out to the rain gauge and found in it fifteen points of rainwater. At what time that evening, do you think, had about half an inch fallen?"

"Ah—um!" The old man pondered. "What do you think, lad?"

"Well, it took almost two hours for fifteen points to register," slowly answered Young Lacy. "I was working in the office late that day, I remember, and when I knocked off about half-past five I stood at the window looking at the rain and thought by sight of it, and by the noise it was making on the roof, that it was coming down harder. My guess is that fifty points registered about seven or half-past seven that evening."

"Yes, lad, I think you're about right," Old Lacy agreed.

"Then," began Bony, "if half an inch had fallen by seven o'clock, at seven o'clock The Black Emperor was just south of our imaginary line when he and his rider should have been home. To-morrow, or some other time, you might make inquiries to ascertain if someone in the district happened to register the rain at that hour. The important point I have to stress is this—when The Black Emperor left his tracks at the place just south of our imaginary line he did not have a rider on his back."

The effect of this assertion on his hearers was peculiar.

Young Lacy stiffened in his chair and his eyes became big. Diana's eyes became small, the pupils tiny circles of violet almost as dark as her eyebrows. Her lips straightened just sufficiently to make her mouth hard and to alter the cast of her face. Old Lacy, with emphatic deliberation, set his cup and saucer down on the arm of his chair and shouted:

"How did you find that out?"

Secretly delighted at the effect of his verbal bomb, Bony

The Bone is Pointed

smiled at them in turn, and noted how the girl's strained expression gave way to one of cool, impersonal interest.

"When people read of a blackfellow being employed by the police to track a criminal, they think that the blackfellow's extraordinary ability is due to his naturally keen eyesight," he said, delighting in keeping his audience in suspense. "Any normally good tracker has served an apprenticeship as long and as thorough as any white craftsman. He begins when a small child, when the lubras take him with them to hunt for food, and when success in the hunt depends on ability to track. Without that apprenticeship the blackfellow would be no superior to the white man who has lived his life in the bush.

"I began my apprenticeship after I left the university, when I went bush instead of continuing my studies, and my aboriginal mentors found me a good student because I had inherited the white man's ability to reason more clearly and quickly than they. The claypans preserved the imprints made by The Black Emperor. Memory of that horse's tracks seen that day I rode him, told me that the tracks on the claypan had been made by him. The outline of the tracks and their spacing satisfied me on that point. Depth, the sludge left in them, the angles of certain facets in conjunction with certain others, informed me what approximate amount of rain had fallen on the claypans when they were made. And the manner in which the animal had made them showed that he carried no burden. It takes many years to make a university professor. How many years would it take to make the professor a tracker like me?"

"Loveacre was right when he told me you were a wizard at the game," asserted Young Lacy. "It seems to me that the more you know about the blacks the less superior to them you feel. Gordon, over at Meena Lake, could write books about them."

"Yes! I understand that he and his mother have been in

close contact with them for years," Bony said. "By the way, to-morrow being Sunday, would you be able to fly me over to Meena? I should like to discuss certain matters with Mr Gordon."

"Certainly. No trouble at all," agreed Young Lacy.

"Might be as well to ring Gordon," suggested the old man.

"Yes. Suggest the middle of the afternoon," Bony urged in support. "There is another matter. What became of Anderson's effects after he disappeared?"

"They are still in his room," answered the old man. "His room hasn't been touched after it was tidied and the bed made the morning he rode away," added Diana.

Bony's expression indicated keen pleasure. He said:

"I should like to examine that room presently. He was, I am given to understand, remarkably facile in the use of the stockwhip. The stockwhip he carried with him that fatal day was never found. Was it the only whip he possessed?"

"Oh, no," replied Young Lacy. "He owned several."

"Where would they be now? In his room?"

"Sure to be—with all his other things."

"Would you bring them here to me?"

Young Lacy at once left his chair. Diana began the movement to rise to her feet when Bony waved her back, saying:

"Eric can bring them, Miss Lacy. I suppose you have some embroidery silk in the house?"

"Yes. Why?" she asked.

Bony smiled at her, and Old Lacy, more often observing his guest than his daughter, failed to note her coldness in opposition to Bony's sunny warmth.

"If you would be so kind as to bring me some—would you?"

"Yes. I have several hanks in my work-basket."

"A matter of interest to me, Mr Lacy," Bony began when the girl had left the veranda, "is that everyone thinks his or her walk of life is superior to others. For instance, I think that the detection of crime is the most important work of any. You, probably, think that raising cattle and growing wool is of the greatest importance. We all appear to fail in giving the other fellow credit for his success which, when all is said, is based only on the keen application to the job in hand. It puzzles me why the getting of coal should be considered so much less important than speaking in Parliament, that the position of secretary to a business man should be thought to be of little account compared with that of, say, the Governor-General. The secretary can be mentally superior to the Governor-General, and the coalminer can be of greater concern to the community than the statesman. That, of course, is by the way. Here are the stockwhips. Thank you, Eric."

Bony accepted four whips varying in length, weight and age. The old man and Young Lacy silently watched the detective whilst he examined each in turn from the handle to the silk cracker neatly affixed to the end of the tapering leather thongs. He was thus engaged when the girl came out with her work-basket. From this examination, Bony's gaze rose to the young man.

"I am sorry to give so much trouble this afternoon," he said. "Is there such a thing to hand as a magnifying glass?"

"Yes, there is. And we have a microscope, too, if you would like that."

"Well—no, not the microscope. The glass will be of use." To Diana, when Young Lacy had left, Bony said: "Ah! The work-basket, Miss Lacy. Now what embroidery silk have you there?"

Without speaking, Diana brought from the basket several hanks of silk—white and black and several shades of blue and of red. These Bony examined for a full minute before looking up and smiling.

"If only the human brain could encompass all knowledge," he complained with mock sadness. "Have you no green silk?"

"No. I never use green or yellow silk for my fancywork."

"Hum! I asked that because I find on each of these four whips crackers made with green silk. Anderson, then, did not obtain his cracker-silk from you."

"No."

"I see that on the slip-over label on one of these unused hanks are the words 'cable silk.' It seems much coarser than that of the other hanks."

"Yes, it is not used for embroidery work but for fancy knitting."

"The word 'cable' reminds me," said Young Lacy, who had returned with the magnifying glass. "I remember ordering green cable silk from Phil Whiting for Jeff Anderson. As a matter of fact Anderson always used green silk for his crackers."

"I wonder, now," Bony said, slowly. "Did Anderson have a special liking for green as a colour?"

"Two of his suits are dark green," replied the young man.

"He must have had a strain of Irish in him."

"What's that!" exclaimed Old Lacy, his body jerking upward.

Bony repeated the remark, and then, accepting the magnifying glass, he studied one of the whip crackers. Several minutes were spent on the study of the four whips.

"Undoubtedly Anderson made his whip crackers with cable silk," he said, breaking a long silence. "Now let us observe with the glass a wisp from the frayed end of this cracker with a wisp of silk I have found."

Bony produced from a long slender pocket-book an envelope, and from the envelope a spill of cigarette paper. Immobile, as though each of them held breathing suspended, the others saw Bony take from the paper a wisp of silk and lay it upon the envelope. No one offered comment when he set beside it a wisp of frayed silk from one of the crackers, and with the glass examined both with studious care. When he looked up at them they saw satisfaction depicted on his face.

"I should like you all to examine these two wisps of silk with the glass," he said, the satisfaction now in his voice. "Both specimens are much faded in colour, but they are sufficiently alike for us to assume that both came from the same material—cable silk."

One by one they accepted the glass and agreed that both wisps of silk were alike in colouring, though both faded.

"What's it all mean, Bony?" demanded the old man.

"One moment, Mr Lacy," said Bony. He returned the wisp of silk to its cigarette paper and the paper to the envelope which he marked Exhibit One. Then he removed one of the crackers and placed this in a used envelope which he marked Exhibit Two.

"I am unable to satisfy your natural curiosity," he told them smilingly. "My own curiosity is not yet satisfied concerning the scrap of cable silk I discovered in a somewhat remarkable position some five months after it was detached from the cracker of Anderson's whip. While I am not sure, I can hazard a guess in which particular square mile Jeffery Anderson played a part in the drama which closed his life."

"Do you really think he was killed by someone?" asked Diana, that hard expressionless mask again on her face.

"Of course he was," interjected Old Lacy. "The blacks killed him for what he did to Inky Boy. I told Jeff to be careful and always to keep his eyes well open."

Bony nodded his head in the affirmative, and neither the girl nor Young Lacy could decide if the affirmation referred to the old man's statement or to Diana's question.

CHAPTER TEN

The Shadow of Civilization

WHEN the maid brought him a cup of early morning tea, Bony was smoking his second cigarette and making notes on a sheet of note-paper, his puckered eyes indicating his displeasure with the progress of this case at Karwir.

After breakfast with the Lacys, during which the case was not mentioned, he rang Sergeant Blake who told of his interview with the Opal Town shopkeeper on the subject of green cable silk, an interview giving no definite results since the storekeeper reported selling green cable silk fairly often. With regard to the time when half an inch of rain had fallen on the eighteenth of April, Blake's news was more encouraging, for one of the Mackays, of Mount Lester Station, agreed that the half-inch had fallen by seven o'clock.

Bony was on his way to join Young Lacy, who was working this Sunday morning on his aeroplane in preparation for the flight to Meena Lake in the afternoon, when he met Bill the Better coming from the cow yard with two buckets of milk.

"Good day!" Bony greeted the little man with the watery blue eyes and the gingery moustache.

"Good day-ee, Inspector! Keepin' dry, ain't it?"

A smile flitted across Bony's dark face, and he said:

"I do not approve of gambling on Sunday, but I'll bet you five shillings even money that it rains before Christmas Day."

The groom set down his milk buckets.

"Lemme see," he said. "To-day's the eighth of October. Yes, I'll take you. Rain to register not less than one point."

Bony produced his long, narrow pocket-book, and on the back of the envelope marked Exhibit One he noted the transaction. As he watched the detective doing this, Bill the Better asked :

"Any chance of you finding the body?"

"Body ! What body?"

"Handerson's body, of course. I don't know of any other likely ones."

"Why are you so interested in the discovery of Anderson's body?"

"Well, you see, I gotta coupler quid on Handerson's carcass. That night 'e didn't come 'ome I bet Charlie a coupler quid he'd be found a corpse. That's more'n five months ago, and the bet's still 'anging fire. Trouble is that Charlie might be left when the carcass is found, and then I can whistle for me money."

"Yes, I can understand how awkward the position is," Bony agreed. "However, I am doing my best. Meanwhile, if you're game, what about another little bet?"

"Too right, Inspector. Anything will do me."

"Good ! I'll bet you a level pound you cannot tell me, without hesitation, just what you did on the eighteenth of April, the day that Anderson disappeared."

The watery eyes blinked.

"Done !" cried Bill the Better. "I'll recite it like a pome. I gets the 'orses in by half-past seven. I 'as me break and then walks over to the wood 'eap. I seen Handerson coming outer the yards with The Black Emperor. 'E walks 'im acrost to the Green Swamp gate, and when 'e gets on inside the paddock the 'orse plays up and Handerson belts 'im with 'is stockwhip. After that he rides east along the south fence."

"Anderson had his stockwhip with him?"

"Too right 'e did. 'E never moved without 'is blinding whip."

"Did you happen to notice what kind of cracker was on the whip that morning?"

"I did. It was a brand new one on 'is newest whip. Thick green-coloured silk 'e always used on 'is whips. I reckon Inky Boy won't ever forget the colour. The nig wasn't awake when the green was changed to scarlet. Well, after I chopped the wood I went out after the ration sheep wot always runs in the night paddock."

"That is the paddock that lies eastward from here and south of Green Swamp Paddock, isn't it?"

"That's it. By the time I'd——"

"You didn't see Anderson when you were out after the ration sheep, I suppose?"

"Cripes, no! 'E'd been gorn a coupler 'ours by then."

When Bill the Better had completed the list of his tasks that day, Bony presented him with a pound note in settlement of the debt.

"You didn't like Anderson, did you?"

The watery eyes peered upward, and in them Bony saw hate.

"No, I didn't," came the assertion. "I'll lay you a whole fiver to a shilling you can't produce anyone who loved the swine. And if you finds 'is carcass, which I'm 'oping you will, I gives the coupler quid I wins from Charlie to St Albans orspital."

"You may have to do that, and I will remind you of the hospital," Bony said. "You don't think, then, that Anderson cleared out of the district for some reason?"

"Cleared out! Not 'im. Why, 'e wanted to marry Miss Lacy to get the flamin' station so's 'e could sack me."

"Indeed!"

"Too right 'e did. But 'e couldn't put that acrost Old Lacy.

Well, I must get along with the milk, Inspector. See you after."

A forthright little man, but hardly a man killer, thought Bony as he crossed the dry bed of the creek above the long waterhole supplying the homestead. Anderson must have been an evil man, a violent man who perished through violence, one who might well have lived to perish at the end of a rope.

A few minutes after three o'clock Young Lacy's plane alighted, with Bony in the passenger's seat, on the wide ribbon of white claypan encircling the lake bed, just below the plateau on which Meena homestead was built. Together pilot and passenger followed the faint path up through the sand-dunes to the plateau where John Gordon and his mother had come to meet them.

Bony took an instant liking to this man and this woman. Young Lacy effected the introduction, and Bony's first impression was confirmed when both accepted him without the slightest hesitation.

"Welcome to Meena, Mr Bonaparte," Mary cried with faint excitement. "We have so few visitors that those we do have are very welcome indeed."

"We expected you before," Gordon said, frankly extending his hand. "It's a pity our lake is dry."

"Yes, isn't it?" Mrs Gordon agreed. "The sound of the waves is just like the surf, and the air is always cool even during the summer."

"I've had no opportunity to come over before to-day," Bony told them. "After what I have heard about your great interest in the aborigines—they occupy a warm place in my heart, you know—this visit gives me very great pleasure."

"We can talk about them for hours, John and I," Mary said, still controlled by that faint excitement. "But let's go along to the house. It will be so much cooler on the veranda."

Chatting to him all the way, she conducted the detective

into the house, and through it to reach the veranda overlooking the great basin of the empty lake. There she made both him and Young Lacy comfortable, before bustling away to prepare the afternoon tea.

"I understand, Mr Gordon, that you represent the third generation of Gordons occupying this country," Bony remarked.

"Yes, that's so. My grandfather was the first to take up this land. We Gordons have clung to it through many bad droughts, and in return the land has given us a living. Grandfather was very Scots, you know, and they say that the Scots are the world's best servants to the land."

"I think so, too," agreed Young Lacy. "But I'm not so sure that the Australian-Scots are such good servants to a netted boundary fence."

The glint of humour in his hazel eyes caused Gordon to smile.

"Don't you worry, Eric," he said. "I've just got all that footing across the Channels completed. Jimmy Partner told us that Mr Bonaparte passed them twice when he and the others were doing it. I haven't seen the job, but I can trust Jimmy Partner to have made it good."

"Doesn't that fence belong to Karwir?" inquired Bony.

"No. It's half and half with Meena," replied Gordon. "Karwir paid to have it built, and Meena agreed to maintain it with materials supplied by Karwir. Where the fence bounds Meena and Mount Lester the arrangement is the other way round."

"Oh yes! By the way, Mr Gordon, if we might get a little business talk over and done with, Blake in his report on this Anderson case says that Jimmy Partner and you mustered sheep away from the Channels where they pass through the fence into Karwir. Were you and Jimmy Partner together the whole of that afternoon of the eighteenth of April?"

"No. We separated, I should say, about three o'clock. I

left Jimmy Partner to drive a mob of sheep towards Meena, and then went on to see if I could pick up another mob. You see, the Channels are very boggy in wet weather, and it was raining."

Whilst listening, Bony's face was bland, and the usual keenness was absent from his eyes. He had been made to feel that he was a most welcome guest at Meena, and his questions were being put with no little diffidence. His first impression of this confident young man was wearing well. He could detect no unease in either his voice or his eyes.

"Did you discover any more sheep near the Channels?"

"Yes. I picked up a mob between that corner right on the southernmost depression and the road gate. It was then, I think, about half-past four."

"Who reached home first?"

"Jimmy Partner got back a little before nine and I reached home shortly after him."

"Neither of you saw Anderson that day?"

"No."

"Or his horse?"

"No. Jimmy Partner and I were several times near the boundary fence where we could have seen him riding it on the far side had he passed when we were there."

"Thank you, Mr Gordon. Just one more question. After Jimmy Partner left you, could he have doubled back to the boundary where, by chance, he might have met Anderson?"

Gordon flushed a trifle. He replied steadily:

"He could but he didn't. The mob of sheep I left in his charge he drove five miles nearer the homestead before leaving them. I know he did this because the next day I went out for them and brought them to the yards here. I found them about where he said he had left them. He had gone off with the tribe on walkabout to Deep Well."

"Thank you."

"There's another thing. At three o'clock, when we first saw

the netted fence that day, Anderson should have reached the gate over the main road and been on his way straight to Karwir. Oh, I've worked out his probable movements that day, knowing the time he left the homestead. He would have been well past the Channels at three o'clock."

"Well, then, what time did you cross the main road when bringing the sheep away from the Channels?"

"I couldn't tell you the time but it was getting dark."

"You didn't see any fresh tracks on that road—horse tracks or motor tracks?"

For the first time Gordon hesitated to reply. Then:

"There may have been tracks of horse or car," he said. "It was growing dark and I didn't notice. But I think I'd have noticed if there had been any because I crossed the road where the ground is sandy, and where fresh tracks would have been plain."

Bony sighed, for at this moment Mary Gordon appeared carrying a large tray.

"Well, I'm glad we have got the business part of our visit over. You know, the warmth of your reception to me, a detective-inspector, on duty as it were, embarrasses me. You, Mrs Gordon, instead of glaring at me and plainly hinting you would like to see the last of me, go to great trouble to give us afternoon tea."

"I think I would offer a cup of tea to my greatest enemy," she said smilingly. "It is a good old bush custom to boil the billy directly anyone arrives."

"How true, Mrs Gordon. How did you and Mr Gordon get along with Jeffery Anderson?"

Now he saw indignation flash into her eyes, and the eyes of her son become agate-hard. It was the son who spoke.

"We never had anything to do with him save on two occasions when he injured our people. I mean, of course, the blacks here. We always call them our people. My father did. So did my grandfather."

Bony rose to accept tea and a cake from his hostess, and, having resumed his chair, he said:

"Tell me about your people, as you so wonderfully call the unfortunate aborigines. I should like to hear about the first and second Gordons, too, if you will."

He noted the flame of enthusiasm leap into their eyes as the woman's gaze met that of her son. It was a torch, lit by the first Gordon, accepted by her from the second Gordon when he died to hand on to her son. He now carried it, but she marched with him. Very softly, she said to the young man:

"You tell Mr Bonaparte, John. You can tell it so much better than I can."

"I don't agree with you, mother, but I'll do my best," the son said, glancing at her and smiling gently. "Of course, Mr Bonaparte, neither mother nor I ever saw Grandfather Gordon. Father told us a great deal about him so that we feel we actually know him. He was a big, hard, raw-boned Scotsman who knew what he wanted and who knew how to keep what he got against all comers.

"Long before he came here, when he was a mere boy, he witnessed the slaughter of a party of blacks near the junction of the Darling River with the Murray. They were all shot down, first the men and then the women and children to the smallest baby. The only crime those blacks committed was to offer objection to their land being taken from them, and the food the land gave them.

"We must admit that then it was an age of brutality. All over the world, in every allegedly civilized country, men were flogged for next to nothing, and hanged for very little more. Millions were enslaved, the stench still clung to the torture chambers, and it was not uncommon for people to die of starvation.

"Grandfather grew to become a tough and hard man, but he was just. When he came out here and found this lake of water and the blacks who had lived beside it for unknown time, he saw that there was plenty of room for both them and him. He became their friend—and that wasn't hard to accomplish, since they had never before had dealings with a white man.

"Of course there were minor troubles in the beginning, but grandfather settled these troubles, not with a gun, or with poison, but with his fists. The Kalchuts were fortunate in having as their chief a man named Yama-Yama, the present chief's father. Yama-Yama was an intelligent man, and he and Grandfather Gordon between them drew up a kind of charter in which it was agreed that grandfather would not hunt kangaroos or other native animals, not shoot the birds on the lake, and not interfere with the blacks in any way. On their part they agreed not to kill cattle, or attack a white man, or interfere in any way with Grandfather Gordon or anyone belonging to him.

"Thereafter life for Grandfather Gordon and his wife ran smoothly until one of his shepherds interfered with one of the lubras. Yama-Yama said they would kill the shepherd. Grandfather told them to carry on, and, after the man was killed, he reported his death as due to accident. Never again did he employ a white man.

"You see, the preservation of the Kalchut tribe has been made possible by the fact that no road passes through the station. Westward of those hills beyond the lake there lies a great desert of sand-dune country, and thus Meena Lake occupies a land pocket, as it were.

"There were many things done by Grandfather Gordon that were wise and far-seeing. He never issued the blacks with rations unless drought destroyed their food-supplies, and then he issued only meat and flour. He and his wife never insisted that the blacks wear white men's clothes: in fact, they frowned upon any alteration in their mode of living. My father continued that policy as far as he was able, and my mother and I have followed it, too, although we have been compelled to go as far as allowing the blacks to wear trousers and shirts when they want to.

"We have made mistakes, not being as wise as Grandfather Gordon and not having his really autocratic power. We have dreaded the coming of a missionary as much as official protectorship and interference. So far the Kalchut has escaped both. To-day our people follow the customs and tribal rites of their ancestors, and they and we have been blessed by an excellent chief in old Nero.

"Some of their customs, of course, we Gordons have had to frown upon, gradually getting them prohibited. Then we have had to meet the ambition of the men of Jimmy Partner's generation who have wanted to go and work on neighbouring stations, but we've got over one of the objections to their doing this by starting a banking account into which their wages are paid.

"The banking account is a communal one administered jointly by mother and me. It supplies cash for bare necessities —for food when it is needed, clothes for the winter and a ration of tobacco throughout the year. The account has been swollen by the tribe's fox hunting and rabbit trapping these last few years. So that the few things the men and women have come to want have been supplied to them through their own efforts. They are far from being mendicants.

"Grandfather Gordon clearly saw that civilization was a curse laid on man, not a blessing. My father saw the shadow of civilization slowly creeping towards the Kalchut tribe, and my mother and I have constantly battled to delay its coming, knowing that the tribe would be overwhelmed, and wiped off the face of the earth. I hope you are not being bored, but you asked me to ride my hobby-horse, you know."

"Bored!" exclaimed Bony, his eyes shining. "Please go on."

Bony's dark and youthfully handsome face was alight. Young Lacy sat without movement. And Mary Gordon stared steadily out over the lake bed towards the distant blue hills, as though she were seeing her husband and son slaying the beast called civilization. John Gordon sighed before continuing.

"We are fighting a losing battle, mother and I," he said as though he too saw the picture Bony imagined his mother was seeing. "These people we call our people have never had the curse of Adam laid on them. They have never delighted in torture. They have never known poverty, for they have never known riches and power over their fellows. They cannot understand the necessity to work when the land provides them with simple needs. The strong succour the weak, and the aged always get first helping of the food. They never think to crush a fellow in order to gain a little power.

"They have known real civilization for countless ages. Before the white and yellow and other black races learned to speak to their kind, these Australian aborigines were conversing intelligently. They practised Christian socialism centuries before Christ was born. They have evolved an apparently complicated although really simple social structure which is wellnigh perfect. They don't breed lunatics or weaklings. They never knew filth and disease before the white man came to Australia.

"And now the shadow of civilization falls on them although they don't know it. Civilization came to shoot them down, to poison them like wild dogs, and then, to excuse itself, to depict the victims of its curse as half-wits in its comic papers, to sneer at them as naked savages, to confine them to reserves and compounds. It has taken away their natural food and feeds them on poison in tins labelled food.

"As I have pointed out, our geographical situation has been most favourable to the Kalchut. Our only serious trouble was with Anderson. My grandfather would have sooled the blacks on to exact their justice, but mother and I dared not do that when he raped a lubra maid working at Karwir homestead and nearly flogged Inky Boy to death. We had to combine with Old Lacy to hush up those crimes against our people, fearing to draw the official eyes of civilization in their direction.

"I don't think, Inspector, that you'll find Anderson dead, and if he is dead, I am certain our people did not compass his death. We knew that day where, approximately, every member of the tribe was. They trust us as much as we trust them, and we would have been told instantly had one or more waylaid Anderson and killed him."

"Then we agree, Mr Gordon, that the only member of the tribe who could have killed Anderson was Jimmy Partner?" Bony asked.

The question caused Mary Gordon to cry, loudly:

"Oh but, Inspector, Jimmy Partner wouldn't have killed him. Why, I reared Jimmy Partner. He grew up with John. He's one of us."

"It was a question I was bound to ask," Bony told her gently.

"Of course, you had to," Gordon agreed. "All the same, Jimmy Partner couldn't have killed him. He was with me up till three o'clock when Anderson should have been miles past the Channels and riding along the road home."

Bony had actually forgotten his cigarettes, and now he abruptly relaxed and felt his clothes for tobacco and papers.

"I'm glad I came," he said quietly. "Why, for a few minutes I think I have been living outside the shadow of civilization. Just think if the world were as pure and life as simple as it was in Australia before ever Dampier saw it. Ah, but then, I should not have been happy, I suppose. There was no crime higher than the elementary crime of stealing your neighbour's wife. No, no! After all, I think I prefer the shadow in which crime and bestiality thrives."

They laughed with him, and Young Lacy's interest was diverted.

"By gum, John, you've got some rabbits over here," he exclaimed.

"Some! We've got millions. I've never seen so many around Meena Lake. They're thicker than they were in 1929. The Kalchuts are doing very well out of them, however, and this summer, if it doesn't rain, will see the end of them."

They all went down to the machine about which the curious aborigines were gathered. Nero was presented to Bony who was not impressed by the chief. He looked for, but failed to see, Wandin and Inky Boy and Abie. Then Mary Gordon was warmly inviting him to call soon and often, and her son was urging him to seek from Meena any help he might require.

And all the way back to Karwir a phrase repeated itself in Bony's mind, the words written with black and evil smoke. The Shadow of Civilization! How real was the shadow to these heroic Gordons, how menacing to the happy Kalchut tribe ignorant of its inevitable doom!

It was full time that the Creator of man wiped out altogether this monster called civilization and began again with the aborigines as a nucleus.

CHAPTER ELEVEN

Menace

THE net gain to Bony from his work throughout the following week was exactly nothing. One full day was spent in the Karwir North Paddock, another day along the west boundary of Mount Lester Station, and a third in examining the Meena country immediately north of Green Swamp Paddock. His reading of the Book of the Bush was fruitless, but even so, at the end of this week he felt still more sure that he was being opposed, actively opposed, in this investigation.

About eleven o'clock this Monday morning he was riding the mare, Kate, northward to the mulga forest in which lay the netted boundary fence, and he was still on the plain when he heard behind him the sound of the Karwir aeroplane. The machine passed him at low altitude. Young Lacy waved down to him and he answered the greeting. In the passenger's seat was Diana Lacy. She did not wave. The pilot was flying his machine above the road to Opal Town, and Bony wondered why he was not taking the more direct route to the township, crossing over Green Swamp four miles to the east.

Diana Lacy was giving much material for speculation. With immense satisfaction Bony was beginning to think that her aloof attitude to him was not based on the fact of his unfortunate parentage; for, try as he might, he had failed to detect in her mental make-up the feeling of superiority begotten by a city education. Nor was she governed by the snobbishness he had so often encountered among far-northern people who employed aborigines as servants. This was not the far north of the continent, where there is a distinct colour prejudice based on familiarity with aborigines debased through association with white people. Here, in this part of Australia, as in so many other inland districts, the sterling character of the full blood and the half-caste was paid reasonable tribute.

Bony was almost certain that it was not because of his birth that Diana Lacy maintained towards him an attitude of controlled hostility. This hostility was a compliment to him. She was not regarding him as an inferior, but rather as an enemy. She feared him, and her fear appeared to have its origin in that meeting at the boundary fence between herself and an unknown man.

It was the subsequent actions of the blacks—the wiping away of all traces of the meeting, the telepathic broadcast, announced by the smoke signal—that made this meeting an important corner-stone in the investigation. He had discarded his theory that the actions of the blacks had been dictated by lovers desirous of keeping their association secret. There was some other reason.

This morning Bony had an engagement to meet Sergeant Blake at the white boundary gate at noon, and now in the mulga forest he was again feeling what he had felt for many days—that he was being kept under constant surveillance. With an hour to spare before meeting the Sergeant, he determined to put this feeling to the proof.

As though casually, he turned his horse to ride back over her tracks, clearly to be seen on the soft sandy surface. Here, but a mile from the boundary, and two from the road gate, the trees were comparatively tall, robust and widely spaced. Lower to the ground grew currant bushes and wait-a-bit, and still lower were the dead filigree buckbush, waiting for the next windstorm to roll in their millions over the dust-masked world. The trees' debris littered the ground, forcing the horse to advance on a winding course—the course just previously made.

For a quarter of a mile Bony made the animal walk back over her own tracks, and then he reined her away to follow the line of an imaginary circle, his eyes small and gleaming as they surveyed the reddish ground ahead and on either side, and peered along the tree aisles for the possible glimpse of a black face or body.

The full circle was completed without his seeing any sign of blacks. The bush was empty, or appeared to be, save for a few robins, two Willie Wagtails busy with their fly-catching, and several sleepy goannas. Tracks there were of an odd rabbit, those left by doves, by reptiles and by insects, but the land was empty of tracks made by possible spies.

Bony was still not satisfied. Arriving at the place where he had turned back, he moved on towards the boundary fence. The day was calm and warm, the cloudless sky appearing to rest on the tree tops. The cawing of a crow at some distance behind him caused him to tighten further his eyes and the frown above them, and when the fence came into sight, he abruptly turned back again and rode in concentric circles.

He now gave less attention to the tree trunks and more to the ground immediately in front of the horse's nodding head. If he was being spied upon by aborigines it would be almost a waste of time trying to see them. And so it was that he saw lying beside a dead leaf a small black feather.

Without sign of haste, he dismounted, stretched himself, then squatted on his heels and rolled a cigarette. The feather was almost at his feet. While he rolled the cigarette he gazed intently at it, observing that it was not black but grey and that it was a bird's breast feather. Having lit the cigarette, he took up a stick and, with apparent idleness, began to draw figures on the sand; and when his pencil passed the feather it was taken up between the ball of his little finger and the edge of the palm of his hand. There was no knowing if a black spy was watching him from round the trunk of the nearest tree.

Along the base of the small feather was a dark-red stain. Blood on a feather! Blood and feathers!

Where Bony squatted was fully three miles from the blood-wood-tree beneath which Diana Lacy had met the unknown, where a man with feathers blood-dried to his feet had obliterated traces of the meeting, and it was improbable that a feather then detached from a foot could have been wind-blown to this place.

The discovery of this feather indicated that the man who was adopting the feathered feet method of leaving no tracks was careless or belittled Bony's bushcraft, because no aboriginal desirous of escaping pursuers would fail constantly to glance behind to be sure that no feather from his feather-encased feet was left to provide a plain clue to his passing.

Still, Bony was not satisfied that one feather gave proof that he was being constantly followed and kept under observation. Although he was instinctively convinced of it, he wanted definite proof.

Mounting again, he rode towards the gate spanning the road to Opal Town, for the first time during his career being the hunted not the hunter. With almost terrible relentlessness he had tracked criminals; and now he was being tracked with that same relentlessness. To escape observation he might gallop the horse, and so leave the unmounted tracker behind. But this would not prevent the tracker following the horse's tracks and eventually reading from the Book of the Bush the tale of Bony's movements. Added to this, was the probability that he was being tracked and observed by more than one spy.

Like every experienced bushman, Bony had acquired the mental trick of registering what the eyes note while the mind is otherwise occupied. Thus, while thinking of the surveillance of which he had become certain, he mentally noted that when he tossed aside the stub of his cigarette it followed the line of an arc to lie in the small shadow cast by a living buckbush.

Why was he being constantly trailed by the blacks? Why, unless in their own interests, or the interests of those directing them? Some connection between the trackers and the disappearance of Jeffery Anderson seemed almost certain.

After his visit to the Gordons, Bony was strongly of the opinion that neither mother nor son knew anything that might help to solve the mystery of Anderson's fate. Both were almost fanatically devoted to the ideal of maintaining the Kalchut tribe in its original state. It was likely that the ideal blinded them to things clearly to be seen by the more worldly-wise, among whom might well be members of the tribe itself. The woman had had no experience of the world beyond the bush, and the young man only that little gained when a boy at school. Like all idealists they would be easy victims to the wily, and who more wily than the aboriginal who had come in contact with the new civilization? Bony was now thinking that the odds favoured some other man than John Gordon being the one who had met Diana Lacy at the boundary fence.

There were so many possibilities that to dwell on them was hardly to put time to good use. The man she had met might have been a member of the Kalchut tribe. He might have been one of the Mackays of Mount Lester Station, or someone from Opal Town. That he wanted Bony to know nothing of the meeting was proved by the removal of all traces of it.

"Yes," he said softly to his horse. "There is ever so much more black than white in this affair. In fact, it might well be all black. There was Anderson, powerful and violent and suffering a sense of injustice after having been forced by Old Lacy to pay compensation to Inky Boy. There was Inky Boy whom Anderson flogged because of the loss of the rams through sheer laziness; Inky Boy would remember the flogging and soon forget the loss of the Karwir rams.

"The Gordons then take a hand in the business. Fearful

that publicity may attack their ideal, they restrain the natural instincts of the blacks to set out for justice; and so Nero and his people plan to act independently of the Gordons. One places the sign at Black Gate saying that old Sarah at Deep Well is dying, so that after the killing has been done excuse for the walkabout can be made to the Gordons, and trackers cannot be called on immediately. The position where I found that piece of green cable silk from Anderson's whip cracker goes far to support the theory that they tied him to a tree and flogged him as he had flogged Inky Boy."

Of the thought of the finding of the cable silk was born another, a thought that made Bony involuntarily rein back his horse and stare up at the brazen sky : If the trackers had been following and observing him ever since his arrival, they would know of his discovery of the odd tracks left on claypans by The Black Emperor. They would know, if not of the cable silk, then of his interest in the tree on which he had found it. If Anderson had been tied to that tree and flogged, and if subsequently Anderson had been killed while tied to it, or close beside it, they would know that he, Bony, was "getting warm."

If it were proved, therefore, that they were planning physical violence against him, it was proof that interest in him had turned to fear of him. They were subtle, these people, and by all accounts they still practised their ancient rites. He was allied to them through his mother's blood. He was susceptible to their magic, and with their magic they would strike at him.

Round came the horse to carry Bony back over her tracks. He now clearly remembered the flight of the cigarette stub that ended beside the buckbush. It was like a picture drawn on the canvas of his mind. On reaching the buckbush, he dismounted and with blazing eyes searched for the discarded cigarette end. It was not there. There were no human tracks, and yet the cigarette stub was no longer where he had dropped it only fifteen minutes before.

CHAPTER TWELVE

Powder of Bark

DESPITE the heat of the day, Sergeant Blake wore his uniform when he drove his car to meet Bony at the Karwir boundary gate. With his red face, grey hair and short clipped moustache, he appeared less at home in a motor-car than he would have been on the back of a horse on parade.

Almost exactly at twelve o'clock he braked the car before the white painted gate near which he saw Bony's horse neck-roped to a shady tree; Bony himself was standing beside a fire in the shade cast by two robust cabbage-trees. The Sergeant turned off the track and parked the machine in the shadow of a mulga.

The appearance this day of Detective-Inspector Napoleon Bonaparte shocked Sergeant Blake. Bony appeared less well-favoured than the usual half-caste stockman, and was obviously not his former smiling self. Without a preliminary greeting, Bony said:

"So Old Lacy telephoned you my message. I didn't think he would forget. Fill your own billy and make tea. We can talk as we eat."

"Good idea!" Blake agreed. "But what's happened? You look shaken by something or other."

The smile that came to Bony's face was forced.

"It is nothing," he lied. "A touch of the sun. I am taking

two aspirin tablets with my tea. Did you see Young Lacy's plane?"

"Yes. He was having trouble and landed at Pine Hut to adjust the carburettor, so he said. The ground south of the hut is quite good enough to make a landing there."

"Indeed! What time did you arrive there?"

"Half an hour back. Eleven-thirty. I stayed with him for ten minutes."

Bony dropped half a handful of tea into the water boiling in his quart-pot and let it boil for ten or twelve seconds before he removed it from the fire. Blake, sitting squarely on the ground, regarded the water in his billy, slowly stirring.

"The plane passed me shortly after ten," Bony said thoughtfully. "Young Lacy would have landed about ten-fifteen. You arrived there at eleven-thirty, so that Young Lacy had then spent an hour and a quarter adjusting the carburettor. Was he still fiddling with it when you left?"

"Oh no! They flew off to Opal Town before I left," Blake replied, wondering at Bony's extraordinary interest. He was, too, most uncomfortable in his tight-fitting tunic, and, when Bony suggested its removal, he took it off with a sigh of relief.

"I wonder why Young Lacy flew over this road to Opal Town instead of direct. Coming this way would add several miles to the journey."

Blake offered no comment. He failed to understand what possible implication lay behind the observation.

"Is there a telephone instrument at this Pine Hut?" inquired Bony.

"Yes. Pine Hut belongs to Meena Station. There was often one or more black stockmen stationed there, but not since the dry season began."

"Then there is communication with Meena homestead. Would one be able to raise Opal Town from Pine Hut?"

The Bone is Pointed

"No. The line is a private one, extending only between the hut and the homestead."

"O! When you reached Pine Hut, what were the Lacys doing?"

"Young Lacy was putting away tools, and the girl was sitting on a case in the shade of the short veranda fronting the hut."

"From my memory of Opal Town," Bony said slowly, "if Young Lacy flew direct from Karwir he would pass over the police station before landing, would he not?"

"Yes, that's so," agreed Blake. "He often does that—comes direct. Goes over the same way on his return flights."

"Now, I should like to know why he came this way. Do me a favour. I want your car to take me to this Pine Hut. You remain here and finish your lunch and look after my horse. I'll not be long away."

Before the Sergeant could speak, Bony was walking across to the car. It was a new machine and Blake was thankful when the detective drove it expertly to the track and expertly changed gears.

"Blest if I can understand him," Blake said aloud. He listened to the dwindling hum of the engine for several minutes until it faded into the silence of the quiet day. He again heard it, like the drone of a distant bee, an hour later, and when Bony rejoined him he said, a little huffily:

"Satisfied that my description of the telephone is correct?"

"My dear man, I didn't doubt your veracity. What I wished to ascertain was if Miss Lacy had rung up Meena homestead."

"Did she?"

"Yes, she did. Her tracks on the earthen floor below the instrument indicate that she spoke for some considerable time to someone at Meena."

"There appears nothing out of place in that," argued Blake. "Remember, they were forced down there. Miss Lacy naturally would occupy the time by talking with Mrs Gordon, or the son."

Bony sighed in his old mocking manner. He said:

"Without doubt, Sergeant, you are right. I am a wicked and suspicious detective, looking for evil where evil doesn't exist." Abruptly the cloud came back into his face, and he asked: "Tell me. Have you ever heard of a fellow named Horace?"

"Horace! Yes, Horace Maginnis keeps the pub in Opal Town."

"I mean the Roman Horace, the philosopher and poet."

"Oh! Yes, I've heard of him. He was a slave or something wasn't he? Kind of raised himself in the community."

"That was he. Horace once said, or wrote, I forget which: 'No matter whether you are high born or low born, there is a coffin waiting for you.'"

"Eh!" ejaculated the astonished Blake.

"Horace wasn't quite correct, Sergeant. Not all men, low born or even high born, are destined to be buried in a coffin. Have you got a new tracker?"

"Yes."

"What's his name?"

"Malluc."

"Young?"

"No. Malluc's getting on in life."

"Sack him."

"What for?"

"For the reason that at this time an elderly aboriginal is a dangerous man to have hanging about a police station. If you cannot get a young man, do without a tracker until I have completed this investigation."

Blake's eyes became big.

"If you say so. But what's the reason? Why don't you take me more into your confidence?"

Almost casually Bony examined the keen face and the

frosty eyes. Blake was a typical outback police administrator
of a huge district. He was naturally stern, and skin-bound
with red tape. When Bony spoke, his face was transformed by
a winning smile.

"I'd like to take you fully into my confidence," he said,
earnestly. "There is a lot to be said in favour of conferences,
but I don't know where this particular investigation is going
to lead me. I intend, of course, to follow it to the end, to find
out what became of Anderson, who killed him, if he was
killed, and how and why he was killed. You knew the man
and his record. You know all the people who knew him. And,
Sergeant, as I have said, I don't know where the investigation into his disappearance is going to lead me."

This somewhat vague generalization merely perplexed
Blake.

"Still——" he objected, and then stopped.

"I would be, indeed, grateful for your assistance, Sergeant,"
Bony said. "We belong to different branches of the Force,
and we unite only on one point, that of making justice swift
and sure. I will confide in you to a certain degree, but not
wholly because I don't know the end of the case. I may need
you more as a human being than as an official colleague.
Did you bring any letters for me?"

"I did. Sorry! I forgot them."

Blake leaned back to reach for his tunic, and from a pocket
produced two letters. Bony first opened one addressed in
handwriting.

"From my wife," he said, looking up. "She tells me that
she and our boys are all well and busy with their respective
careers. They live just out of Brisbane, at Banyo, you know.
Superintendent Browne has been out there. He told my wife
that I was expected back at headquarters on the seventh of
the month. He said, too, that Colonel Spendor is very angry
because I did not report, and that this time the Colonel in-
tends taking drastic action concerning my disobedience.

Browne asked her to write urgently and plead with me to return at once. I like Browne although he does not understand me; he persists in his belief that I am a mere policeman—if you will excuse me, Sergeant. And now for this official letter. I will read it to give you an insight into what I have to put up with."

Blake wanted to smile and dared not. Secretly he was a rebel against the authority that kept him roped to a place like Opal Town. Bony began to read the typescript he had withdrawn from the long official envelope:

Ninth October—Prior to your assignment it was made clear to you that the exigency of the Department required you to report back not later than October the seventh. Former latitude extended to you could not in this instance be granted. Therefore, as from the seventh instant you are granted leave of absence without pay until October the twenty-first. Should you fail to report for duty on or before that date, the Chief Secretary will be advised to terminate your appointment.

Blake's face was serious.

"Better report on time," he said. "You have only six days of your leave left."

"But, my dear Blake," argued Bony, becoming at once grandiloquent. "If I had thrown up my investigations at the orders of headquarters, how many of them should I have successfully finalized? Why, about three per cent. The Commissioner has sacked me at least five times for refusing to relinquish an investigation. Then, I have had to give a detailed explanation and get myself reinstated without loss of pay. Since this present investigation will not be concluded in time to permit me to report on the twenty-first I shall again be sacked, and again have to trouble myself to get reinstated. One would think that no successful investigator of crime would have to suffer such pin-pricks. However, we will forget it. Did you make any further progress with the inquiry into the local sale of green cable silk?"

Again Blake wanted to smile but dared not.

"A little," he replied. "Whiting says that he has not sold green cable silk to the Gordons for a very long time, and that he doesn't remember ever having sold cable silk, green or any other colour, to the Mackays. What's the strength of this cable silk?"

"The tensile strength?"

"No. You know what I mean."

"I will tell you that, and several other things, for I think I could rely on you should the necessity to do so ever arise. I found a wisp of green cable silk adhering to the trunk of a tree at about the height of a man's head. It was detached from the cracker of Anderson's stockwhip, and I think it was so detached when he was about to thrash a man as he once thrashed Inky Boy. Immediately afterwards he was killed.

"The situation of the tree indicates the approximate locality where Anderson was killed—always assuming he was killed. It might well have been he who was tied to the tree trunk and flogged to death with his own whip. I have been prevented from making a minute examination of the tree trunk, and the locality, by the constant surveillance maintained by one or more aboriginals who have adopted the blood and feathers method of leaving no tracks. Do you think you could get me two dogs?"

"What sort of dogs?"

"Mongrel cattle dogs for preference. I must become a huntsman. Could you bring me out two?"

"Yes, I could borrow them from the butcher, I think. When will you want them?"

"I'll let you know. In a day or so. By the way, how long have you been stationed here?"

"Eleven years. Ten years too long."

"I have been instrumental in having two senior police

officers stationed in outback districts promoted to eastern districts. If you want a thing done, remember always go to the wife of the man who can do it. Who was the officer stationed here before you?"

"Inspector Dowling, now stationed at Cairns. He was here eight years."

"Oh. He won't do. Find out for me who was stationed here thirty-six-seven-eight years ago. The officer at that time is certainly now retired, but he may not be dead. If he is alive, get in touch with him, and ask him if he remembers an Irish woman, probably cook, employed at Karwir. Got that?"

"Yes."

"Then that will be all to-day. Have the two dogs ready to bring out here when I call for them. Be discreet."

For some time after Blake had left, Bony squatted beside his lunch fire smoking the eternal cigarettes. Now and then he moved to ease his legs, but not once since the policeman had left him did he look up or about. He knew, because his scalp and back informed him of it, that he was being watched, and he thought he knew the position of the watcher by the constant chattering of two or three galahs in a tree somewhere beyond his horse.

He was well aware that to pursue the watcher amid the close cover provided by the mulga forest would be fruitless, and that a search for his tracks would also be fruitless. Squatted there in the shade cast by the cabbage-trees, he was assailed by temptation. He was probably facing grave danger to his life; and he knew that there could be no possible reflection on his career if he at once threw up this case and obeyed the order to return to Brisbane. By refusing to abandon this investigation, he might well be dismissed from the service, for on former occasions when he had disobeyed a similar order the Chief Commissioner himself had added the threat of dismissal in his own handwriting. There was nothing personal in the typewritten communication he had just received.

Yet he knew he would never succumb to the temptation. Pride was his weapon; his reputation his armour. He would go forward even if he lost his official position, even if he lost his life. Once he failed to solve a case, once he was conscious of failure, it would be the beginning of the end for him. And for Marie, his wife, and for the boys, too. For they and he owed rank and social standing only to his invincible pride.

This day he was very different from the man who walked the earth as Detective-Inspector Bonaparte. Within Bony's soul constantly warred the opposing influences planted therein by his white father and his black mother, and according to external influences of the moment, so did the battle favour one side or the other. To the fact of his alliance with the aborigines he had blinded Colonel Spendor, many of his colleagues, and many people like the Lacys and the Gordons. But he had not blinded these Kalchut blacks. They knew him, knew that never with the hammer of pride and the file of success would he break the racial bond. Their blood flowed through his veins. Their beliefs and their superstitions were implanted in the very marrow of his bones, and all his advanced education could not make him other than what he was.

And now his soul was swiftly becoming ruled by his mother and her people, the rule hastened by the Kalchut tribe. Their shadow had fallen upon him, a half-caste, when it would have failed utterly to touch a white man. A white man would never have suspected himself of being watched and tracked by people who were never seen and who left no sign of their movements on ground that showed the imprint even of scorpions.

Yes, they could kill him as it seemed certain they were about to do. They could demand his body and take it. He could never be free of the blood, never escape them. Ah—but he could! He could escape them before they struck. He could return to Brisbane, and there rant and rave at being ordered to return and so claim that he was officially prevented from successfully completing this case. Yes, he could do that. But he himself would know it for an excuse. Defeated by fear, within six months he and his would become bush nomads. Detective-Inspector Napoleon Bonaparte would indeed become poor old Bony. Better death than that. Compared with that what would be death?

His unseen trackers had retrieved his discarded cigarette ends, because they had once been one with his person. No longer was his trackers' attitude towards him a negative one. They had resolved on action. They, or someone who controlled them, determined to deal with him, to remove him because he was dangerous. And he, being what he was, was open to receive their magic with which they would kill him.

They were preparing to point the bone at him.

The act of pointing the bone was, of course, merely a theatrical show, having a psychological effect both on the bone-pointers and the victim. The power to kill lay not in the outward show but in the mental willing to death conducted by the executioners. Bony knew that the pointing bone could be used by any male member of nearly all the Australian tribes, but its success in killing depended on the mental power of the pointers. If the victim could conquer inherited superstitions, and then if his mind were stronger than the minds of the bone-pointers, he might escape death long enough for his relations to find out who was pointing the bone and at once exact vengeance.

Once the bone was pointed at him, Bony, his escape from death would depend on his ability to resist the minds willing death long enough for him to finish his job and return to Brisbane where the white men's influences, plus the service of a hypnotist, would free him of the magic.

A light, cold finger ran its tip up Bony's spine and touched the roots of his hair. The pointing bone had killed that Dieri

man away at the back of Lake Frome. Bony's mind recalled
the fellow's terror-stricken face on which was written the
awful knowledge of his doom. Five days he had lived before
he died in convulsions—the eagle's claws buried in his kidneys and the bones piercing his liver and heart. There had
been that half-caste just over the southern Queensland border,
he who had run away with a chief's favourite lubra. A
pointed stick had been aimed at him, and he had taken two
months to waste away to death despite a white doctor, a
squatter and his wife, and Bony. The doctor had said it was
the Barcoo sickness.

Bony's eyes closed. Doubless it was the heat of the afternoon or, perhaps, the smoke of the fire. Or was it? Bony's
subconscious mind urged him to stand up, urged him to race
to his horse and ride like the wind to Opal Town to hire a
car to take him to the distant railway. He ought not to feel the
need to sleep. He never slept during the daylight hours. He
should not want to sleep now when his mind was so occupied
with this case, and so influenced by the menace crowding
close.

Was the idea of sleep being suggested to his mind?

For five or six long minutes Bony fought the demon of
panic, while his motionless body rested on his heels. Little
beads of moisture glistened on his broad forehead and at the
corners of his mouth. His will eventually beat down the panic.
Now he knew that he could and would pretend to submit
to the suggestion to sleep. Uncertainty in the immediate
future would be unbearable.

In simulation Bony rose to stretch his arms and to yawn.
He made a little hole in the soft sand of the ground to take
his hip and settled himself so that he lay on his left side facing
the horse, his head resting on his left forearm and his right
hand tucked away under his body, the fingers firmly curved
about the butt of his automatic pistol. His eyes partially
closed, and his mind at work countering the suggestion to

sleep, he maintained a steady watch on the dozing horse, while listening to the chattering galahs.

The minutes passed in slow procession. The invisible birds screamed once and then flew to another tree to continue their chattering in which now was certain anger. Then the horse awoke to toss her head, then to stand without movement and to stare at a point beyond Bony's range of vision.

Slowly now she began to move the angle of her head, and to Bony it was obvious that she was watching something moving, something that was approaching him. Then he saw it. A tall black figure slowly became detached from the trunks of a tree standing in shadow. The man was entirely naked save for the masses of feathers about his feet.

It was Wandin. His hair was glued with clay and encircled with a ring fashioned from canegrass. He carried no weapon, neither waddy nor spear. He carried, like any one might carry a saucer filled with tea, a curved piece of bark. When he entered the sunlight Bony saw clearly his face fixed by the expression of hatred, his eyes alive like black opals.

How carefully he carried the piece of bark in his right hand! It might have been filled to the brim with liquid, but, as Bony knew, it contained not liquid but powder. Without sound, the aboriginal drew near and nearer to the recumbent man so sorely tempted to shoot with the weapon he kept hidden beneath his body. What Wandin was going to do could be prevented now, but not for always. What he did not achieve now another would achieve in the future.

And so Wandin came to stand close to Bony. His right hand carried the bark over Bony's body and tilted it so that the powder fell in a mist upon him. That Bony continued inactive, that he did not spring to his feet and shoot down this sorcerer carrying out a further step in the boning, said much for the half-caste's courage and power of will. He began to tremble when Wandin retreated, but gave no sign that he was awake.

So the blacks had been tracking him for weeks, and intuition had again served him well. The Kalchut were behind the disappearance of Jeffery Anderson, and knowing Bony to be a danger to them, they were preparing to remove him.

Well, they could get on with their boning. He would fight it with all the strength of his mind, and again he would triumph over his aboriginal ancestry as he had so often done before. He would put on the armour of the white man and carry the weapons of mockery and cynicism. By the shade of the Little Corporal himself! Was he a savage? Was he an ignorant nomad of the bush? Was he a child to suffer palpitation of the heart because a black ghost had appeared in broad day? Was he a mental weakling to suffer evil born in lesser minds, to be frightened away from this absorbing investigation by the mental power of a people free of the curse laid upon Adam?

He pretended to awake. He sat up, stared about, scrambled to his feet and gathered sticks with which to replenish the fire. He knew the worst now, and now he felt strong.

CHAPTER THIRTEEN

Pointed Bones and Eagle's Claws

THE most potent magic is that brought from a great distance.

When the world was young, when the white men, probably, were gug-guggering like apes, an old Pittongu man left the Murchison Range to travel far to the north. Like a knight of a much later age, he was well armed, carrying with him stone axes, stone knives, barbed spears, and a particularly deadly magic called *maringilitha*.

One day, when well forward on his journey, he dropped some of the *maringüitha* which, on striking the ground, caused a great explosion. The old Pittongu (bat) man was blown into dust, as were all his weapons, and on the place arose a great stone surrounded by very many little stones. Into the big and all the little stones entered the bat man's *maringilitha* magic, so that these stones became of great commercial value to the tribes who owned the land, the Worgaia and the Gnanji.

The most daring members of these tribes from time to time collected little stones and sang into them their own particular curses, then wrapped each stone in paper bark and tied the bark with human hair string. To all the tribes far south and east this new form of magic, called *mauia*, came to be considered one of the most potent forms of magic that could be employed against an enemy.

Several of these stones had in the course of inter-tribal trade come into the possession of the Kalchut tribe, and were safely kept, with the sacred articles used in initiation ceremonies, in the secret storehouse situated somewhere among the hills east of Meena Lake.

Previous to Bony's visit to the Gordons, Nero and several of his older men had travelled to the storehouse, from which they had taken one of the *mauia* stones and the pointing bone apparatus. Subsequently Wandin had set out with the *mauia* stone in the dilly-bag suspended from his neck, to await a favourable opportunity of "opening" Bony's body that the magic of the pointed bones might more easily enter it.

Seen only by the galahs, he had watched the meeting of Bony and Sergeant Blake, and then, when the policeman had departed, he had sat with his arms rested on his hunched knees and his forehead pressing down upon his arms, and willed Bony to sleep. Thinking he had achieved this, he scraped particles off the *mauia* stone on to a piece of bark, carried the bark to the recumbent form of the half-caste, and spilled over him the dust of the magic stone.

Having then retreated to a secret camp, he made a fire and placed on it the piece of bark, watching to see how the bark would burn. It burned slowly, telling Wandin that the prospective victim would die slowly.

Out of the tribe's sight that night he and his chief held a conference about a little fire. It was decided to perform the boning during the night of the full moon, when, it was thought, the dreaded Mindye, so fearful of the light, would tarry at his home.

Thus, when the full orb of the copper-coloured moon rose above the sharp rim of the uplands east of the lake, Nero and Wandin stole from the camp, regarded fearfully by the men and the women who suspected a deed of magic was to be committed this night. They passed the Meena homestead almost immediately below the veranda on which John Gordon sat reading to his mother who was knitting. On went Nero and Wandin, their naked feet making no sound, their black bodies covered only with trousers, until they stopped before a tree killed by lightning and never since used by the nesting birds.

It was Nero who knelt before the tree and Wandin who climbed on his broad back to reach a hand into a great hole in the trunk. From this hole he brought out the pointing bone apparatus which he thrust into his dilly-bag.

Neither man spoke and, turning away, they began the journey to the secret camp. Nero walked first, taking unusual care never to touch a fallen stick with his feet, careful to follow claypans as much as possible, Wandin walking in his tracks so that it would appear that only one man walked abroad this night.

The moon had reached the meridian when they came to the road at a place midway between the Karwir boundary gate and Pine Hut. Nero selected a claypan crossing on which the tracks of motors were hardly discernible in broad daylight. It was two o'clock in the morning when they arrived at the secret camp beside the banked fire. Nero gave his orders. One broke down the banked fire and added fuel, and on it placed an old rusty billycan. The other brought a kangaroo, the hind feet of which were tied together.

"Cut his throat and bleed him on to the bark," instructed the chief in the Kalchut language.

This the second fellow did, using a curved sheet of bark already fouled with congealed blood. He and his companion were entirely naked save for their feet that were encased with feathers. Obeying another order given by Nero, the man who had replenished the fire brought a striped linen mattress case still containing a large quantity of feathers.

By now both Wandin and Nero had removed their trousers and had taken a dust bath. They sat on the ground, and, when the bark carrying the fresh blood was brought to them, each in turn plunged his feet into the blood. Then they sat together with their feet buried among the feathers in the mattress. Tea was made and given them in jam tins instead of pannikins, and, in order that their "insides" might be strong to project magic, they ate strips of kangaroo flesh, raw and bloody. Said Nero:

"Where that Bony feller camped to-night?"

"He's camped on the veranda of Green Swamp hut. He always camps on the veranda, never inside the hut."

"You pick up any more cigarette ends?"

"Not for many days. Bony feller knows we picked them up. He's a cunning feller. So he puts his cigarette ends in his pocket and burns them when he makes a fire."

"What Bony feller do all day?" continued Nero.

"He track about sandhills and then all along both sides of boundary fence crossing the Channels."

Wandin chuckled, saying:

"Bony feller won't track much longer. Before the moon grows round again he'll be dead. The *mauia* bark said so when I burned it."

The eyes of the two camped here flashed whitely in the firelight.

"What you do—bone him?" one asked, his voice fearful.

Nero nodded, replying:

"Bony feller come to know too much. Presently he get to know more. That's no good to the Kalchut. When me and Wandin gone, you two will lie down and sleep and forget us, eh?"

It was an order, and the campers nodded understandingly. Then Nero and Wandin withdrew their feet from the mattress and detached from the masses about them all those feathers not securely glued. Great care was exercised in this; and then, satisfied that none would become detached from those remaining, they arose and walked into the moonlit night, Wandin following his chief.

Eventually the pair arrived at one of the depressions or channels on which no herbage or scrub grew, and they advanced boldly along this depression until the netted barrier was reached. They were most careful in climbing the barrier, both pausing to be sure that no feather had been detached by the wire barbs. And so, presently, they arrived at the western extremity of the high ground on which were the Green Swamp hut and well.

Now the moon's light fell strongly upon the front of the hut, glinted in bars on the iron roof, fell upon the motionless figure lying on the veranda floor covered with a blanket. Nero and Wandin crouched on the warm moonlit ground less than two hundred yards from the sleeping Bony. With his hands Nero pushed the sand before him into a long ridge to serve as a protection to him and his companion, and to prevent their victim from dreaming of the ancestral camps in which lived their respective mothers, for such a dream would tell him who the bone pointers were.

On their side of the sand ridge Wandin buried the six bones and the eagle's claws of the boning apparatus. Nero from his dilly-bag took a ball of porcupine-grass gum and proceeded to knead it into the form of a plate. Having done this he took from his dilly-bag a full twenty of Bony's discarded cigarette ends, placed these on the gum plate and then turned up the circular edge to enclose them into a completed ball. With the ball of gum, containing matter that had once been one with the victim, on the ground between them, the two men crouched over it and began to "sing" it with their magic.

"Bony feller may you die," muttered Nero.

"Bony feller may you die sure and slow like the bark said," muttered Wandin.

"May you groan like a bull-frog."

"May your liver bleed and be drowned in its blood."

"May your bones become like sand."

"May you sick when you eat."

"May you be hungry and still sick when you eat."
"May you howl like a dingo."
"May you groan like a bull-frog."
"May you sit down and roll on the ground."
"May you die thirsty."
"May you die with blood in your mouth."

Each man spat upon the gum ball. Nero dug from the ground the buried boning apparatus—five sharply pointed little bones attached to one end of a long length of human hair string, and one small pointed bone and two eagle's claws fastened to the other end of the string. And while Wandin repeated all the curses they had sung into the gum ball, Nero forced the point of each bone and the tip of the claws into the ball, so that claws and bones might take from the "sung" gum ball the curses to be transmitted to the victim. Thus was the evil magic sung into the cigarette stubs, that once had been in contact with the victim, to be sent through the bones and the claws into the body opened to receive it by the *mauia* stone dust.

Nero passed the eagle's claws to Wandin, himself retaining the five pointed bones. He knelt facing the sleeping Bony, and Wandin took a similar position behind him. With the human hair string connecting the five bones and the single bone and the claws, as well as connecting the two men, they pointed bones and claws at Bony and solemnly repeated all their curses. So from the tips of bones and claws their magic sped through the air to enter the body of the man asleep.

For a full quarter-hour they repeated their curses, after which Nero placed the boning apparatus in his dilly-bag and then gravely handed to Wandin the ball of gum in which were embedded the cigarette ends.

Wandin rose to his feet to walk away in a wide circular course that took him to the rear of the hut. A soundless black shadow casting on the ground a shadow as black, he cautiously moved round the hut wall, reached the end of the veranda, edged close and closer to the sleeping Bony, and deposited the gum ball on the ground a few inches from his head.

As it had come to the hut, so the shadow departed to rejoin the chief of the Kalchut tribe.

CHAPTER FOURTEEN

The Bomb

IT was the third Friday in the month, a day when Old Lacy sat on the bench in the small courthouse at Opal Town, and this particular day in early summer was windless and heavy with heat. The birds inhabiting the vicinity of the Karwir homestead drowsed in the bloodwoods lining the creek, their calls and their chatterings stilled by the necessity of keeping wide their beaks. All the morning the musical ring of hammer on iron and anvil had issued from the blacksmith's shop, but this, too, ceased when the cook beat upon his iron triangle calling the hands to lunch. The ensuing silence was disturbed only by an occasional blowfly beyond the fly-netting of the long veranda where Diana Lacy sat in a lounge chair pretending to read.

The luncheon table had been prepared on this same veranda—for two. Already the house gong had sounded, and the girl's slim fingers beat an impatient tattoo on the arm of her chair. Except for this nervous betrayal she appeared calm and, as usual, mistress of herself. Yet she was feeling slight excitement as she awaited the person who was to lunch with her.

When the door at the far end of the veranda was opened, the drumming of her fingers instantly ceased, memory still vivid of that occasion when she had first met Mr Napoleon Bonaparte at the horse yards. Her blue eyes with the violet

irises continued to stare at the printed page, and did not
glance upward to meet the eyes of the Karwir guest until he
came to stand before her.

"I hope I have not delayed lunch over long, Miss Lacy,"
Bony said, gravely. "It was a little difficult to take the first
step from under the shower."

Almost impersonally she studied him: his suit of tussore
silk, his white canvas shoes, the entire polished grooming of
him. It was as though her mind was still commanded by what
she had been reading. Before rising, she said:

"You have caused no inconvenience, Mr Bonaparte. The
weather dictates a cold lunch. My father and brother have
gone to Opal Town to-day, so you will have to put up with
my demands to be amused. Will you take that chair?"

"Thank you."

Bony assisted the girl to be seated at the table, before he
took his place opposite her and then moved the vase of flowers
lightly to one side.

"I met Mr Lacy and your brother on the road this morning," he told her. "Evidently your father prefers a car to an
aeroplane. He takes a great interest in court work, I understand."

"Yes. He likes to feel he's a dictator. I have often sat in
court and watched him. He fines all culprits two pounds and
costs, and, should one attempt to argue, he shouts him down.
I suppose you are accustomed to being a dictator all the time."

"A dictator! Why, Miss Lacy, I am the victim of several
dictators. Colonel Spendor, my wife and my children are to
be numbered among them."

"But what of your victims? Don't they regard you as a kind
of dictator?"

Bony smiled. "Their nemesis, perhaps," he corrected, adding
as an afterthought: "And then only when they've been apprehended. Before being apprehended they think they are the
dictators, issuing orders for me to follow. Then they reveal

astonishment when they are informed that, as the old song puts it, their day's work is done."

For a little while they gave attention to the food, and then Diana, setting down her knife and fork, said, slightly frowning:

"You know, you puzzle me. I've heard you say that you never fail to unravel a mystery. Is that really so, or were you boasting?"

"Since I became a member of the Criminal Investigation Branch I must have conducted at least a hundred investigations," Bony replied. 'Some were quite trivial; several were very involved. No, I have not yet failed to complete satisfactorily any case I have taken up."

"Do you really think you will succeed in completing this one?"

"I can see no reason why I should not."

Again Diana gave attention to her plate. She did not look at Bony when she put her next question.

"May I assume from that that you are—what shall I say? —well forward in your investigation?"

"Er—hardly. As a matter of fact, I have made very little progress. This disappearance case, taken up so long after it actually began, is proving to be most difficult. Even so, I see no reason why I should not succeed in finding out what happened to Jeffery Anderson. Success depends only on the factor of time."

"And luck?"

Bony considered, Diana regarding him with her eyes turned slightly upward as her face was turned down to her plate. She was very much mistress of herself and inclined to underestimate the man she could not bowl out socially.

"And luck," Bony repeated. "Yes, I suppose a little depends on luck, if coincidence may be regarded as providing an investigator with luck. I think luck plays only a small part, certainly a much smaller part than the mistakes committed by the criminal. Even in my present investigation, I have been favoured by one bad mistake made by someone."

"One bad mistake!" the girl echoed. "What was that?"

"As I have said, time is the only practical factor on the side of the investigator, Miss Lacy," Bony went on, gently ignoring her inquiry. "Given unlimited time, no investigator need fail."

Perhaps Diana suspected a trap, or perhaps she feared rebuff if she pressed her question concerning the mistake he mentioned.

"The sole basis of my reputation for uninterrupted successes is my inability to leave an investigation once I have begun it," Bony said. "I suppose I have conducted at least a hundred investigations as I think I mentioned. The majority of them were completed within a week or two. Some, however, occupied my attention for many months, eleven months being spent on one. I hope you will not become bored with me should I have to spend eleven months on this Anderson case."

She raised her head and actually smiled at him. It was as though strain had relaxed. She said:

"Eleven months is a long time, Mr Bonaparte. Wouldn't your wife and children come to miss you?"

"Alas! I fear that my unfortunate wife, and my no less unfortunate children, have formed the habit of missing me. Still, were I a sailor they would be even more unfortunate. Then, of course, there is another side to these prolonged absences from home. We are an affectionate family, owing probably to the effect of absence on the human heart."

"Now you are being cynical."

"They say that the cynic is one who never sees a good quality in a man, and who never fails to see a bad one," said Bony, smiling. "That being so, I am no cynic."

Diana appeared to think the conversation was drifting, for she said:

"From what you tell me you seem to have a free hand with regard to the time taken in your investigations."

"Yes. Oh yes! I see to that. Punctually at the end of the first fortnight that I am away from home my wife writes imploring me to return, and my immediate superior demands to know what I am doing. Then, after the first month, Colonel Spendor writes to announce that he has given me the sack, the word 'sack' being his. Having received the sack, I then have to interview the Commissioner and have myself reinstated without loss of pay. Colonel Spendor is the kind of man who likes to sack me, and then likes to feel the glow of generosity when reinstating me."

"From what you, say, Colonel Spendor must be more or less like my father."

"More, Miss Lacy, much more. Pardon me for seeming familiarity, but you and I have something in common. We both know how to manage human lions for their own good."

Bony's effort to warm the girl towards him failed. The barrier she had erected between them refused to give to his assault. For a second or two he gave attention to his food, while his mind worked at this problem of the immovable barrier.

That his reading of this charming Australian girl was at fault he declined to admit. She was a little white aristocrat; he an Australian half-caste. It was not, he felt sure, a sense or knowledge of racial superiority that formed the unbreakable barrier, else she would not have been here sitting at table with him. He had never seen her smile with real warmth, nor detected warmth in her voice. And yet she was warm, a chip off the old block. No, it was not racial superiority that had built the barrier. There was an entirely different explanation, possibly knowledge of secret events, or a suspicion of them, which affected her or those to whom she was loyal.

Loyalty! That was it. This vivid young woman was opposing him because of loyalty to someone his presence at Karwir might ultimately affect. There was no hint of admiration in his eyes when he raised them and spoke to his hostess.

"I like lions, human lions," he told her. "When one has removed a lion's skin one finds a new-shorn lamb. My chief blasts and damns me, his face scarlet, his eyes globes of ice. He shouts. Yes, he likes to shout. He shouts at me, telling me to get out of his sight. He loves to tell me I'm no policeman. He tells me I am a rebel who ought to be shot for insubordination. But, Miss Lacy, he has never said I was a fool. Tell me, please, whom it was you met at the bloodwood-tree on the boundary fence that day I arrived here."

"Whom did I—I beg your pardon?"

Bony's voice remained mildly conversational when he repeated the question. He had timed his bomb to explode at the close of luncheon, and now he leaned forward over the table and offered her a cigarette from his open case. Her gaze centred on his guileless eyes, her hand gropingly extracted a cigarette and then a match flared and was held in service. She accepted the service before rising indignation took her to her feet to stare at him, as he, too, stood up.

"I consider you to be impertinent," she cried. "You ask a question smacking of innuendo."

"Indeed no, Miss Lacy. I asked a quite straightforward question. I'm sorry, but I must press for the answer."

"I refuse to give it, Mr Bonaparte."

"After that meeting between you and someone who came from Meena, the blacks most thoroughly wiped away all traces of it," Bony said, well satisfied with the effects of his bomb. There was less anger than mortification in her eyes. "The action of the blacks indicates, or appears to indicate, that either you or the person you met desired that I should not know of the meeting. Apparently the object of the meeting was a secret to be kept at all costs. Were I sure that the meeting was a quite harmless one between, let us say, two lovers, I should certainly not even have mentioned it. Since I am not sure, I must continue to press you for the answer to my question."

Now anger held full sway in the blue eyes, and furiously the girl cried:

"I still refuse to answer your question. It does not concern you."

After this declaration they stood on either side of the table, Diana with her head thrown back, her breast quickly rising and falling, her eyes blazing; Bony passive, his eyes lakes of blue ice. He wished ardently to break her, to smash down the barrier she had erected between them, to know her true self.

"Might it be that your answer would implicate the person you met in the disappearance of Jeffery Anderson?" he said in an effort to obtain an admission of the name of the person she had met. "Recent events point to the fact that the people who wiped away traces of the meeting have come to fear me for what I will discover concerning Anderson's fate."

"You are quite wrong. I will not answer a question that concerns my private life only. Whom I meet is my affair, not yours."

Bony sighed in mock defeat and, bowing stiffly, turned and walked away to the far veranda door. Having placed his hand on the brass knob, he left the door and returned to the girl's side. She stared up at him, her breath held, her lips parted. She heard him say, his voice still provokingly calm:

"The next time you use the telephone at Pine Hut, remember to refrain from making in the dust on the note shelf many little crosses."

"Crosses! Little crosses!"

"Little crosses, Miss Lacy. When I was very young I used to place little crosses at the bottom of letters I wrote to a young woman."

And then swiftly, without another word, he turned, crossed the veranda to the door, leaving her speechless.

Half an hour later she saw him, dressed in his old bush clothes, leave the house and pass out through the garden gate. She was then in the garden, and through a gap in the canegrass hedge she saw him go into the office, come out with the key of Anderson's room, unlock its door and enter. He was there only a minute, and then he returned to the office where, presumably, he left the key. Ten minutes after that she saw him leading his horse to the Green Swamp Paddock gate, saw him mount on its far side and ride away along the road to Opal Town and the boundary.

Even then she was still biting her lips in anger.

CHAPTER FIFTEEN

The Time Factor

BONY rode away from Karwir with a shadow in his eyes and a faintly grim smile about his mouth. He had paid the call at the homestead only for the purpose of learning a little more about the meeting of the riders of the white and brown horses, knowing that Old Lacy and his son would be absent at Opal Town.

Like almost every man living in solitude, Bony found pleasure in talking aloud to his horse. And now he said to her:

"Making crosses at the end of a letter, indeed! As though I, Napoleon Bonaparte, would ever have done such a thing, when I could and did pen poetry about my love. Ah, youth is Life, but age is Triumph, triumph over Life, mocking youth and tormenting it. If you possessed a human brain, my dear Kate, you would agree with me."

The mare softly snorted, tossed her head and increased her pace. It was as though she did understand and appreciate her rider's confidences. Bony continued:

"I suppose, Kate, that hunting evil-doers and associating with detectives and policemen have gone far to making me a fearful liar. Who was it who said: 'Liars are verbal forgers'? Hum! That hints at crime. I must tread more circumspectly else I become a moral criminal. Still, I suppose there are occasions when the end does justify the means. Those imaginary crosses drawn in the dust thick on the telephone instrument at Pine Hut did produce a result, a negative one possibly, but one which my imagination can make positive. That very nice and wholesome young woman, who actually thinks she is smarter than poor old Bony, answered my question so clearly by refusing to answer it at all—with words. She admitted that she had met John Gordon at the boundary fence, that she loves him and he her; and she now thinks that she unconsciously drew little crosses while talking to him on the telephone to Meena.

"The odds greatly favour that meeting being arranged between lovers for the purpose of a little innocent love-making. We know, Kate, that Old Lacy thinks he's a wise father, thinks that his daughter hasn't a lover and never had a lover. We know that he desires his daughter to marry well, that is to say, to marry a man of position in the social and financial worlds. Doubtless the girl knows that too. Yet she falls in love with a man who is nobody in the social and financial worlds. Not her fault, of course. John Gordon has much to commend him to any woman, and a very great deal to commend him to me and to people like me. He is respected, and admirable in all things except wealth.

"Like me, the girl is a real lion tamer. I am sadly mistaken if she couldn't tame Old Lacy sufficiently to make him consent to her alliance with John Gordon. But, Kate, she is not yet of age; and there is the possibility that she so loves the old lion that she could not bring herself to desert him by marrying Gordon. She may argue that, being only twenty, she can wait several years; for her father is over seventy and his life may end before she is thirty.

"I wonder, now. I wonder if I have entered a maze, if I have imagined that the traces of the meeting were wiped away to prevent *my* seeing them, when the object might really have been to prevent *anyone* seeing them, anyone who could have read their meaning and talked about the meeting. If that is so, then the meeting can have no connection with the disappearance of Jeffery Anderson. If that is so, then the disappearance is all black, and to the blacks only can I look for a solution of the mystery."

Oblivious of the hot sunlight striking upon his left cheek, neck and hand, Bony was carried at a quick walk over the slightly undulating plain country towards the far distant mulga forest through which passed the netted boundary fence. The depressions were filled to the brim with mirage water, as though this world of colourful space were composed of treeless islands dotted upon a vast lake. The gum-trees marking the creek and the Karwir homestead had already risen above the "water" to become waving coconut and date palms, and now were swiftly being dwarfed by distance. Now there emerged from the "water" ahead to cross an "island" a shape like that of a beetle on stilts. The beetle sank again into the "water" with a deep humming, finally emerging to crawl up upon the "island" on which Bony himself was the castaway mariner. He urged the horse off the track, when the car halted and from it issued Old Lacy's booming voice.

"Was hoping you were going to stay the night, Bony," he said, before clambering out stern first. Then, when he had reached the horse's side and was resting a great hand on its neck: "I was looking forward to a pitch with you. What's taking you away?"

"Duty, Mr Lacy. I called at the homestead to inspect Anderson's whips again. Miss Lacy provided a delightful luncheon. Now I have to get back to work without having the pleasure of spending the evening with you, because my chief has written to the effect that if I have not reported back at headquarters by to-morrow I shall be sacked."

"Sacked! Sacked!"

Bony smiled with his face only and nodded impressively.

"I was given a fortnight to investigate this case—as though I could complete it in two weeks. Now, because I have not given it up and reported as instructed, my chief is angry and threatens the sack. Of course, Mr Lacy, I shouldn't dream of giving it up until I have concluded it to my own satisfaction."

"Of course you wouldn't," agreed the old man, his eyes gleaming. "And don't you worry about the sack. I'll have something to say about that, if it happens. How are you fixed for rations and horse feed at the hut?"

"Plenty of everything, thanks. Oh, but if you could send out some meat."

"Right! I'll send it to-morrow. That do?"

"Very well. And by the way, would you lend me your microscope? I'd take great care of it. I may want it. I hope I shall."

"Yes, too right! The lad can fly it and the meat out some time to-morrow. Anything else, now?"

"No, I think that will be all."

The old man smiled in his grim manner and stepped back from the horse.

"Don't you let your boss take you away from here until you can tell us what happened to Jeff Anderson," he urged. "And don't you worry about getting the sack. I can make things jump around down in Brisbane when I want to."

He went backward into the car, slammed the door and waved a hand—a man whom age could not dominate nor men subdue.

Bony was further delayed, this time for half an hour, by an ant battle, so that when he arrived at the boundary gate he saw beyond it Sergeant Blake and his car. The Sergeant had been asked to leave Opal Town half an hour after the chairman of the bench. Blake straightened up from the task of making tea, two dogs tethered to trees having announced the arrival of the horseman.

"So you managed the dogs, Sergeant?"

"They're pretty rangy and only good for chasing rabbits," Blake said, doubtfully.

"They will suit my purpose."

"Your trouble will be keeping 'em with you."

"Presently you will see how I make a dog stick closer to me than a poor relation. You know, Blake, when making my report on the termination of this case I am going to give you an excellent notice." The Sergeant grinned with quick pleasure. "If there is a man I like better than a good colleague it is a man with a swift perception of the needs of the moment. You have the gift of making good tea when tea is to be valued like a costly gift."

The smile faded from the weather-beaten face, and the short grey moustache settled again into its official angles. Bony, having brought the cup of his quart-pot, filled it from the billy and helped himself to the sugar in the Sergeant's tin. Blake fell to loading his pipe and watching Bony manufacture cigarettes. He offered no comment about perception of the needs of the moment.

"This case is becoming increasingly interesting," Bony said, with a slight pause between each word. "Assigned to this case, any one of the world's great investigators would have become hopelessly bushed, literally and practically. It is an investigation to be successfully conducted only by me, on several counts. I am, of course, familiar with drawing-rooms, but they are not my natural background. This world of the bush is my background, my natural element. The bush is like a giant book offering to me plain print and the language I understand. The book is so big, however, that I require sometimes a great deal of time to find in it the passages interesting me at the moment. And finally, as I think I have told you, time is my greatest asset; without it I am as ordinary men."

"The last day of your leave is up to-morrow, isn't it?"

"I am not concerned about that, Sergeant. Official action taken in Brisbane is of less importance than a recent development here at Karwir. Do you know what this is?"

Before Sergeant Blake Bony set on the ground the ball of

gummed cigarette stubs he had found beside him when he awoke that morning. Blake peered down at the gum ball, then gingerly took it up the better to examine it.

"No, I don't know what it is," he admitted.

"The latest development in this case has deprived me of my greatest asset, the unconsciousness of the value of time. Patience is a great gift, Blake, the greatest. Unfortunately neither Colonel Spendor nor my immediate chief, Superintendent Browne, has that gift. The Colonel, like all self-important big business men, constantly yells for results. I give results, but in my own way and in my own time.

" 'Report!' they yell, like babies yelling for a bottle of milk. Am I to report every other day that I did this and did that, that I found a certain track here and a wisp of cable silk there? That a crow gurgled like a man being strangled, and that one night someone left at my side a ball of gum and cigarette ends? That I began work at such and such a time in the morning and left work at such and such a time?"

Blake was astonished by the rising anger in the voice of this man, usually so calm. He noted that anger did not make the voice louder in volume.

"When I am on a case nothing outside interests me. I don't work for so many hours a day. I work all day, every minute I'm awake. The Commissioner has sacked me before, in his own way, and I have reinstated myself, in my own way. This time, however, the Commissioner means business, thinking that he can bring me to heel, as I will presently show you I can bring those dogs to heel. As you say, to-morrow is my last day. And you know I could not reach Brisbane by then, even if I wanted to—which I don't.

"Sack me, would they! I—don't—think! I won't wait to be sacked like an errand boy. Here, I have an envelope! It will do fittingly for the occasion. Now watch me sack myself. I'm finished with the Department that I've served so well. Here's my resignation. I write it on the back of an envelope.

Take it, Sergeant. Mail it for me to the Chief Commissioner."

Blake was forced to accept the split-open envelope on which Bony had written his resignation. Bony's outburst had made him uncomfortable, a sensation that was increased when the half-caste raised his knees and pressed his face between them. Quite deliberately, Blake dropped the resignation into the fire. Presently Bony lifted his head to stare beyond the fire at the dozing horse standing in shadow.

"Yes, I have been deprived of the exercise of my greatest gift, unconsciousness of time, infinite patience. Neither Browne nor the Commissioner could deprive me of that; they could not rivet to my legs the irons of limitation.

"Look all about you, Sergeant. You see but a fraction of a great area of land in which eight months ago a man was destroyed and buried. I know, approximately, where he was killed; but as yet I don't know where he was buried and by whom. I have to find where he was buried, who buried him, who killed him—within the next three weeks, at the longest a month. I may be able to extend the limit to six weeks, but I gravely doubt it. I may not need six weeks, or even three weeks, but the time limit is now my master. Because it has never before been my master I have always succeeded. Now that it is my master I may well fail for the first time. What do you make of the ball of gum in which are embedded a mass of my discarded cigarette ends?"

"I don't know. What does it mean?"

"It is the announcement to me that I have been boned by the blacks."

"What's that!" almost shouted Blake.

Bony turned slightly to regard the policeman who saw in his eyes blue pools of horror.

"Oh, that's it, is it?" he said, and whistled.

"I see that you realize the seriousness of the threat behind the boning," Bony said.

"Realize it! I realize it all right," Blake replied. "I've

never seen the thing done, but I have known men who have. Old Lacy knows of its deadliness. He once told me that he warned Anderson to be careful or he'd be boned. The old man's a believer in the magic. Said he saw a white man die of being boned. Why don't you give up the case and get back to Brisbane as soon as you can?"

"Give it up!" shouted Bony, springing to his feet. "What of my reputation, my personal pride?"

"Well, no one's going to blame you for giving it up. You've been ordered to, remember. Anderson disappeared six months before you came here. It's not as though his body was found and examined by you the day after he disappeared, when you might have discovered a dozen clues, when the scent was hot. Anyway, who's to know that the man is dead?"

Bony's body sank upon his heels, and for a moment he was silent and motionless. Then he said:

"But I know. I was sent here to find out what happened to him, what was done to him and by whom. Ha—um! It would be easy to follow your road. Away from the bush I might defy the magic, most likely I should escape it. But your road would be signposted 'Failure.' No one would blame me for obeying orders to give up the case; but I should know, I'd always know that I gave it up because I was unable to carry on, unable to solve it. No one would blame me but myself."

Sergeant Blake did not speak when Bony finished, the index finger of his right hand pointing at himself. He still failed to understand the basis of Bony's pride in accomplishment, although now he was sure it was not mere vanity. The Sergeant felt as one of an audience waiting for the curtain to go up. And now up it went.

"No, Sergeant, I couldn't bear failure. Being what you are, you could never clearly understand what I am. You can have no conception of what I am, what influences are ever at war within me. Once I failed to finish an investigation, I could no longer hold to the straw keeping me afloat on the sea of life, beneath the surface of which the sharks of my maternal ancestry are for ever trying to destroy me. Once I am unable to admire the great Detective-Inspector Napoleon Bonaparte, I become parted from my straw. Down I go into the sea to be claimed for ever by my mother's race.

"Don't for one moment think that I despise my mother's race. At a very early age I was offered a choice. I could choose to be an aboriginal or a white man. I chose to become the latter, and have become the latter with distinction in all but blood. To fail now would mean to lose everything for which I have worked, and the only thing which enables me to cling to what I have is my pride.

"You cannot know of the eternal battle I fight, to lose which means for me and mine what we should regard as degradation; my family and I should fall to that plane on which live the poor whites and the outcast aborigines. Failure! No. Surrender to the fear of death by boning! No. The white man might say, surrender. My wife, who understands, would say, no. And so, Sergeant, I must go on. I must for the first time triumph over the absence of my greatest asset. I must work against time as well as against the insidious mental poison now beginning to be administered."

Sergeant Blake regarded Bony with steady eyes. He saw clearly enough that in Bony's attitude and speech there was no melodrama, no conceit or flashy show. The half-caste's sincerity was beyond doubt. Blake had heard of the efficacy of the aborigine's power to will death and achieve it in others. Now the Sergeant understood the basis of Bony's reputation for success in his chosen work. He felt this late afternoon the shock of the battle Bony had mentioned, the battle which was a clash of inhibitions, loyalties, superstitions, instincts, love, pride and ambition. There sat a man of great courage, and almost eagerly, he said:

"You haven't made much use of me, sir. Let me help more. Two's better than one any time. Let me inquire among the blacks who's doing the boning. It could be stopped. Why, the Gordons would stop it."

"Thank you, Sergeant," Bony said very softly.

"Good! Now let's get going. What shall I do?"

"You will not make inquiry of the blacks, and you will not mention the fact of the boning to the Gordons. I will tell you why. My impression of John Gordon and his mother is excellent. My admiration for them is unbounded, for what they are doing for one Australian tribe is unique. I do not think that John Gordon was in any way concerned with the death of Anderson, or that he knows any particular of it. I think him innocent, but I have no proof. Until I have proof of his innocence I cannot permit myself to be beholden to him for any service whatsoever.

"Supposing you went to him, supposing I went to him, and asked him to intercede with the blacks for my life, and then I discovered that he had killed Anderson. Think of that situation. Neither you nor I would ever discover by inquiring among them which of the blacks were doing the boning.

"You have offered to co-operate with me, even after I have written out my resignation from the Force. You are whiter than your skin, Blake. I accept your offer, but still you must be patient with me, be content with the part I shall allot you. Oh, I shall want your assistance all right. Above all I shall want the contact with all that you represent. Will you try to meet me here at six o'clock every evening from now on?"

"Yes, I can do that."

"Then I will be waiting for you. If I am not you need not wait for me, for I will be detained on my work. On your way back to-night I want you to stop at Pine Hut and there smash the battery jars inside the telephone box."

A quick frown came into, then passed from the military face.

"Very well, I'll do that," assented Sergeant Blake.

CHAPTER SIXTEEN

Things Below the Surface

BONY made the two dogs his willing slaves by a method known to the aborigines. They were friendly animals, two rangy members of the great canine League of Nations. One looked something like a Queensland heeler, and in the other there was a distinct strain of the bull terrier. After making a fuss of them, Bony gently forced the nose of each up and into an armpit. Having freed them, he turned to the interested Sergeant, the dogs leaping about him.

"They'll do," he said. "They are of the mixed breed I wanted, intelligent, loaded with stamina and hunting mad. For weeks I have been the hunted; now I become the hunter. *Au revoir!* I'll expect you here to-morrow evening at six. Remember to smash those batteries inside the telephone box at Pine Hut, and then be indignant at the vandalism should questions be asked. Nothing of the boning to anyone, remember, and find out, if you can, who is the Kalchut medicine man. You will do all that?"

"I will. You can depend on me."

And so Bony walked over to his horse and led it to the Karwir boundary gate, the two dogs jumping about horse and man, the horse obviously pleased by the companionship. Blake watched until they all disappeared among the trees beyond the fence.

At a walking pace, Bony rode for two miles towards Green

Swamp when, abruptly, he swung his horse round, urged her into a gallop back over her own tracks, and shouted to the dogs. The mare snorted, and the dogs yelped into excited frenzy.

"Hool 'em Sool 'em!" shouted the half-caste.

The enthusiastic dogs raced ahead of the galloping horse. They wanted no urging to enter into this new game with their new master. For a while the hunting pack raced back towards the boundary fence, and then southward of it to sweep in wide semicircles through the mulga forest, Bony constantly urging the dogs to "Sool 'em!"

An observer would have thought he had taken leave of his senses. The road to Karwir was crossed several times; the boundary fence appeared more than once to block them. Then the chase would swerve from it and head southward, then to the east or west, the dogs constantly urged to "Sool 'em up." They startled a kangaroo, they put up a dozing rabbit, they chased goannas into trees, and always Bony cried to them, and they followed him. Thus, like a mad huntsman, Bony hunted the black spies who moved without leaving tracks, who could easily defy him but not the dogs.

"Either the blacks cleared out when they saw Blake unload the dogs and guessed their purpose, or they have given up spying on me, being satisfied that after their boning I will no longer be dangerous," he observed to the horse when he was standing beside her and the panting dogs lay stretched on the ground. The dogs yelped when they heard his voice and the winded horse raised her drooping head.

"Yes, my friends. I thought it was so, because for the first time for weeks I do not feel that sensation of cold at the back of my head and neck. And now for camp and dinner and bed."

They were on the branch road to Green Swamp, and Bony walked leading the mare, the dogs trotting wearily beside him. The galahs were coming from and going to the water in the sheep troughs beside the well at Green Swamp, some to chatter, others to scream defiance as they passed overhead. When the man and his companions entered the line of box-trees surrounding the swamp, the sun was resting on the western scrub line and the soft wind carrying Bony's cigarette smoke before him promised a cool night.

Now the box-trees thinned as Bony walked beneath them to their southern edge where the ground rose sharply to the low plateau on which were situated the hut, the well and the windmill. He saw with quickened interest the column of blue smoke slanting away low over the ground to the eastern boundary, then saw that the smoke column was based upon a mound of smoking debris marking the site of the hut.

The dogs, smelling the water in the troughs, raced away towards them. The horse whinnied and nudged Bony's back to hurry him. He took her to the nearest of two troughs; and while she drank, he gazed a little blankly at the smouldering debris two hundred yards distant from the well, the gloom deepening among the lower lying box-trees, the sky swiftly being painted with bars of red, green and indigo blue.

It was useless to search for possible tracks; there was little doubt that the hut had been deliberately destroyed by people who would have been careful to leave no tracks. No one, other than the blacks, would have had cause to commit such an act of incendiarism.

Bony's mind went back to the early morning of that day. He recalled having heaped white ash over the glowing red embers of his breakfast fire on the wide hearth before closing the door and leaving for the day's work. Any fire insurance man would have agreed that he had done everything needful to prevent fire. There had been no wind this day till late evening; but there had been several whirlwinds marching drunkenly across the land, and one of these might have passed over the hut and, with its back draught, scattered the embers over the hut's wooden floor.

The odds in favour of such a happening were small; those in favour of deliberate incendiarism very many. The hut was a white man's home. It was, too, Bony's temporary home. Its destruction would not only greatly inconvenience Bony when time had become of vital value; it would drive him closer to the bush and to the influences of the bush that were to assist the aborigines in their boning. It would be all to their advantage to delay him in his investigation by making him journey daily to and from the homestead, twelve miles to the south. As a matter of routine, Bony searched for tracks and found none.

The advancing night was sliding across the sky, pushing down to the sun's couch the colourful draperies of departing day, when Bony took the mare to a patch of dry tussock grass and there hobbled her short. Then he made a fire beneath one of the box-trees and heated water in his quart-pot, while the dogs watched him with eyes saying plainly that they were hungry. And when they came to understand that there was nothing to eat they lay down beside their new master while he dined on hot water and cigarettes.

For several hours, Bony squatted on his heels to ponder on this latest development and to plan for the future. He felt tired and safe from observation, and yet he could not free his mind of an unease akin to that of approaching death.

It was after ten o'clock when he removed his riding boots, added wood to the fire, scooped a hole in the ground to take his hip, and composed himself for slumber, the dogs curled at his feet. Yet sleep was denied him. Imps pricked his skin, and when his mind was losing consciousness vague and terrible shapes rushed at him to awaken him fully with cold shock. Fear was like a devil that came to gloat over him every time the fire died down, and at one o'clock he began to feel severe abdominal pains that kept him awake until the new day dawned. Only then did he fall into an oft-interrupted sleep from which finally he was roused by the barking dogs and the roaring hum of an aeroplane engine.

With eyes heavy from lack of sleep and muscles protesting against the torturing long night, Bony arose to watch the plane arriving from the homestead many hours before he had expected it. The machine circled once before dropping beyond his view to land where the several depressions became one to enter Green Swamp. Bony's gaze swept southward to where he had hobbled his horse, and although he was unable to see her, he could hear the tinkle of the bell suspended from her neck. He met Young Lacy coming from the plane, carrying a fore-quarter of mutton in a calico bag and the microscope in its wood box.

"Good day, Bony!" he was greeted by Young Lacy, who added: "Why, you've been and gone and burned Green Swamp Mansion!"

"It was burned down when I arrived here last evening. I don't know how it happened, and I am sure I left the small breakfast fire safe on the hearth," Bony explained. "It's most unfortunate."

"For you it must be," came the cheerful agreement. "Anyway, it's no loss to Karwir. I've been wanting the old dad to pull it down and build a decent place here. How did you get on for tucker?"

"Hot water and cigarettes. I am glad you flew over this morning: we'd all have been pretty hungry by this afternoon. Did you happen to bring any tea?"

"You bet. I never fly without tea and a billycan and a tin of water. Oh, and a tin of plain biscuits. Here, you take the meat and get going on some chops. I see the axe beside the alleged woodheap wasn't burned. I'll go back for the tea and things."

Five minutes later the dogs had been fed, chops were grilling on the coals, and water was beginning to stir in the new billycan.

"I'm sorry about this place being burned down," Bony was saying. "I'm responsible, you see."

"Oh rot! Good job the joint did burn. Did you lose much in it?"

"Only toilet gear and underwear."

"Bad luck. What do you intend doing now? You look like a feller who's been on the ran-tan for a week."

Bony sighed, saying:

"I feel it. Do you think Mr Lacy would be generous enough to send me out camp gear and horse feed? You see, I have reached the conclusion that this part of Green Swamp is of the utmost importance to my investigation, and to ride to and from the homestead every day would take too much time."

"Of course it would," Young Lacy promptly agreed. "I came this morning because this afternoon the old man wants me to take a truck into town and bring out a load of paints and other stuff. I can bring out all you need this afternoon, and then go on to town. What about your personal wants?"

"Well, Blake is coming out this evening and he could bring the things I require. I'll make out the list for you to take to him. As for the camp gear, I wonder, now. Could you bring a small tank for water? You see, having to put up a camp, I'd like to have it at the foot of the dunes where the north fence runs down to the flat country bordering the north channel. If you could——"

"Of course! I could truck the camp gear to where you want it, bring a tank over here and fill it and then leave it at the camp. No trouble."

For the first time this day Bony smiled.

"You are most helpful and I thank you," he told Young Lacy. "Ah, I'm feeling better already. I had a rotten night. A touch of the Barcoo sickness. You might bring out some aspirin and a bottle or two of chlorodyne. This case is begining to open up and I cannot afford to fall sick. By the way, how long now have your sister and John Gordon been in love?"

"About a year, I think. John's a decent sort but—I say, how did you know—about them?"

"Guessed it," Bony replied, casually.

"Well, don't mention it to the old dad, will you? He thinks the sun shines out of Diana, and he'd go to market if he knew. You see, John's comparatively poor to what Diana and I will be some day. He's hoping that Diana will marry a duke or something, although how he can expect her to meet a duke here on Karwir I don't know. And then, there's another thing. Mother having died, the old man would be ditched without her, you understand. Things being as they are, Diana and John want to keep their affair quiet for a few years."

"Yes, I understand," Bony said, softly. "I have thought it might be that way. If your father would readily consent to their marriage, would they marry, do you think?"

The fingers of a brown hand combed the unruly red hair and hazel eyes regarded Bony frankly.

"I don't know how to answer that," replied Young Lacy. "If they married it would mean Diana going to live at Meena Lake, and she won't leave the old dad. Karwir is willed to me, so John couldn't very well come to live at Karwir. And there's his mother."

"Of course! I appreciate the situation, but matters will come right in the end. I had no authority to mention the affair, and I trust you will forget I did mention it."

"Oh, that's all right. Well, I suppose I had better get back. I'll have to pack up the camp gear you'll need. I'll be out about three o'clock."

They rose together from about the fire, and Bony accompanied Young Lacy to the machine; expertly turned into the light wind, it rose to fly away towards the homestead. As Bony walked back to his fire depression sat upon him, and, spiritually, he cried aloud against the fate that had made him what he was and not as the young airman to whom life was a living joy.

It would be at least five hours before he could expect to hear the hum of the truck engine; and, as men in Australia have done for countless ages, Bony squatted over a little fire and now and then absently pushed inward the burning ends of little sticks. He squatted in sunlight, and it seemed that he squatted in shadow cast by a bloodwood-tree. It was his mind that was in shadow, this he knew. He could not force it into the sunshine, the spectrum of which contained the rays of hope, health, and ambition. He knew himself to be stricken with an illness not to be conquered by medicine. Hypnotism might succeed, but only in circumstances and in a place far distant and different from this.

Almost all his life this man of two races had sailed a sea over which he had been blown by the wind of ambition towards the Land of Great Achievement. But below the surface of the sea lurked monstrous things, shadowy things that waited, waited always to drag him under and down to a worse existence than that known by his maternal ancestors. And now his craft was discovered to be unseaworthy and was floundering, and the monstrous shadowy shapes were close to the surface waiting patiently to claim him.

The phrase "I am boned," was hammered upon his mind. It was exactly the same as the phrase "I am sentenced to death." His mind was ruled by the hideous implication of the idea expressed by the word "boned." In sympathy with his state of mind, his nerves and muscles were beginning to rebel against normal unconscious control. He felt tired and ill, as a man does who is due for a bout of influenza. But the will to live, the will to achieve, was still strong, and with devastating suddenness it rebelled against the inevitability of the boning.

Bony was on his feet, as though lifted there by the sight of a death-adder. His handsome features were distorted by impotent rage, and facing towards Meena he began to shout:

"Kill me! Go on, blast you, kill me! I defy you to do it. You can't do it to-day, or to-morrow, or next week or next month. I'm going to live long enough to finish this job. You kill me, you black swine! You can't do it. I'm half white, d'you hear! I'm a million miles above you, and you can't drag me down. I'm going to find Jeffery Anderson, and you càn't stop me finding him. I'll find him. I'll make him walk the earth and stalk about your camps and point a fleshless finger at you all. Go and tell that to old Nero and Wandin and all the others. You fools! You can't beat me down, not Detective-Inspector Napoleon Bonaparte. Go on, do your worst and be damned to you. Go and tell Nero——"

As though a shovel-nose spear had entered his back, Bony collapsed to the ground. He writhed and moaned as though, seized by the shark-teeth of despair, he were being pulled down beneath the surface of this brilliant and colourful day. There was none to comfort him, to encourage him, in this land so empty of human beings. None watched, not even the men with blood and feathers on their feet. They knew; they did not have to watch. The dogs had stood stiffly to look in the direction to which Bony had shouted, hoping he was urging them forward to the hunt; but detecting the fearsome ring in his voice, they came to him, softly whimpering, one to lick his neck, the other to bury a cold nose in the hot palm of a hand.

And like a light penetrating the fog, the touch of one dog's tongue and the other's nose, and the sound of their soft cries, guided Bony back. He ceased his moans and the writhing of his body. He heaved a long-drawn sigh. He sat up to hug the dogs close to his sides with his arms, and the two mongrels whimpered their pleasure and wanted to lick his face. Presently Bony spoke:

"We mustn't let go like that again," he said. "No, not like

that. Oh no! We mustn't let the old bone take full charge like that ever again. After all we are men and we can die like men if and when we have to. To go down like that is just what the bone-pointers are trying to make us do. They want us to lie down and slowly perish without making an effort to resist them. We will resist them, won't we? We've got to find Anderson who is lying somewhere not a great distance from us at this moment. We've got to find those who killed him. We've got to think not of ourselves but of the investigation, of Marie, of the boys, of old Colonel Spendor, who is my friend although he sacks me sometimes—the old Commisioner who has always believed in me, always secretly acclaimed me as the best detective in Australia, who has helped me to become what I am.

"Find Anderson, that's what we've got to do, my dear old Sool-'Em-Up and Hool-'Em-Up. We've got to smell him out of his grave, raise him up and make him tell us who slew him and why. We've got to work, to hunt day and night, to find Anderson and beat the bone. Oh curse the bone! Let's forget it! Come on, let's to work!"

CHAPTER SEVENTEEN

Steps of Progress

BONY's new camp was established just south of the Karwir-Meena boundary fence where it left the sand-dune country to run across flat land for three-quarters of a mile before turning southward to cross the several depressions or channels. To the west from the front of the camp, which was splendidly shaded by two cabbage-trees, the eye was at once attracted by the netted barrier passing north of the camp. Beyond it some fifty yards a fine specimen of mulga grew in solitary state on the wide ribbon of claypans that separated the sand-dunes from the flat grey country.

Adhering to the trunk of that solitary tree Bony had discovered the wisp of green cable silk.

It was now the second afternoon following that on which Young Lacy had brought out the gear and assisted Bony to make this new camp. Throughout the preceding day Bony had hunted for aboriginal spies and had found none. From the fence round to Green Swamp, he had examined the claypan ribbon fronting the dunes, hoping to pick out on the surface traces of one or more tracks made by The Black Emperor when it rained six months before. During the first part of the second day he and the dogs had ranged over adjacent Meena country, examining sand-dunes and flat lands. Bony had found no further clue; but still he was certain that this area of country could provide him with all the pieces of the jig-saw puzzle if only he could delve beneath the surface laid by the rain and the wind and the heat of the sun.

After breakfast he had been violently sick, and for lunch he had been satisfied with a few plain biscuits and a pannikin or two of tea. Feeling now a little better, he decided again to examine that solitary mulga-tree. Before, he had been reluctant to spend time here lest he should betray his interest to those watching spies.

When he climbed over the barb-top barrier, the dogs followed, refusing to remain in the camp shade despite the heat of the day. The mare standing in the improvised yard near the camp raised her head to watch, but soon began again to doze, grateful for the spell from work.

Bony came to a standstill before the tree. Yes—there was the faint dent on the bark he had made with his thumb-nail to mark the exact place where he had found the wisp of cable silk. On a former visit to this tree he had walked round and round it for several minutes without seeing anything to arouse his interest. And now as though the trunk were the hub of a wheel, line of vision a spoke, and himself a section of the rim, Bony again slowly circled the tree a bare two feet from it. Finding nothing abnormal when making a general examination of the straight trunk, he decided to look for clues in support of his theory of the wisp of cable silk.

It was not until he had closely examined the base of the trunk for several minutes that Bony decided that an area of faint discolouration, in the centre of which was a curved line some two inches long, was a bark bruise. Any man with less bush erudition than Bony would never have seen the mark, and would certainly not have guessed what had made it—the heel of a man's boot. It was immediately below his own mark where the wisp of cable silk had been.

Twenty minutes later he discovered another bruise, this one being opposite the mark made by his thumbnail and some sixty-two inches from the ground. It extended half-way round the trunk and was about five inches wide. Bony sighed his triumph before turning to the bored dogs to whom he said:

"We progress, my canine friends. To-day we have taken a further step, a confident step. I have now proof of my theory of what happened to Anderson, the theory that I built up from the wisp of cable silk. From this side of the fence a party of aboriginals doubtless saw Anderson riding down the slope of the sand-dune on the other side of the fence. Probably insults were passed over the barrier, and then, enraged, Anderson jumped from his horse, neck-roped it to a fence post, leapt the barrier and rushed about the blacks intending to whip them.

"Remembering what their race had suffered at his hands, they declined to be whipped and decided to give him the father of a hiding. There was a fierce struggle until the white man was knocked unconscious. He was dragged to this tree. One of the blacks went to the horse and removed a stirrup-leather; with it Anderson was made a helpless captive, the long strap being passed round the trunk and his neck and buckled where his hands could not reach it. The wound made on the tree by the strap is approximately sixty-two inches up from the ground, because Anderson was a six-foot man and his knees were slightly relaxed.

"On regaining his senses, Anderson faced his enemies, one of whom had his whip with the green cable silk cracker. Probably they told him what they were going to do. The fellow with the whip made a trial cast to learn its exact length, and the silk cracker smacked the trunk above Anderson's head. After that the flogging began in earnest, and continued until the captive again became unconscious. His body slumped downward and he was hanged by the strap.

"Yes—that's about how it happened, Hool-'Em-Up and you, you imitation bull terrier. An ugly affair altogether. Now we'll give the trunk of this tree another overhaul. We'll examine the bark square inch by square inch just in case it has caught anything else on its raised and serrated edges."

Going to ground, Bony began to circle the tree. He took it in successively higher layers until at last he came to stand on his feet. An hour was spent thus, his eyes small and steady, his brows knit and the whole of his mind directing his eyes. And when he stood before the mark he had made with his thumb-nail, he brought his eyes close to the bark several inches below the mark. Then quickly he moved his head to either side and squinted diagonally across the place, for only now and then when the soft wind moved it, did the light fall glintingly on a human hair. Like the silk it was caught fast by the bark.

"So—another—step—we—take—to-day!" he cried so loudly that the dogs rushed to jump up about him. "We find a hair of the man who was strapped to this tree, doubtless caught by the bark as he made a frantic effort to escape the whip lash. It is light-brown in colour, and, I should say, two inches in length. Anderson's hair was light-brown. There in that single hair, to be seen only when light strikes upon it at an angle, is the final brick of the building of my theory. I'm lucky, I'll not deny. It is the only tree within many yards. It is not a smooth-skinned leopardwood-tree, but a mulga-tree, the bark of which is rough and hard. Nero, and Wandin, and Malluc—you scoundrels—as Dryden wrote, beware the fury of a patient man."

Bony successfully detached the hair and imprisoned it within a cigarette paper which he placed in an envelope, later to be marked Exhibit Three.

"Oh yes, we now know that Anderson was strapped to this tree and flogged with the whip he himself used to flog Inky Boy," Bony remarked to the dogs. "There he hung suspended by the stirrup-leather. Then what happened? What happened then? Why, the blacks had to conceal the body. They must have been confident before they killed

179

Anderson that John Gordon was riding away from the Channels with a mob of sheep, but even so they must have seen the danger to themselves in the possibility that Gordon might return to the locality in search of other sheep. Thus they would not have carried the body away to another place.

"They would have done one of two things. With pointed mulga sticks they would have dug a grave out there in that soft, flat ground. Or they would have carried the body up among the dunes and buried it at the foot of the eastern slope of one of them, knowing that the prevailing westerly wind would push the dune farther and farther over and on it. Ah—yes—I can see a lot of manual labour in front of me."

For two hours the menace of the boning had been banished from Bony's mind, and, calling the dogs, he climbed back over the fence to his camp and put on the billy to boil for tea. He was elated by his discoveries, and hope burned brightly that he would complete his case before physical illness mastered him. At long last he possessed a lead. He had correctly placed sufficient pieces of the puzzle to enable him to see almost the entire picture.

At six o'clock, when Sergeant Blake reached the boundary fence, he found Bony waiting with the tea newly made, the mare neck-roped to a tree and the dogs tethered to other trees. Bony's eyes were bright, but his cheeks were a little sunken and his lips appeared to be much thinner.

"How's things?" asked the policeman.

"I was sick again this morning," replied Bony. "However, I managed a few biscuits for lunch, and I am feeling much less depressed because I have made several important discoveries."

"Good! Let's have some dinner. I've brought it. The wife says that if I won't get home in time for dinner, then I must take it with me. There's cold beef, a salad and an apple pie with cream."

"What a feast!" Bony exclaimed. "My bread is rock-hard, the meat has become fly-blown, and the cow has bolted."

Blake set the food out on a square of American cloth, and Bony, tempted, ate while he told about his work that afternoon.

"Anderson's hair was light-brown, wasn't it?" he asked.

Blake nodded, saying:

"It was. And he always wore it fairly long."

"Still, Sergeant, it has yet to be proved that the hair I found attached to the bark came from the head of the missing man," argued Bony. "Er—excuse me. I am very sorry. It is an insult to your wife's excellent cooking."

He hurried away to the trees and Blake heard him retching. It was the Barcoo sickness all right, or was it? The previous evening when they had eaten at this place, Bony had done this very same thing. As Blake well knew, the Barcoo sickness strikes quickly and without warning, and if this was the Barcoo sickness then its following so closely on the boning was an extraordinary coincidence.

"Rotten luck," he said when Bony returned.

"You've said it, Blake. I quite enjoyed the meal."

Bony helped himself to tea, added milk from the bottle Blake had brought, but did not take sugar.

"As I was saying," he continued, "we have yet to prove that the hair I found caught up by the bark of that tree came from Anderson's head. Fortunately, we have an excellent chance of proving it. The Karwir people have never disturbed Anderson's room, and, when there the other day, I noticed that his comb and brushes contained several of his hairs. As I have the microscope, will you run me in to the homestead?"

"Certainly."

"Then we'll get along. For a detective I am going, this evening, to be communicative. I will invite the Karwir people to be present when we examine under the microscope the tree-caught hair, and a hair from one of Anderson's brushes.

I want you to observe carefully the reaction of each member of the Lacy household. Say nothing. Note and tell me afterwards what you observe, if anything. Now let's go. The animals will be safe enough."

Half an hour later the car was braked before the gate in the canegrass fence, and Blake followed Bony to the door in the long south veranda where they were welcomed by Old Lacy himself.

"Why, Bony, it's you! Hullo, Blake!" he boomed.

"Good evening, Mr Lacy," Bony said in reply. "Sergeant Blake came out to see me this afternoon, and I have persuaded him to run me in. I can now personally state my regret at the destruction of Green Swamp hut. It must have been due to my carelessness."

Old Lacy stood aside from the doorway.

"Go in! Go in! Don't let the firing of that hut worry you. It was past time that I built another out there, and save for a few rations the only articles of value in the place were a crowbar and a couple of shovels. Hi, there, Diana! Is there any dinner left? Here's two visitors."

Bony hastened to assure Old Lacy, and Diana who appeared from the house dining-room, that he and the Sergeant had dined, and he was about to state the reason for the call when the squatter commanded them to sit down and have a peg. Never a drinker, Bony sipped a glass of whisky and soda with real gratitude.

"You're not lookin' too well, Bony," observed their host.

"No, I am not well. I have a touch of the Barcoo sickness."

At once Old Lacy was concerned, saying:

"That's bad. Not many complaints worse than that. Chlorodyne and brandy's about the only thing for it, with a feed now and then of potatoes steeped all night in vinegar. You must take some out with you, unless, of course, you'd care to camp here a few days."

"You are more than kind, and I should like to accept your

suggestion; but this case is at last moving and I may complete it more quickly than I anticipated."

"Ah—ah! That's good. What have you found? Anything important?"

"It may be of great importance," Bony replied cautiously. "You will remember that I told you I found a wisp of green cable silk, believed to have come from Anderson's whip cracker, caught by the bark of a tree. To the bark of that same tree I have found a human hair still clinging after all these months. It is of the same colour as Anderson's hair, but we cannot be certain that the hair I have found came from his head until we compare it with one known to have come from it. I have brought the microscope, and I suggest we all go over to Anderson's room to compare the hair I found with one taken from his brushes."

With remarkable agility Old Lacy sprang to his feet. Blake rose next and then Bony before Diana Lacy. After his first bow of greeting, he had not looked at her, and now he stood aside to permit her to pass on behind her father.

"We'll soon decide the matter," remarked the old man. "If the hair you found is Anderson's, what will it prove?"

"That he was tied to a certain tree and flogged with his own whip."

"I thought it was something like that. Those damned blacks treated him to the medicine he gave to that loafer, Inky Boy," the old man said triumphantly, triumphantly because his own baseless theory promised to become fact.

The girl, Blake and Bony, halted outside the door of Anderson's room in the office building while the old man entered the office for the key.

"Yours must be an extraordinary interesting profession, Mr Bonaparte," she said, tonelessly.

"Sometimes, Miss Lacy. There's a lot of routine work, however, in every case. Perhaps the most interesting part of an investigation is provided by clues such as human hairs, finger-prints, tobacco ash and the manner in which a man wears out his boots."

Old Lacy emerged from the office, followed by his son who cheerfully greeted the callers, and, the door having been unlocked and thrown open, they trooped into the room that had not been occupied for six months. One open door of the wardrobe revealed suits hanging within. On a hook beside the window were Anderson's several whips. The bed was made, but red dust lay lightly on the coverlet. On the chest of drawers were the missing man's toilet articles arrayed before a wide mirror.

"Now, I'll set up the instrument and we'll see what we see," Bony said quietly, and the others stood back without comment. "Could we have the office petrol light?"

Young Lacy hurried out to the office. Through the single window the glory of the departing day tinted their faces with scarlet, giving soft russet tints even to Bony's black hair as he manipulated the microscope set upon the dressing chest. The lamp was placed beside it, pumped and lit, and the red oblong within the window frame became purple. Having arranged side by side between two plain glasses the hair he had found adhering to the tree and one he took from a hair brush, Bony adjusted the mirror and focused the instrument.

"Ladies first! Miss Lacy, will you kindly give us your opinion on these two hairs?"

"I hardly think my opinion will count, Mr Bonaparte, but I cannot refrain from looking at them."

"Thank you. As a matter of fact, Miss Lacy, I am relying on your feminine powers of colour matching."

Silently the men stood regarding the girl's shapely back while she peered through the instrument. She appeared to take quite several minutes in her examination, but the period was much less. Then she said:

"They look alike to me."

This was Old Lacy's verdict. Blake was much less sure, and

his opinion was backed by Young Lacy. Bony demanded a full five minutes for his investigation; then he turned to face them, his brows contrated by a slight frown.

"They are not from the same head," he said slowly. "I grant you the great difficulty in judging the colour of those two hairs. The colour of that taken from the tree, however, is lighter than that of the hair just taken from the brush. This difference could be attributed to the bleaching action of sunlight on the hair found on the tree. The difference is so slight, however, that we cannot accept colour as a basis for judgement. The difference I observe between those two hairs lies in their size or thickness. The hair taken from the tree is smaller than that taken from the brush, it is finer. You will see that the hair taken from the brush is coarse. The hairs have come from two men, not one. I may have to send them to Brisbane for a more expert examination which I feel sure will bear out my opinion. Take another glance at them and note the difference in size. In colour both hairs are light-brown, but with a slight difference in shade."

Blake examined the hairs and agreed with Bony concerning their difference in size. Diana stated that their sizes were equal, to which her father agreed. Young Lacy could not be positive.

"Well, we must await the expert's opinion," Bony told them. "My opinion is that not Anderson but another man was secured to the tree, and the hair of that man's head was similar in colour to Anderson's."

"That being so, d'you think Anderson tied a fellow to the tree and flogged him?" asked Young Lacy.

"I don't now know what to think," Bony admitted. "It is all most puzzling. I must examine the tree again, and follow certain theories I have evolved from the examination of the hairs. Excuse me."

Turning his back upon them, he carefully replaced the hair found on the mulga-tree in its envelope marked Exhibit

Three, and into a second envelope to be marked Exhibit Four he placed several hairs taken from the brushes. After that he became obviously anxious to depart from the homestead.

Old Lacy wanted him and the Sergeant to stay the evening, and, when he begged to be excused, the old man insisted that he take a bottle of brandy and a bottle of vinegar in which to steep sliced potatoes as a cure for the Barcoo sickness.

"Well, what do you think of the three Lacys?" inquired Bony, when they were on their way back to the boundary gate.

"The old man was quite at sea about the hairs, and a little disappointed that you seemed confused by their difference," replied Blake. "Did the hairs really confuse you?"

"No. I wanted to avoid refusing to answer questions. What of Young Lacy and the girl—their reactions?"

"The girl seemed to be suffering strain. Young Lacy was merely interested. Miss Lacy seemed to dislike you."

"Why?"

"Well, maybe——"

"She doesn't dislike me by reason of my birth. She dislikes me because she fears me," asserted Bony. "There is a distinct difference of shade in those two hairs, and yet she said they were alike. In one respect I am not at all disappointed that those hairs are not alike, that they both did not come from Anderson's head. Anderson was not the man tied to the tree, but Anderson flogged the man who was tied to it, and that man had hair much like Anderson's. John Gordon's hair is light-brown, is it not?"

Blake frowned, then nodded slowly.

"I believe that now I could give a logical outline of what happened that afternoon of rain six months ago," Bony said, breaking a long silence. "There is, however, a further step I must take to prove that Gordon was tied to the tree. If he was not, then we must look for another man. It is strange how an investigation will sometimes hang fire for weeks, then suddenly be rushed forward by one small and not so very important clue. This evening you have seen me throwing a spanner into the theoretical machine I built up. I may have something further to say to-morrow evening when you come out."

CHAPTER EIGHTEEN

Rising Winds

At the Karwir homestead breakfast was at eight, permitting Old Lacy to meet the homestead hands outside the office and give them his orders for the day, then to talk for ten minutes by telephone to the overseer at the out-station.

The Lacys met at the breakfast table set out during the hot summer months on the long south veranda. As was ever the case, Old Lacy was in a hurry, though there was rarely necessity for haste.

"I'm going out to take a squint at Blackfellow's Well," he announced, serving from a dish of lamb's fry and bacon. "Fred says he's noticed that the shaft has got a bad bulge half-way down. Due to earth slip, or a tremor, I suppose. Knew a well once that got like a corkscrew inside a week. Might have to get another well sunk at Blackfellow's. No might about it. Will have to sink one, just because this dry season we need all the spare cash for feed for the sheep! Shouldn't have any sheep on the place! You coming out with me, my gal?"

"Well, I was thinking of running in to Opal Town," Diana replied, reluctantly. "Shopping, you know."

"Oh, all right! I'll take Bill the Better. He can drive and lay bets that we'll find Fred down the well. Cheerful lad, Bill the Better. Anyway, he can go down the shaft and report.

Fred's like me, stiff in the knees. How about you, lad? Want to come?"

"Sorry, but I've got a deal of book work to do. Those returns for the Lands Department," answered Young Lacy. "It's funny about the 'phone. It's working all right now. I rang up Phil Whiting just before I came over from the office."

"Must have been a stick or something on the line that the wind has blown off," commented Old Lacy. "I couldn't raise a thing when I wanted to get through to Mount Lester last night."

Diana herself saw to her father's lunch basket, and saw, too, that it was packed on the old car used for the run work. She gave Bill the Better the usual instructions how to make tea weak enough to prevent the squatter from having indigestion for a week. The old man liked tea jet-black.

At nine o'clock she was on the road to Opal Town, driving her own smart single-seater. The day gave promise of being gusty and dusty and altogether unpleasant. Already the mirage water, gathered over claypan and depression, appeared not to have its usual "body," to be attenuated, unreal. The sky was stained by a dull-white, high-level haze that, unable to defeat the sun, gave to its rays a peculiar yellow tint. Before half-past nine, she reached the boundary gate.

For miles she had steered her car in the wheel tracks last passed over by the car owned and driven by Sergeant Blake. Getting out to open the gate she saw, bush girl that she was, the small boot marks made by Bony when he had opened the gate to permit them to pass through from Karwir country. It was when beyond the gate that she saw the larger imprints made by the Sergeant, and on both sides of the fence there were many imprints of dogs, how many dogs she was unable to decide. These tracks mystified her, for Young Lacy had not thought it worth while to mention Bony's acquisition of dogs. There was much else to interest Diana Lacy. She ex-

amined the temporary camp used by Bony and the Sergeant
when they met every evening.

The pupils of her eyes were mere pin points when she drove
on to Opal Town. The lines about her mouth tended to
straighten out its delightful curves. Her mind was flooded
with questions, and in her heart was a vast unease.

Where had that man obtained the dogs? Why did he have
them with him? He had not got them from Karwir, and as
far as she knew he had not gone to the township. Sergeant
Blake must have brought them out. Why? Hardly for company.

If the wind failed to reach gale strength before it moved
round to the south, that man would read her own tracks, read
in them her interest in him and his dogs. What eyes he must
have to have found that tiny fibre of cable silk and the hair
attached to the bark of one tree out of countless numbers of
trees! And now he knew that the hair he had found had not
come from Anderson's head. And he had let her understand
that he suspected it had come from John Gordon's head.

This extraordinary half-caste seemed to be growing bigger
and bigger, or was it because he was occupying an increasingly large space in her mind? In all her twenty-odd years
Diana Lacy had had her way with men. She looked upon
men, the nice men, as having been especially born to amuse
her, to grant her wishes, to make the wheels of her life go
round. Only one man had she ever found a little difficult—
her father, in whom she suspected volcanic depths. Only one
man she feared, and she had come to fear him quite recently
—this strange man from the Criminal Investigation Branch.
She ought, she was sure, to despise him for his birth, to regard
him as she had always regarded half-castes, as unfortunate
people, but, well, not quite nice. And she was angry with
herself, and angry with him that his personality made it impossible for her to despise him.

Her feminine instinct informed her that Mr Napoleon

Bonaparte was "a nice man," not unlike a white man a little too deeply tanned by the sun. She did not fear him, physically. Physically he attracted her. She liked his face. She liked the way he smiled. She liked his eyes that were so blue and candid and friendly. It was his mind that she feared. He was the first man she had ever met who had demanded from her and received, recognition of his mental superiority.

All men she had come to look upon as subject to her feminine charm and wit, even her own father. No man had ever rebelled against her rule until this Bonaparte man had arrived. He conceded her charm, and this she had been quick to see. He would have paid tribute to her wit had she not from the first withdrawn herself from him. But not for a moment had he admitted any inferiority on his part. Her world had been calm and safe and sure before his arrival at Karwir. He had come to find out certain things and, despite her, he had found out certain things, and he would go on finding out other things—if the Barcoo sickness did not force him to give up.

Stopping the car outside Pine Hut, Diana remained seated, lighting a cigarette and quietly smoking while she carefully examined the building for sign of a chance swagman in occupation. No smoke rose from the iron chimney. The door was latched. She had noted the tracks made by Blake's car passing by along the road. There certainly were no tracks of dogs about this place.

The wind was carrying little dust eddies across the wide, clear, flat area of land stretching away from the front of the hut, and it sang in small high notes about the building, but she was confident, when stepping to ground, that it was not sufficiently strong to prevent ample warning of the approach of a car.

Oh, she knew the place well enough! Countless times had she stopped her car here to spend half an hour talking to John Gordon. To-day she was hoping desperately that she would hear his voice and not the voice of his mother saying that John was away out on the run and would not be home till late.

Before entering this one-room stockman's house, she surveyed its interior from the open doorway. There was the usual dust on the long table and the form flanking it. The usual sheets of newspaper littered the floor and unburned, charred wood rested on top of the white ash in the wide hearth. There, affixed to the wall just inside the door, was the telephone instrument with its small shelf for the writing of notes. There was dust on this shelf and on top of the box, the dust in which she had been charged with drawing little crosses.

Diana's face flamed. She knew she never had drawn crosses, and she knew that Bony knew she had never drawn crosses. Every time she thought of that luncheon she felt like shedding tears of vexation. To think that he could so successfully spring that on her, so take her by surprise that she was helpless to deny it—she a woman of the world and over twenty. His open suggestion of her secret meeting with John she had, of course, valiantly and resolutely defeated, but she had gone down like a simpleton before his crafty flank attack.

No, there was no defeating that mind behind the bright blue eyes. She believed what he had told her about his never failing in an investigation. A man with a mind like that could not fail. He wouldn't fail here at Karwir—unless the Barcoo sickness conquered. All that could be done was to retreat, to delay revelation, to smother up still further the thing that time should have successfully buried for ever.

Diana twirled the handle protruding from the box affair and lifted the horn monstrosity to her ear. No voice interrupted the song of the wind. Replacing the horn she rang again, and again lifted the horn to her ear. Only the song of the wind reached her. It came humming along the wire. It came in through the door in shrill cadences.

It was now that she saw the discolouration on the earth floor immediately below the instrument, and with sudden suspicion she raised the little clasp and pulled the front back from the box. Within, the two glass cells lay wrecked.

Without haste, her mind governed by a strang fatalistic calm, she stepped from the hut, latched the door after her, and walked to her car, there to sit and put a match to another cigarette. As her father sometimes said: there was nothing for it but hard smoking.

So he had broken the cells to prevent her from ringing up Meena! He knew it was John she had met on the boundary fence. He knew she had talked to John that day her brother flew her to Opal Town. Now he guessed that the hair he had found on the tree trunk had come from John's head. He had only talked about those hairs to lure her into another trap, knowing that she would try to communicate with John to tell him about the hairs. Well, she had fallen into the trap, as he would well know, because she couldn't wipe out the tracks like the blacks could. He knew she would try to tell John not to leave his hair on his comb and brushes or towels. Well, she wasn't beaten yet. She would go to Meena to tell John in person.

Down went the toe of the fashionable shoe to stamp hard on the starter button. The engine purred into life, and she swung the machine round to take the track to Meena homestead. The road was like a snake's track. She accelerated across the claypans and the hard areas of grey ground. She was forced to brake hard before reaching the sandy areas, fearful of a skid much worse than any produced by a slippery road. Twice she was stopped by a gate.

Mary Gordon came hurrying to meet her from the direction of the cow shed. She was carrying a heavy bucket of milk, her spare figure encased in a print frock and her head protected from the sun by a blue scarf.

"I heard you coming," she cried excitedly to Diana. "John's

out, and I've been out all the morning watching the blacks drive rabbits into a yard. The fire will be dead, but it won't take long to boil the kettle. I've got a new tin one that comes to the boil in a few minutes. I suppose you rang from Pine Hut and couldn't get us."

Diana, shorter than the elder woman, her youth and supple grace making striking contrast, said simply :

"I'd like a cup of tea. I'm sorry John is out. I wanted to see him most importantly."

"Well, come along in. The place will be upside down, but you mustn't mind. I went out before John left." Mary Gordon bustled on ahead through the wicket gate and along the cinder path to the veranda door, across the veranda and into the kitchen-living-room. There she turned to her visitor to say: "Well, I never ! I told John not to bother with anything, and he's washed up and tidied and actually re-set the table for me. Now you sit there on the couch while I make up the fire. And off with your hat. It'll cool your head."

With her hands raised to the task of removing her hat, Diana glanced about this pleasant, plainly furnished room that always gave the impression that it was thoroughly cleaned at least six times every day. It enshrined the family life of the Gordon clan. The modern sewing machine and the radio cabinet contrasted with the old muzzle-loading muskets left by John the First. The new tin kettle squatted beside the great iron ones brought here from outside in those years when utensils were made to last. The grandfather clock, the pride and affection of the first Mrs Gordon, gleamed not unlike the slender mulga shafts of the aborigines' spears. Table and chairs, pictures and ornaments represented the fashions of a hundred years. There were no flowers, but the floor exuded the refreshing smell of carbolic.

"The rabbits here are terrible," Mary rattled on. "I've never in all my life seen so many. What they're living on I don't know. I've got to stand over the hens while I feed them to stop them being robbed by the rabbits who don't fear me any more than the hens do. The cats and the dogs won't look at them, they're so sick of the sight of them. Jimmy Partner says they mayn't stay here much longer, and he and the blacks have been working at the skin getting. Yesterday he and the blacks built mile-long netted fence wings in the form of a great V, and at the point of the V they built a large trap-yard.

"Last night they lifted the netting off the ground and just hung it atop the temporary posts so that the rabbits from the warrens could run out on to the lake and feed on what's left of the rubbish in the middle of it. Then, before dawn, they went along the wings and pegged the netting to the ground. I went out while they were doing it, and afterwards we all walked round the lake to the far side where we waited till daybreak.

"My, it was exciting! We stretched out like a lot of Old Country beaters, and marched across the lake towards the trap beating tins and things. Oh, Diana! You ought to have been there. It was marvellous. The rabbits streamed towards the trap before us like a huge flock of sheep, all making for the warrens beyond the wing-fences. The eagles came down low and flew so close that you could see their beady red eyes. When the rabbits reached the wing-fences they ran along them in to the V point just like two rivers of fur. There must have been thousands and thousands. Thousands of them escaped by running back past us. Thousands more wouldn't go into the trap-yard, but in the yard, when we got to it, Jimmy Partner estimated there were five to six thousand. The blacks are all down there now skinning them. And skins are such a good price this year, too."

"The Kalchut banking account ought to swell this month if the blacks can trap them like that," Diana said, smiling at the other woman's enthusiasm.

"It will, dear, but if they catch as many every morning for

twelve months it won't make any difference to the horde."
Mary abruptly sat down on the couch beside the girl. "I'm
sorry John isn't at home. He'll be ever so disappointed when
he knows you came."

"I suppose he will be away all day?"

"Yes, he will so. He and Jimmy Partner have been cutting
scrub for the ewes away over at the foot of the Painted Hills.
Jimmy Partner ought to have been with him to-day, but Nero
and the others didn't quite know how to make the trap-yard."

Diana nodded. Mary saw her disappointment.

"John has never told you about what happened to Jeffery
Anderson, has he?" Diana softly questioned.

"What happened to him! No. What did happen to him?"
Mary's expression of pleasure at the visit changed swiftly
to one of alarm.

"Would you be a brave dear woman and not question me?
You see, I can't say anything because John made me promise
not to. I have always thought he ought to tell you, but he says
it would be better for him and everyone for you not to know.
Things are better forgotten. I've come over chiefly to get him,
or you, to collect every hair of his that may be on his comb
and brushes and pillows and towels."

"Mercy me, why?"

The girl made a slight despairing motion with her hands.

"I can't tell you. I promised John I wouldn't without his
permission. You've just got to trust me and him, too. He'd
be angry with me if he knew I had said anything to you at
all, but I can't help it as he is away and we must gather up
any hairs he might have left."

Mary glanced helplessly out through the window. When she
encountered the violet eyes again there was horror in her own.

"I—I—have sometimes wondered," she said slowly. "I
can't forget that night of rain when I waited here listening for
them to come home, and then went down to the blacks' camp
to get them to go and search. They were very late. Jimmy

Partner was talking to Nero, and the next morning all the blacks went off on walk-about. Then John came home, and he had a blue bruise across his throat, and he said it had been done when he rode under a tree branch in the dark. I—I—won't ask questions. But please answer this one. Is there any danger to John—through Inspector Bonaparte?"

Diana nodded and sighed softly.

"Yes. The detective is finding out about things. Oh, I wish John had been home, and then I should not have had to upset you. I wish he had confided in you. But it's too late to wish that. We've got to work to protect him. We've got to be very careful. I can see now that John was very wise not to tell you anything at all, because, should Inspector Bonaparte come again and question you, you can tell him nothing because you know nothing."

"But I do. I know about——"

"You know nothing, dear. Just remember that you know nothing. You can help him by knowing nothing. Don't you see that?"

Mary Gordon stood looking down into the troubled eyes, and slowly her mouth became grim and her own eyes determined.

"I shall give nothing away, Diana, and I shall never question John. He will tell me when he thinks it proper. I know how to fight. I've had to fight all my life. There now, the kettle's boiling, and after we've had a cup of tea we'll hunt for every blessed hair."

Turning, she walked towards the stove, then stopped to stare at a striped linen mattress cover neatly folded and resting on the dresser.

"That's funny!" she exclaimed, crossing to the dresser and taking up the mattress cover. Permitting one end to fall to the floor, she shook it out, and discovered that the end on the floor was cut right across. Reversing it, she held the striped cover like an open sack. Diana watched, a frown puckering her eyes. She saw one brown hand slip down and into the cover and then come out with a black feather held between forefinger and thumb.

"What is there peculiar about it?" asked the girl.

Mary uttered a little sharp laugh of bewilderment. Then she said, looking at Diana over the mattress cover:

"Years ago, when my husband was alive, the lake was crowded with birds, and one winter he and the blacks shot enough of them to fill two mattresses with their feathers. One mattress John has always slept on. The other was always on one of the spare beds. About four weeks ago I found the mattress on the spare bed missing. I asked John about it and he didn't know anything. I asked Jimmy Partner and he didn't know about it. The blacks have never once robbed us. And now here's the mattress cover with all the feathers gone."

"Someone must have taken it. Perhaps John found it in the bush somewhere."

"But he would have said something about it last night when he came home. Unless he found it this morning, perhaps in the harness shed."

Diana's face had become strained and pale.

"What time was John to leave this morning," she asked.

"What time? Oh, early. About six o'clock."

"And you were away from before daybreak?"

"Yes. Why?"

"No one else was here? All the blacks were away at the rabbit drive?"

"All of them except Wandin. I saw him on my way back home. He was sitting before a little fire all by himself, and he looked like a praying mantis."

"Then it must have been John who found the cover."

"Yes, of course. There could be no one else. My, it's going to be a nasty day. And here am I forgetting all about the tea."

Diana drank her tea appreciatively despite her worrying thoughts, and afterwards the two women passed along to the short passage and entered John's room. Determination overcoming her diffidence, Diana thoroughly searched the pillows and sheets for hair and found two on a pillow, while Mary took the brushes and the comb to the kitchen and burned every hair on those articles. Satisfied now that Mr Napoleon Bonaparte was checkmated, Diana put on her hat preparatory to leaving for the township.

"You needn't tell John what we've done, dear, but you must watch his toilet things and his pillows in case that detective should come over. I don't think he would dare to ask John directly for one of his hairs."

"Don't you worry, Diana," Mary said, her mouth still grim. "I was nice to Mr Bonaparte when he came in your brother's plane, and I'll be nice to him again, but he'll get nothing out of me."

"I thought you would be sensible," the girl said softly, and then hugged the older woman and kissed her with deep affection. "Tell John that the telephone jars at Pine Hut are somehow broken and want replacing. And I'll meet him at the burnt tree on the boundary at eleven to-morrow morning. Don't forget to tell him that, will you?"

"I'll not forget. Good-bye, and leave me to do the fighting at Meena."

Mary accompanied her guest out to the car, then stood watching it slide noiselessly away into the rising dust, the wind-hiss over the ground subduing the hum of the engine.

Diana had covered seven of the twelve miles to Pine Hut when she saw far ahead a horseman, also riding to Pine Hut. Not until she was close behind him did he hear the engine of her car. He reined his horse off the track and looked round. It was Bony.

He was riding to Pine Hut. He could have come from nowhere save the Meena homestead.

CHAPTER NINETEEN

Seed Planting

DIANA stared through the red, dust-laden air at the man seated on the brown mare. She knew him to be Detective-Inspector Bonaparte, but he was in the light of day so changed in physical aspect as to astonish her. The previous evening she had seen him in the dull glow of departing day, and subsequently in the white light of the office petrol lamp, when he had looked both tired and indisposed. But this morning she could the better compare his appearance with what it had been that luncheon hour on the Karwir south veranda.

Though this man was her enemy, Diana's feminine sympathy claimed her heart as she watched him lift his hat to her, then slide down from the horse's back, and advance with peculiar gait, leading the mare.

She did not get out of the car. Switching off the engine ignition, she leaned a little over the sill of the door window. Somehow she thought of a Chinese lantern wind-blown in the morning after a night of gaiety. The lantern of this man's personality, so clearly to be seen in his eyes, in his smile, had gone out. Debonair, suave, naturally courteous, she had known him. Now he stood within a yard of her, his eyes afire with a strange light, the wind ruffling his straight black hair, his hat still held in his left hand. He seemed to be smaller in stature, and it was as though the wind were swaying his body.

Then he smiled, and that was the completing line in a caricature.

"Good morning, Miss Lacy!" he said, his well remembered voice still pleasing when she expected it to be harsh. Her own voice sounded small and distant.

"Good morning, Inspector. You look ill this morning. Is the Barcoo sickness as bad as ever?"

"I fear so. I have come to regard it as a competitor in a race. It and I race to the goal represented by the end of this investigation. Which will win is at present uncertain."

"You certainly look very ill. Don't you think you ought to see a doctor?"

"A doctor would say: 'My man, because you have the Barcoo sickness, you must at once get away from the back country, and the medicine I shall prescribe will then defeat the cause of the malady.' My own condition interests me much, for it is not unlike that of a victim to the pointing of the bone by wild aborigines. I saw a man die of being boned. He, too, was unable to retain food, and he told that nightly he had fearful dreams so that he could not properly sleep. In the end he died, after having complained of bones constantly being thrust into his liver, and his kidneys being constantly lacerated by the eagle's claws. I am suffering pains in those organs."

"But surely you don't believe that your illness is due to the blacks having pointed the bone at you?" Diana said, her brows raised in incredulity.

"I have the Barcoo sickness, Miss Lacy. It is unfortunate, but I will not permit it to interfere with my work—yet. I trust you were more fortunate in your visit to Meena. There was no one at home when I called."

Diana plunged recklessly:

"Why did you call?"

She could have bitten out her tongue after putting the unwarranted question, and she was still more furious when he replied politely and without hesitation:

"I rode over to return a mattress cover I found in the bush, knowing by the marked tag that it originally came from Meena. I expect the blacks required the feathers and took it without understanding they were committing a white man's crime."

"Oh!"

"They use feathers on their feet, you know, when they wish to escape an enemy by leaving no tracks—and to wipe out tracks that they do not wish to remain in evidence."

The suggestion she ignored.

"Was it you who smashed the telephone jars in the instrument at Pine Hut?"

"No. Why should I do that?"

"I don't know really. Our telephone to Opal Town was out of order, too, from eight o'clock last night to nearly eight this morning. You are such a queer man, and so many queer things have happened since you came to Karwir."

"Indeed!"

"Yes, indeed! Little crosses made in the dust on the telephone instrument at Pine Hut was one of the queer things. I could not see any crosses there this morning when I stopped."

"I wiped the instrument clean after I had observed them," Bony countered gravely. "The dust there now has accumulated since I cleaned the instrument. So you didn't notice any more crosses this morning?"

"I think I had better be getting along, Mr Bonaparte," Diana said a little sharply, almost betraying herself by laughing. And then she sprang her little trap. "Did you find any of Mr Gordon's hair at Meena?"

Now his eyes became as large as saucers.

"Mr Gordon's hair! Why do you think I should be interested in Mr Gordon's hair?"

"Just to compare some of it with the hair you say you found clinging to a certain tree."

"Ah! Now why didn't I think of that? Mr Gordon's hair is light-brown, I am told. It is not dissimilar to that of the missing man. When I see Mr Gordon again I must ask him for one or two of his hairs and compare them under the lens of the microscope."

There was no catching this man in a verbal trap. There was no getting round corners to see into his mind. Ill he certainly was, but he was still master of his mind.

"Well, good-bye!" she called to him. "You really ought to see a doctor, or you will come to believe that you've been boned by the blacks. Anyway, follow dad's prescription of the sliced potatoes steeped in vinegar. Dad's a good bush doctor, you know."

Bony bowed his head to indicate that he heard her above the whine of the wind, and stood watching the car glide away with its escort of following dust.

"The Barcoo sickness is what he's got," she was saying aloud, a habit easily formed by one travelling alone. "The pointing bone business is all tosh. John would never get the blacks to do such a thing. I can't think that he would, although he and his mother would go far. No, it can't be that. Anyway, pointing the bone wouldn't be effective against a man like the Inspector. He's educated. He's ever so much more highly educated than I am."

She drove all the way to Pine Hut with the dust clouds raised by the wheels behind her. The hut came out of a red murk to meet her, silently to salute her as she passed it to reach the Karwir road to Opal Town. Here at the road junction she stopped the car, undecided whether to go on to the township or to return home. Again she spoke aloud.

"Oh yes, that man went to Meena hoping for the opportunity of getting some of John's hair. The opportunity was just waiting for him. In one of his pockets at this moment some of John's hair is wrapped up in a cigarette paper or an envelope. Ye gods! That man's as deep as the ocean. Oh! I wonder now! Yes, that might work. There can't be any harm in trying it. An acorn planted may become a giant tree."

Diana reached Opal Town at exactly twelve o'clock, and there standing outside the police station was Sergeant Blake.

"Good day, Miss Lacy!" he shouted above the wind. "Bad day to come to town."

"Yes, isn't it, Mr Blake?" Diana agreed, sweetly. "I have to shop and couldn't delay doing it. You know, dad's quite worried."

"Oh—what about?"

"He's worried about Mr Bonaparte. He says that if Mr Bonaparte really has got the Barcoo sickness he should leave at once and see a doctor. He feels that he is in some way responsible for anyone working on his run, you see. Although Mr Bonaparte is not actually working for dad, he is on Karwir. It would be terrible if Mr Bonaparte became so weak and ill that he died in his lonely camp, wouldn't it?"

"He won't do that, I think, Miss Lacy. I go out and meet him every evening. He's very keen to finalize his case, and from the way it's going he mightn't be long in doing that."

"Well, let's hope he does it soon and then seeks medical aid. I met him this morning. He looks really ill. He told me that his illness was not unlike the effects of being boned by the blacks. Surely he doesn't thing the Kalchut blacks have boned him?"

"I wouldn't put it past some of them," Blake countered, cautiously. "Are you going to run in and see the wife? She'd be happy to make a pot of tea."

"I know she would, and I will go in and ask her. I'm as thirsty as a cattle dog after a day's work. Now you stay out here and keep your eyes open for escaping criminals. You wouldn't be interested in our gossip."

Blake smiled and opened the door for her, and then glanced

at her flying feet as she ran into the police station. He stared down the dust-painted street and frowned. It would be awkward if Bonaparte did die out there on Karwir. There might be hell to pay over it.

In the living room the large Mrs Blake was fussing about her visitor.

"You go into the bedroom, Miss Lacy, and wash the dust off your face and hands. You know the way. I'll make the tea. My, what a day!"

Diana hurried with her toilet, indeed grateful to Mrs Blake, but frantically hoping that Sergeant Blake would not come in and ruin the chance for a little gossip.

"How's your father?" asked Mrs Blake when Diana joined her. "He's a wonderful man for his age and all. Pity the country hasn't more like him."

"Oh, he's quite well, thank you. Of course, he refuses to give up or even to think he's getting old. He's a little worried about Mr Bonaparte, though."

"Yes, the Sergeant said Mr Bonaparte was poorly," Mrs Blake remarked. "What a wonderful man he is to be sure. So polished, so unassuming."

"They think a great deal of him down in Brisbane, don't they?" suggested Diana, still frantically hoping that this *tête-à-tête* would not be interrupted.

"The Sergeant says that they think the sun shines out of his boots," replied Mrs Blake. "How is your tea?"

"Lovely. I was so thirsty. It's a beast of a day. Yes, that's what dad says about Mr Bonaparte. That's why he's so worried, in a way. You see, if anything happened to Mr Bonaparte, if he became so ill and weak that he died out there in the bush, dad would feel himself partly to blame. They'd say, down in Brisbane, that he ought to have done something to make Mr Bonaparte give up."

"Hm! They might do that, Miss Lacy. Still, Mr Bonaparte is not that ill, surely?"

"I met him this morning on the road. Stopped to talk to him for five minutes. He looks positively awful. He cannot keep any food down, he says. Well, you know, he can't go on like that, can he?"

"No, that's so," agreed Mrs Blake, her brows drawn close in a frown.

"I think that Sergeant Blake ought to urge him to go away and receive medical attention. It's none of my business, I know, but if anything happened to Mr Bonaparte they might blame Mr Blake for allowing him to go on when he's so ill. I don't know what to do. Neither does dad. Well, I must be going. I must hurry through my shopping and get home before the dust gets much worse. Thank you for the tea. It's really kind of you. When are you going to make that husband of yours bring you to Karwir in the new car? You make him."

Mrs Blake smiled. "He's always too busy—so he says," she answered, a little grimly.

She followed the girl out to the car, and Diana was thankful that the Sergeant was nowhere in sight. Having again urged Mrs Blake to make her husband take her out to Karwir, Diana set off on her shopping excursion, which, surprisingly, was very quickly completed.

When she left the town the bush on the Common was lashed by the dust-laden wind and the undersides of the blue-bushes were brillian purple. Into the teeth of the hot wind she sent the machine, now less pestered by the dust that rose in a long slant behind it.

"An acorn becomes a giant tree in favourable circumstances," she said aloud. "The little acorns I planted in the minds of Sergeant Blake and his wife might well grow to big trees. He'll urge Bonaparte to give up the investigation and retire. She'll urge her husband to write to headquarters about his illness, if he won't give up. And headquarters will do something about it, for sure. And then John will be safe."

She saw nothing of the brown mare and her rider on the

drive back to Karwir, where she found it impossible to take her lunch with her brother on the south veranda. The dust compelled them to eat in the morning-room, and after lunch Young Lacy returned to his work in the office. Diana retired to her room, partly undressed and donned a dressing-gown before settling to write letters.

It was a little before four o'clock when she heard the car returning from outback. Two minutes later Young Lacy burst unceremoniously into her room. Calamity was written plainly on his boyish face.

"Bill the Better is home. The dad has come a cropper. Bill says he's broken a leg. Went down the well and slipped."

"Broken a leg! Where is he?"

"Out at Blackfellow's. Wouldn't let Bill and Fred put him on the car. Sent in for the truck. We're going out for him. We'll want a mattress or two."

"And Dr Linden," added Diana, white-faced but calmly courageous. "You call him and tell him to come out at once. I'll see to the things we'll want. I'm going with you."

"All right. Rush. We can't lose time."

Diana ran into the passage and shouted for Mabel the maid. She was flinging on her clothes when the girl appeared.

"Tell the cook to make tea in the thermos flasks. We'll want a bottle of milk. Get the bottle of brandy from the chiffonier. Bill the Better can take the mattresses from the beds in the two single rooms."

"All right, Miss Lacy. Is Mr Lacy badly hurt?"

"Yes, very, but don't stand there talking."

When Diana went out to the truck it was loaded and her brother was waiting at the wheel. She climbed into the seat next to him, Bill the Better beside her. He was red with dust, but his watery blue eyes were at the moment strangely clear and hard.

"The boss would go down the flamin' well," he shouted to beat the roar of the engine and the wind lashing the passing trees. "I went down and told 'im and Fred what was wrong and where it was wrong. Fred tried to stop 'im goin' down, but 'e would go down. Why does 'e think 'e's a bloomin' three-year-old? 'E slipped off the ladder and ended up on the pump platform. Busted a leg down there, 'e did. I went down after 'im, and lashed 'im to the windlass rope and held 'im while old Fred pulled us up."

"Where is the leg broken, do you know?" Diana asked, wondering why her brother didn't drive the truck all out as she would have done.

"Dunno properly. In the thigh it looks like. The boss 'e yells at me and says: 'You tell 'em back at the homestead not to send for no flamin' quack till I say so.' We lays 'im out on the ground, careful like, and Fred got 'is straw mattress for 'im to set 'is head on. Then 'e says: 'Wot in 'ell are yer gapin' at me like that for? Get goin' in the car and don't drive fast or you'll bust the big ends and the station can't afford a new set with the dry times on us."

A few minutes later, he said:

"Me and old Fred done our best, but 'e would go down the flamin' well. You know how 'tis. There ain't no 'oldin' the boss when 'e's set on doing anythink."

Diana laid a hand on his grimy forearm, saying:

"Don't you worry, Bill. We know you did your best. Everything will be all right."

They found Old Lacy lying on the ground near the well coping, his head resting on a straw mattress, a billy of jet-black tea and two pannikins beside him. Fred rose from squatting on his other side. He was a wild-whiskered nugget of a man.

Diana ran to her father and knelt at his side. She stared down at him with tear-filled eyes.

"Oh dad, is the poor leg broken, d'you think?"

" 'Fraid so, my gal, but don't you fret. It was me own fault. Bill was doing all right, but I went down to check up on him, old fool that I am. You brought the mattresses? Good! Set em out on the floor of the truck. Fred's taken the door off the hut to roll me on and to lift me up on to the truck."

Diana offered him brandy but he refused it. They lifted him on to the door, and he instructed them how to raise him carefully and then to slide him off the door on to the mattresses.

"Have a peg before we start?" suggested Young Lacy.

"No, lad, I'm all right. Give a stiffener to Fred and Bill. Where the devil have you got to, Fred? Oh, there you are! Don't you go down that flaming well, now. I'll send out to have the cattle shifted until we can put another shaft down. I think I will have a peg, lad. I got sort of shook up."

It was noon the next day when Diana remembered her appointment with John Gordon fixed for eleven o'clock.

CHAPTER TWENTY

Colonel Spendor

THE well nourished and still erect figure of the Chief Commissioner of the Queensland Police passed through the outer office to that inner room in which even the walls exuded police history. He was white-haired and white-moustached; his feet trod lightly, bespeaking training as a cavalry officer; his lounge suit of light-grey tweed fitted admirably, but a uniform would have fitted better.

"Good morning, sir!" said the secretary, having come to attention from bending over the huge table desk set in the middle of the large room.

"Mornin' Lowther!"

Off came the Chief Commissioner's hat, to be flung into a chair as he passed behind the desk to the comfortable swivel affair in which he did his daily work. Lowther retrieved the hat and hung it on its peg inside a wall cupboard. He had shaken the cushion in the swivel chair, but Colonel Spendor punched and belaboured it further till he was satisfied. Then with many snorts and hmffs, he sat down.

The morning had begun.

Two pink, plump hands went out to draw a pile of opened correspondence nearer their owner. A pair of dark-grey eyes directed a flashing glance to the secretary still standing beside his chief.

"Well, what the devil are you standing there for? Got a pain or something?"

Long association with Colonel Spendor had given Lowther mastery over his features.

"Superintendent Browne is anxious to see you as early as possible, sir," Lowther murmured.

"Browne!" The Colonel swung a little sideways the better to deliver a frontal attack. He repeated the name as though it had been that of a famous ballet dancer, gave a terrific snort, and propelled himself round again to the table with such violence that the chair revolved almost in a complete circle.

"Superintendent Browne hinted, sir, that the urgency of the matter was dictated by a communication concerning Detective-Inspector Bonaparte."

Two plump hands swept aside the pile of correspondence, then they fell to the chair arms and grasped them, so that when the Colonel rose the chair rose with him. When he relaxed the chair thudded heavily on the carpet.

"A deserter, Lowther. I ordered Bonaparte to report by a certain date. He said he would before he left on that assignment. He didn't report on the date named. I wrote saying that if on the expiry of the term he had not reported he would be dismissed. He hasn't reported. He flouts my authority. Dumbly tells me to go to hades. He's unreliable, Lowther. I'm tired of him. Now, no more about Browne. I'll see him at the morning conference."

Colonel Spendor dragged the pile of correspondence tempestuously to him.

"Inspector Bonaparte is too much a Javert, sir. I wouldn't like him on my tail."

"I'm not interested in your tail, Lowther. I am trying to be interested in this correspondence, trying to earn my salary. I'm the only one here who is trying to do that. How many times have I had to sack Bonaparte? Tell me that, as you seem to ache for a back-yard gossip this morning."

"Six times, sir. You have reinstated him without loss of pay on six occasions."

"Just so, Lowther. I'm soft. But I'm not going to be soft any more. Discipline was becoming so bad that it would have been only a matter of time when every constable on the beat would have thumbed his nose as I passed by. What progress is Askew making on the Strathmore case? Did Browne tell you that?"

"He didn't mention it, sir."

"He wouldn't. Why? Because Askew is a fool. Why? Because Browne would sooner waste my time than take an interest in his department. Bonaparte should have been assigned to that case, and, Lowther, Bonaparte is mooning about the bush looking at the birds and things and explainin' to people what a damned fine detective he is." Up rose the Colonel and the chair to fall again with a thud. Police typists in the office below looked at each other and grinned.

The courageous Lowther persisted.

"The matter concerning Inspector Bonaparte is one of life and death, sir."

"Life and death!" shouted Colonel Spendor. "Aren't we all alive to-day and dead to-morrow? What the devil's the matter with you this morning? Blast you, Lowther, you must be sickening for something."

"Maybe, sir, but I would urge you to see Superintendent Browne. I wouldn't dare to urge it, but the Superintendent stressed the importance of the matter."

Colonel Spendor sighed as though he had held his breathing for five minutes. Again he looked directly at his secretary.

"It's well for you, Lowther, that I'm a meek and tolerant man," he said, without sign of humour. "I'll see Browne. Send him in."

The Officer in Charge of the Criminal Investigation Branch

was waiting in the outer office. A large man in his early fifties, Browne looked precisely what he was—a bulldog. Long before he could reach the Colonel's desk he was asked, firmly:

"What the devil d'you want to interrupt me at my routine work for? You know I never grant interviews before I clear my desk. Sit down—there."

A pudgy pink forefinger indicated the chair placed opposite the Chief Commissioner.

"Thank you, sir. When you have heard me you will probably be glad that I insisted on seeing you so early," Browne said, before sitting down. "I have had a personal letter from Sergeant J. M. Blake, stationed at Opal Town. Mrs Blake is related to my wife, and on that score Sergeant Blake has written privately to me instead of through the ordinary official channels. You will remember, sir, that Inspector Bonaparte went to Opal Town several weeks ago to investigate a disappearance."

"Yes, yes! Get on with it. What's it all about?"

"I'll read you Sergeant Blake's letter. He writes:

Dear Harry—It is only after much hesitation that I am writing to you on a subject that ought probably to be dealt with officially. On the other hand to write officially might get me into hot water because my position is very awkward; and it might be thought that I had no right to interfere in what concerned your Branch and about an officer in your Branch who is my superior. So please understand that I am writing privately and not as a policeman.

Here are certain facts and certain opinions concerning D.-I. Bonaparte now investigating the disappearance of a man named Jeffery Anderson.

When D.-I. Bonaparte began his investigation, five months had passed since Anderson disappeared. He came to believe that the local tribe of blacks had had something to

213

do with it, because some of them kept watch on him and used feathers on their feet to prevent him knowing it.

On 19 October one or more members of the tribe pointed the bone at D.-I. Bonaparte when he was asleep on the veranda of an old hut, leaving at his side a ball of grass gum in which were embedded a number of his discarded cigarette ends, this being a kind of notice of the boning. Shortly afterwards D.-I. Bonaparte complained of being unable to sleep at night, of his skin being irritated by pricking, and of pains in his liver and kidneys. Then, he got so that he was unable to retain food.

When I suggested that he give up the case, *pro tem*, and return to Brisbane, he raved at me and said he wouldn't think of giving up the case until he had finalized it, that he had had no failures and he wasn't going to have a failure this time. His nerves seemed shot to pieces, and he complained bitterly of having been put on leave without pay, and of being interfered with as though he were an ordinary policeman. Then he split open an envelope and wrote his resignation on it and gave it to me to forward. When he wasn't looking, I dropped it into the lunch fire.

On subsequent dates when I saw him he appeared increasingly worse. He is unable to retain food, and his strength is being sapped, but his mind is as keen as ever and his determination to finalize his case, or die in the attempt, is unshaken. Kate has cooked special food for him which I have taken out every evening, but D.-I. Bonaparte is unable to retain it although he feels hungry.

His illness is similar to what is called the Barcoo sickness, but for several reasons I don't think it is that. He hasn't been long enough outback this time to have contracted the Barcoo sickness. The sickness came immediately after the boning. And there is no pain in the liver and kidneys of the sufferer from the Barcoo sickness.

When I suggested that I take a hand and try to discover which of the blacks had done the boning, D.-I. Bonaparte would not hear of it. Nor would he allow me to interview a Mr John Gordon who has great influence over the blacks, arguing that should he have to pull in Mr Gordon he would be embarrassed by the fact of Mr Gordon's having acted on his behalf. You understand, D.-I Bonaparte took me into his confidence only after I had promised to respect it and do nothing without his permission.

I am writing to you without his permission, and I don't feel too good about it. But, as Ida says, if D.-I. Bonaparte should die before he winds up his case we would feel responsible, and the police heads might hold it against me. Anyway, we both like D.-I. Bonaparte, and his present condition of health is felt by us as a personal matter.

I think that D.-I. Bonaparate was boned, and that he is not suffering from the Barcoo sicknes. A lot of ignorant people would laugh at the very idea, but I've heard things, and Mr Lacy, of Karwir, tells of bonings that have come within his experience. Then again, the local blacks are not de-tribalized. The Gordons have done and are doing everything in their power to keep white influence from destroying the Kalchut blacks, so that these people still practise their ancient customs and initiation rites.

You may or may not know that the actual act of pointing the bone is only show. The thing lying behind it, that does the killing, is the mental power of thought transference, the organs of the victim reacting in accordance with the thought-suggestions received from the executioners. D.-I. Bonaparte, being a half-caste, is more liable to be affected by this magic than a white man would be. And in Mr Lacy's experience even a white man was boned to death.

Miss Lacy and her father, as well as myself, have urged D.-I. Bonaparte to retire from his case and see a doctor. But the Lacys don't know of the boning and D.-I. Bonaparte argues that, since he was boned, no treatment for the

Barcoo sickness would be any good. He says that the boning is being carried on to force him to give up his case, and that if he completes it, or if he consents to retire (which he won't) the boning will stop and he will automatically recover.

The point is that he won't retire, and it looks as though he may die before he can finish his investigation. Doctors would be unable to cure him. The arrest of the entire Kalchut tribe, besides going against D.-I. Bonaparte's wishes, would not have the effect of stopping the boning; moreover it would be next to impossible, for at Opal Town there is not nearly sufficient jail accommodation.

Well, Harry, there are the facts. You will understand my position. I know something of D.-I. Bonaparte's investigation, and I don't think he has a chance of finishing this job. Only this evening when I was out there to see him he had barely the strength to get on his horse. All he can take is brandy and water. He can't go on long like that. It seems to me that the only thing to do is to remove him to Brisbane by force.

Superintendent Browne looked up from the letter and encountered the wide eyes of his chief. "Well, what do you think, sir? Gastric trouble or black magic?"

Colonel Spendor had become remarkably passive.

"Causes don't matter two hoots, Browne," he replied. "It's the effects we have to combat. We have to fight the effects and to save Bonaparte for years of service to the State. Blast him, Browne! We both like the fellow; we both acknowledge his remarkable gifts and charm of manner, and now we've to take off our hats to him for his pertinacity and courage. Hang it, I'd sooner lose you than him."

"And I'd sooner lose you as my chief than Bony," flashed Superintendent Browne.

"That's right! Argue!" shouted the Colonel. "Waste time

arguing when that poor fellow's out there in the back of beyond dying. By gad, Browne, it's terrible. Let me see! Yes,
you send Sergeant—No, that won't do. Ah—what about you
going out to Opal Town? You could bring Bony back, arrest
him if necessary. Trip would do you good. Buck you up.
You're getting too easy with the men. Charter a plane. Go
on, do something instead of gawking at me like that."

A snort. Browne was on his feet. The Colonel pushed his
chair back so forcibly that it turned over.

"Money! You ring up the aerodrome about the plane. I'll
see to the money."

As Browne and his chief moved towards the door, Colonel
Spendor bawled for Lowther. Lowther opened the door before
Browne could do so.

"You called, sir?"

"Called, Lowther? No, I was singing a tune. You sit down
and write a draft letter to the Chief Secretary saying that our
advice about the termination of Bonaparte's appointment was
based on wrong premises. You know, much regret and all that
foolishness."

"It's not necessary, sir. The letter referring to Inspector
Bonaparte's appointment was never sent."

"Never sent! Why?"

"I forgot to send it, sir."

Lowther was standing erect, his face a mask.

Slowly the grim expression of the Colonel's brick-red face
faded, and slowly into the dark-grey eyes crept a furtive gleam
like sunshine seen through falling rain. Out went one plump
hand to grasp Lowther's forearm and squeeze it. Colonel
Spendor knew that his secretary never forgot anything.

CHAPTER TWENTY-ONE

Facets

ON the morning of the first of November Sergeant Blake received this telegram:

> Superintendent Browne leaving by plane to-day for Opal Town. Try to obtain Inspector Bonaparte's consent to camp with him. Do all possible assist valued officer of the Department. Your action commended. Spendor.

Mrs Blake read this message twice before looking up to encounter her husband's eyes.

"I said you would be doing the right thing by writing to Harry," she said, very much the woman. " 'Your action commended.' It might mean a transfer east, or even promotion. Anyway, you're relieved of responsibility, or very soon will be. Harry ought to be here when?"

"Late this evening. That's if he leaves early to-day. Don't think he will, though, otherwise I wouldn't have been urged to get Bony's consent to camp with him."

"When are you leaving for his camp?"

"About eleven," Blake replied. "I've a few jobs to do in the office."

"Well, I'm sending out a billy of fresh milk and some coffee. You try to persuade Bony to drink some. It'll be better than only the brandy and water. Thank the good God that Harry is coming west to take him away. Such a nice man, too, in spite of his birth. What about taking a mattress and blankets in case Bony consents—?"

"It'd be no use. He won't let me stay with him."

Blake hurried back to the office to answer a telephone summons. He stepped smartly, for the load that had ridden him since he had written his letter to Superintendent Browne was now lifted. "Your action commended" sounded good. To his surprise he heard the voice of Old Lacy when he answered the call.

"Good day-ee, Sergeant. No, I'm not up. The leg is still ironed in plaster and the women won't leave me alone. The lad has put an extension of the phone through to my bedroom so's I can talk to the hands and shake 'em up. How's Bony?"

"No better, Mr Lacy. He's becoming very weak."

"Has he still got the pains in his kidneys and where his liver ought to be?"

"Yes, gets them bad at night. He can't sleep, and then when day comes he won't, saying he mustn't let up on his work."

"Humph! Well, he's got plenty of guts, that feller, I must say. I've been thinking about him a lot, and I'm getting damned worried. You remember when you came out here and I told you that a man suffering from the Barcoo sickness wouldn't get pains where he's got 'em?"

"Yes."

"Well, as I said, I've been thinking and worrying a lot about Bony. I don't believe he's got the Barcoo sickness. I think he's been boned by some of those Kalchut blacks. Stands to reason that having killed Jeff Anderson, as I've always thought, they would try to prevent anyone from sheeting the crime home to them. Bony being a half-caste gives them a pull."

Blake raised the old argument of the triumph of education over such superstition.

"Education makes no difference, except that the boning takes longer to accomplish, Sergeant. Either he's being boned or he's being poisoned. The blacks would even do that, even poison the water when he was away from camp. I'm voting for the boning, anyway. He will have to clear out. There's nothing else for it. If he doesn't the bone will finish him. You'd better report his condition and advise his removal if he won't go."

"Yes, I suppose that is what had better be done," agreed Blake, and added: "Miss Lacy been talking it over with you?"

"Well, yes, she mentioned that one day she met Bony and he told her his condition was something like the effects of being boned. She's a bit worried, too. Now, look here. You being under Bony in rank, and probably not wanting to interfere, what if I write to Brisbane and tell 'em what we suspect?"

"Might be a good idea," conceded Blake, thoughtfully.

"All right! I'll write to-day, now. The lad is flying to town this afternoon with the mail. I'm sorry to have to do it, but we can't let Bony die in trying to clear up what most likely will never be known. So long!"

"How's the old leg?" Blake managed to get in before Old Lacy could hang up.

"What's that? Oh, the leg! Gives me jip. They've got it hoisted to the roof, and the women won't let me move. Linden says I'll be here for weeks yet." There was a throaty chuckle. "The quack wanted me to go to the hospital where he'd have me under his eyes, but I'm not havin' any. When a man's got to leave his home he can leave it in a box. I'm staying here so's I can keep a tally on things. I'm a long way from being dead or disinterested in my job."

"There's nothing like keeping cheerful to live long," Blake said, himself cheerful.

He arrived at the Karwir boundary gate a few minutes before twelve o'clock. This place of meeting had had to be abandoned because of Bony's increasing physical weakness. Blake drove on towards Karwir another mile and took the branch track to Green Swamp. Three miles from the main road he came to the southern edge of the southernmost depression on which stood the corner post where the netted barrier ran north for two miles to turn east again opposite Bony's tent camp. By now Sergeant Blake's car had laid a trail over the several depressions and the narrow sand-banks separating them, and to-day when he sent the machine across each depression it was not unlike driving through lakes of water, so heavy was the mirage. The car's tracks on the wide, flat depressions were barely discernible, but they could be seen crossing the sand-banks that appeared like a distant shore.

When he had crossed the northernmost of the depressions and was moving over the flat land towards the towering dunes of sand at the edge of which smoked Bony's fire before the white tent, two dogs came racing to welcome him. They barked frantically about the car until it stopped a little distance from the fire.

Detective-Inspector Bonaparte was sitting on an empty petrol case in the shade of one of the two cabbage-trees. As Blake alighted from the machine, he rose to his feet, drew water from the nearby iron tank, and carried the billy to the fire. Bony looked an aged man. His body was bent. His face was a travesty, the cheeks being sunken, the eyes lustreless, the mouth a fixed grin. Only the voice was unaltered.

"Good day, Sergeant," came the soft tones and pure accent. "It is good of you to come out this hot day."

"Oh, the heat's nothing. I'm used to it. How're you feeling to-day?"

"Not good, Sergeant. Another bad night. I have just awakened from an uneasy sleep. I felt work beyond me this morning, but we will get to it again this afternoon. Anderson lies near here, I am positively sure. He cannot be beyond a mile away. As I told you yesterday, I have only to find his grave and then my investigation is complete."

"Righto! We'll get on with the burrowing among those dunes after lunch. I've brought out some milk and the wife says I'm to try you with some coffee. Think you could eat a little? What about a nice thin slice of ham and a lettuce salad?"

"I couldn't eat, Blake. The coffee I will try. Kindly convey my thanks to Mrs Blake. Say to her that I should like to accept her delicacies, but I fear to do so. I've been keeping off the brandy as much as possible, too, especially during the day. Spirits depress me, and I cannot afford to be mentally depressed just now."

Blake had milk heating in a saucepan.

"Old Lacy rang up just before I left," he said, trying to speak lightly. "The old man had the telephone extended to his bedroom, and he's happier now that he can ring up his overseer and stockmen. I'll bet the nurse and Miss Lacy aren't having too easy a time with him."

"No, he would be a bad patient. How goes his leg?"

"Oh, just going on the same. Time is the only very important part of the cure. Old bones won't knit fast, you know. He told me he was worried about you. It seems that the girl and he have been talking a bit, and the old man now believes that you haven't got the Barcoo sickness but have been boned by the blacks."

"Indeed!"

"Yes. It appears you put the idea into Miss Lacy's head that day you met her coming back from Meena. I'm thinking she knows something about the boning and why it was done."

"I have thought that, too. I told her I felt much like a man who was boned in order to let her know I suspected it. What makes you think she knows all about it?"

Blake related the gist of Diana's conversation with him and with Mrs Blake.

"It seems to us that she wanted to impress us with the danger of your pegging out here alone, and she suggested that

I should report your illness to headquarters so that they would insist on your retiring from the case. She seems anxious to get you out of the way, and now she has told Old Lacy what you said about feeling like a boned man, and she's urging him to write to headquarters."

"Really, Blake, that is too much," Bony exclaimed. "Am I to be prevented from completing my case by the very man who wrote to headquarters so often insisting that the investigation be begun?" Blake's ears were shocked by the terrible laughter. "I can just hear and see Colonel Spendor when he receives Old Lacy's letter. 'Damn and blast Bony! He rebelled against my orders. He's got himself boned by the blacks, or is up against some other tomfoolery, and now he can stew in his own juice. He's sacked and he has resigned, and now he can go to the devil. Write to Lacy and tell him that he's got his detective and he can damn well keep him.' That's what Colonel Spendor will say when he receives Old Lacy's letter."

"Still, Miss Lacy's interest in your position appears to indicate that—"

"She knows of the boning," Bony carried on. "That's no news. I know it, and I know she would like very much to have me removed by force in case I solve this mystery before I die. Oh, I've got them all cut and dried. I know as much about the killing of Anderson as though I had witnessed it, but what they did with the body I don't know and cannot think. My brain won't work."

Blake stood up from brewing the coffee. He said:

"Well, it appears to me that finding a body in this country after it has been planted six months is too much to hope for. It is harder than going through a haystack to find a needle."

"It is no more difficult than going through a haystack for a needle with an electro-magnet," Bony objected. "The extent and variety of the country doesn't matter. The time factor is of little account. My mind ought to be the electro-magnet in attracting the body of Anderson. Failure to discover the

needle cannot be credited to the amount of hay or the little-
ness of the needle. It is my mind that fails, and my mind
fails because it is upset by the boning. The object of the boning is to drive me away, but the object it has actually
achieved has been to blunt my mental power. Without Anderson's remains to prove that he is dead, all my work amounts
to nothing, all the clues I have discovered are valueless."

"Well, what about giving it up and returning at a later
date when you have recovered your health?"

"We have so often argued the matter, Sergeant, that you
begin to weary me. I will not give up. I have explained why
I dare not give up. Once I let go my pride in achievement I
become worse than nothing. This coffee is delicious. If only I
can keep it down."

"Sip it slowly," urged Blake.

Four minutes later Bony was dreadfully sick. Blake held
him, himself shaken by the terrible convulsions. He carried
the emaciated body into the tent and laid it on the stretcher,
and had almost to use force to persuade the detective to drink
a stiff tot of raw brandy. Bony's breath was painfully
laboured and his face distorted by pain.

" 'May the bones pierce your liver and the eagle's claws
tear your kidneys to string,' " quoted the sick man, slowly
and softly. "The bones keep thrusting through my liver and
the eagle's claws keep clamping on my kidneys. They stop
my breathing, the eagle's claws."

"Lie quiet," Blake entreated.

"That I mustn't do. I must not give in."

"Lie quiet for five minutes," Blake said firmly.

Slowly the laborious breathing eased. The lids covered
the blue eyes that once reflected the virile mind of a virile
man in the prime of life. When was that, considered Blake?
Only a week or two ago. Thank God, Browne was on his
way by now. And when he had taken this wreck away the
Kalchut blacks would be dealt with. Be gad, he would deal

with 'em. 'Bout time they were split up and civilized and the magic knocked out of them.

"Your five minutes are up, Sergeant," Bony said, unsteadily. "I mustn't give in. I think I want to smoke a cigarette. It's a good thing the boning doesn't stop the ability to smoke."

"Have a drop more brandy?"

"No. I'll be all right now. I should not have succumbed to temptation, but the coffee smelled delightful."

Despite Blake's urgings to remain on the stretcher Bony rose and walked shakily to the petrol case. Blake helped himself to more coffee and loaded and lit his pipe.

"Success in crime investigation, Sergeant, depends on the ability of the investigator to put himself into the mind of the criminal," Bony said, after a few minutes of silence that emphasized the stillness of the day. "Supposing you had seen Anderson riding down from the dunes that day it rained, and that after an argument you killed him. What would you have done with the body?"

Blake pondered before replying:

"I think, like you, that I would have taken it to the side of a sand-dune that looks like a wave about to crash on a beach and there at the foot of it I would have scooped out a hole and pushed the body in, knowing that the next wind would push the dune farther over it."

"Wouldn't you have seen the rain falling, the sky promising more rain, and known that when the sand of the dune was wet it would be a long time before the wind exerted its power over it again?"

"Ah—probably I would," agreed the policeman.

"I think we have been wasting time among the dunes."

"Then Anderson must lie out on that flat, soft ground bordering the depression."

"Yes, he must," Bony said. "And yet—— Try to see yourself standing somewhere near here, with the body at your feet, and the problem of its disposal hammering at your brain. You have been riding all day and you have no digging tools with you. All you have is your hands and the ends of sticks with which to make a hole."

"Why are you so sure that Anderson was buried here and not taken a good way away?" pressed Blake, as though he wanted time to conceive himself faced by such a dilemma.

"Because the men who killed him would know what every bushman knows—that no matter where a man may be, no matter how far he may be from human habitation, when in the bush he can never know when he will be met by someone. No, Anderson's killers wasted no time in burying him, and ran as little risk as was possible. Here they could see to a great distance on all sides; and since there were more than one, one could watch from the summit of a dune while the other dug the grave."

"Could they have ridden across to the Green Swamp hut and got a shovel or even a crowbar?" inquired Blake.

He did not see the faded blue eyes flash into momentary brilliance. When he did look at Bony, the dark lids hid the blue eyes.

"One could have ridden over to the hut and brought back a shovel and even a crowbar," Bony answered. "That seems unnecessary, though."

"Yes, I suppose so, when there's so much soft ground available. How are you feeling now?"

"A little better but I do not feel able to do any work. This afternoon we'll just sit and talk, if you will be good enough to keep me company for an hour or two."

About the time that Sergeant Blake left Bony's camp, Diana Lacy and John Gordon met some two miles westward of the bloodwood-tree on the Karwir boundary. Not since that day Bony arrived at Karwir had these two met, and this meeting had been delayed by Old Lacy's accident, which had vastly added to the girl's household tasks. Her increasing alarm at the reports of Bonaparte's health had at last dictated an appointment arranged through a discreet person in Opal Town.

"Oh, John I've got so much to tell you and so little time to do it in, as I must be home by five o'clock," Diana cried. "Let me go and please let me talk."

"Very well," reluctantly assented her lover. "Let's sit on that tree trunk over there in the shade. I've been wondering about you, aching for your kisses. Afterwards, I guessed why you didn't turn up the day following your visit to Meena, but it was a fearful disappointment."

In the tree shadow they sat, John's arm about Diana's slim waist, her head resting against his shoulder, his lips caressing her dark hair. She told of Bony's discovery of the piece of green cable silk, of the hair found on the tree trunk, the hair that had not come from the head of Jeffery Anderson. Then she told of her meeting with Bony after her last visit to Meena.

"I gave the feather-filled mattress to Jimmy Partner," Gordon admitted. "I had to know what this detective was doing, and there were no birds on the lake to provide feathers for the blacks' feet. They should have burned the case. I suppose they didn't trouble even to obliterate the camp."

"Yes, that might be so, dear, but don't you see, the Inspector found no one at home when he visited Meena. He went inside to place the mattress case on the end of the dresser. I'm sure he went into your room and took some of your hair from your brushes. That's what he went there for. I could see that he suspected you when the microscope proved that the hair he had taken from the tree wasn't Anderson's. He must know by now that it wasn't Anderson but you who was tied to the tree that day."

"We know that Bonaparte found the piece of cable silk," Gordon said calmly, so calmly that Diana twisted her body in order to look at him. "After he got the dogs, the blacks were forced to keep well wide of him, but we know that he found marks on the tree trunk that interested him enormously. It doesn't really matter what he finds and what he learns so long as he doesn't find the body, and he won't find that."

"But, dear——"

"Supposing he has found sufficient on which to reconstruct the affair, what can he prove from what he has found? Nothing of any importance. He can't prove that Anderson is dead. We know that he has been walking about all over the place, digging into the base of sand-dunes, and that sometimes Sergeant Blake has been helping him. He knows he can't do anything until he finds the body, and, as I have just said, he'll never do that."

A silence fell between them for a little while. Then the girl sighed and said :

"I wish I were not so worried about it."

"I'm not greatly worried about it, sweetheart," Gordon told her. "I'm worried only about the possibility of Bonaparte putting in a confidential report that may affect the Kalchut in a roundabout manner. Neither mother nor I want to see official interference with them. That would mean their swift de-tribalization and inevitable extinction. No matter how kindly officialdom might deal with them, once they are interfered with it is the beginning of the end."

"But the time must come when——"

"Yes, dear, that too is inevitable, but we Gordons are going to delay the inevitable as long as possible. This Anderson business is going to make matters doubly hard for us. In death, Anderson will do the Kalchut more harm than he did when alive."

"And you feel really sure the Inspector won't find him?" pressed Diana.

"Quite sure."

Again they fell silent, and again the girl broke the silence.

"Well, the Inspector can't last much longer. He'll have to go away soon."

"Go away soon What do you mean?"

"Don't you know he's very sick?"

"No."

"You don't? Didn't the blacks who have been watching him tell you?"

"No."

"That's strange, dear. The Inspector has been frightfully ill with the Barcoo sickness. Sergeant Blake says he's so ill that he can hardly walk at all. Are you sure you don't know anything about it?"

"I've said so. The blacks never mentioned it to me. They would have known. How long has he been ill?"

Violet eyes searched deeply the hazel eyes regarding her beneath puzzled brows. Gordon saw in the violet eyes a dawning horror, and then he was listening to her account of Bony's attack of the Barcoo sickness, of Bony's reference to the likeness of his symptoms to those suffered by the victim of the pointed bone, of her father's conviction that Bony had been boned. And while she recited all this her heart was lightened of its load of suspicion that her lover had induced the boning, for in his eyes horror and anger swiftly blazed.

"The blacks did bone him," she cried, just a little shrilly. "That's why they didn't tell you he was so ill. Oh, John, and I've been thinking you might have got them to do it to drive the Inspector away from Karwir."

"Of course I didn't. If they have boned the detective they did it off their own bat, knowing quite well I wouldn't stand for it." Gordon pursed his lips, worry now settled upon him in earnest. "D'you think Bonaparte knows he's been boned?"

"Yes, John, I do. I—I think he's the bravest man I've ever met. He'd sooner die than give up. Oh, I've done what I could to get him away, indirectly, of course. I suggested to Mrs Blake and her husband that the Sergeant should report

Bonaparte's illness to his headquarters, and I've persuaded dad to write down to Brisbane about it."

Gordon was still frowning when he said:

"Do you think that was wise? Bonaparte is bound to hear of all that eventually, and then he'll bring you into it."

"Oh, I'm brought into it already." And Diana told of the trap Bony had set for her baited with imagined kisses on a telephone instrument, and his knowledge of their meeting near the bloodwood-tree. Despairingly, she cried:

"He finds out everything, John. Nothing can be kept from him. Our only hope is that he will be forced to give up."

The man's arm tightened about her waist, and the added pressure broke the straw of her composure. She clung to him tightly.

"Oh, John, what will they do when he finds out everything, finds Anderson?" she cried.

"They will probably be most dramatic," was his answer. "But I keep assuring you that he won't find Anderson. Without proof that Anderson is dead, Bonaparte, or his superiors, can do nothing. Now, sweetheart, don't you worry so. There's no real reason to worry. You know, you haven't once to-day told me that you love me."

"Oh, but you know I do. I wish I could stay here with you for ever. I'd like to ride away with you to the fabled Inland Sea and there find an island off its shore where you and I could find our bower house. Instead—I must go. Look at the sun. It's getting late."

Gordon watched her ride away homeward until she was engulfed by the coldly indifferent trees. Then he vaulted the barrier and strode, his eyes blazing with anger, across the half-mile of country to where Jimmy Partner and Abie were waiting with the horses—Abie with thick masses of feathers on his feet. At Gordon's approach they arose. They saw anger in his face.

"What's the matter, John?" inquired Jimmy Partner.

Gordon came to stand immediately before the man who could put him on his back with one hand. His voice was brittle when he asked:

"Do you know anything about the boning of the detective?"

Jimmy Partner's gaze fell to his feet. Then:

"Yes, John," he said softly. "I thought it a good way to get rid of the detective. He's been finding out too much. I wongied with Nero and Wandin, and they agreed to get the bone——"

Gordon's right fist crashed between the downcast eyes. Opportunity was his to measure distance, and Jimmy Partner was looking down at the ground. The black wrestler collapsed. Furiously Gordon turned upon the shrinking Abie, shouted at him to get busy wiping out the traces of the meeting at the fence; and when Jimmy Partner rose unsteadily to his feet, he saw as through a mist his friend and boss riding away towards the Meena homestead.

Since the day Diana Lacy had visited Meena, and had assisted in the salvaging of John's hairs, Mary Gordon had daily guarded his comb and brushes and the pillows, and had kept watch on the house even while she milked the cows.

Unsatisfied curiosity regarding what had really happened that day of rain when her son and Jimmy Partner had not returned home till an agonizingly late hour, was now balanced by the thought that, knowing nothing, she could admit nothing. What she thought and guessed were little secrets of her own, and her faith in her son was untarnished.

This afternoon of the lovers' meeting at the boundary fence, she expected John and Jimmy Partner home at six o'clock, and by half-past five the meat was brown in the oven, the peach pie cooked and being kept hot beside the stove, and the potatoes in their jackets were just put on to boil. She heard the wicket gate click and then jar shut, and, knowing it was neither John nor Jimmy Partner, she stepped to the door—to be confronted by Wandin.

Gaunt but stately, this personage of the Kalchut tribe was unusually excited.

"Johnny Boss him not home, missus?"

"No, not yet, Wandin. What do you want?"

Wandin's eyes were wide, his breathing fast. He grinned and said:

"You come with me, eh? All rabbits they go walk-about. They clear outer here. They go quick, too right."

"The rabbits going, Wandin?"

"Too right, missus. They go walkabout. Bimeby no rabbits here Meena Lake. You come see, eh?"

Mary gave a swift glance to the cooking dinner, hastily removed her house apron, tossed it on to the couch, and hurried after the tall, stalking figure of Wandin. He led her southward of the house for some two hundred yards and then up to the summit of the lake-encircling dunes.

The hot sun streamed over the vast empty bed of the lake, casting the long shadows of the dunes across the little valley to the lesser dunes merging into the base of the upland. The end of the tree-belt was a further hundred yards south of Mary and Wandin, and they could see for miles from the south round to the north-east. From the south-east came a cool and strangely fragrant wind.

"Look, missus!" urged Wandin. "See, the rabbits clear out on walkabout. Look at that feller."

He pointed, and Mary watched a rabbit pass over the dune on which they were standing. It passed only a few feet from them, unafraid, as though utterly unconscious of them. It ran down the steep lee-side slope, crossed the little valley and ran up the slope of the lesser dune. Its progress was unnatural, as Mary observed.

She watched others pass on either side, all running in the same direction, the progress of each unnatural. Normally a rabbit, even when hungry and making out for feed, always runs in short spurts, with a period of sitting up for observation at the end of each run. This evening there was no stopping for observation. The rabbits evinced no sign of fear, either of those who stood on the summit of the dune, or of the carrion birds whirring above them.

The birds knew of this abnormality, especially the crows. Of recent months the crows and eagles had increased enormously, and now the sky was filled with them. The crows were cawing vociferously, and the eagles were planing with seldom a wing flap, some low to ground, the higher birds like dust motes against the sky.

Mary turned full circle, slowly, spellbound by this genesis of a rabbit migration. Wherever she looked she saw running rodents. They were crossing the lake, coming towards her, passing her, running away from her to the south-east whence came the strangely fragrant little wind. All were running into the wind and in the same direction, all running in that unnatural, purposeful manner.

"Bimeby no rabbits at Meena," Wandin predicted. "Plenty feed bimeby after rain come. Long time now 'fore rabbits so thick at Meena."

Mary quite forgot her cooking dinner. When she turned again to the lake the sun was appreciably lower above the smoke-blue Meena Hills. Low upon the barren dust plain of the lake bed and coloured by the sun, hung a film of scarlet gauze created from dust raised by the running rabbits. Each rabbit was the point of a dust-spear; each rabbit was like a speck of flotsam carried by a strong current to the south-east, a current never varying in its movement.

Wandin drew Mary's attention to the horseman coming from the south, riding fast down the long ground slope. Although he was a mile distant she recognized the horse and her son who rode. Remembering the dinner, she uttered a little exclamation, but found herself unable to be drawn from this vantage point that offered a grandstand seat for the opening of a mighty drama. She could hear the excited cries of the aborigines and their children, cries sometimes drowned by the cawing of the crows. A rabbit passed so close to Wandin that he was able to kick out at it and send it rolling down the slope. It continued on its course as though unaware of the interruption. The sunlight falling obliquely upon the eastern land rise was painted scarlet by the dust following the leaders of the horde, and the far edge of this dust was creeping to the land summit as though a red coverlet were being drawn across the world.

"Blackfeller go walkabout to-morrow p'raps," Wandin said. "Blackfeller like rabbit, rabbit like blackfeller. Stop one place long time goodoh. Then little wind come and he no longer stop one place. He go walkabout or he sit down long time and die. Johnny Boss he leave Jimmy Partner and Abie in bush. Look, missus, Johnny Boss he hurry. Waffor?"

When John Gordon was a hundred yards from them, Mary waved to him to join them on this grandstand of fine red sand. She saw the evidence of the horse's pace in the white foam flecking its shoulders, and then she saw her son's face made almost ugly with anger. He sent the horse up the yielding slope of the dune and leapt to the ground before them. The horse neighed and, because the reins were not trailed to the ground, turned away and trotted to the yards and the drinking trough.

"All the rabbits are going," Mary cried excitedly.

Gordon glanced at her, and she received a small thrilling shock at sight of his blazing eyes. To Wandin, he said:

"Have you and Nero been boning that beeg feller blackfeller p'liceman?"

Without hesitation, Wandin replied:

"Yes, Johnny Boss. Him find out too——"

A clenched fist, from the knuckles of which the skin was stripped, crashed to the point of his jaw, and Wandin spun round and fell on his face and chest upon the soft sand of the dune.

Mary stood quite still, her work-worn hands clasped and pressed to her mouth to stifle a scream. Gordon nodded to her, his face a grin of fury, and then ran down the dune and vanished beyond the house. Wandin, sprawling at her feet, called up to her:

"Waffor Johnny Boss do that, missus?"

Gordon ran to the gate beyond the house, cleared it like a racing dog, and continued to run along the winding path to the aborigines' camp. It was deserted, all were away watching the rabbit migration. From the camp Gordon hurried on round the lake shore, and so found Nero squatted over a little fire, an ebony gargoyle and as motionless as one.

Nero did not hear the white man's approach. He did not even hear the snap of the stick trodden upon by Gordon. His mind was concentrated on the terrible work of killing a man miles away. He toppled over and sprawled beside his little fire when the side of Gordon's riding boot connected with his stern quarters. As one awakening from a pleasant dream, with his hair and beard dripping red sand, he was picked up and shaken till his eyes appeared likely to drop from their sockets. Then he was flung backward to the ground; and, when he regained his breath and conquerred his dizziness, he saw John Gordon squatting beside his little fire and rolling a cigarette.

"Waffor you kickum like that grey gelding?" he whined.

"Go along to the house and bring Wandin. Run, you devil."

Nero was long past the real running age, but he made a valiant effort to move faster than his usual gait, his mind most uneasy, his body a little tired from the enforced exertion. The minutes slipped by and Gordon smoked and seldom moved. The rage gradually subsided and left him a little ashamed. He did not look up when the soft crunching of naked feet on soft sand reached him.

"Sit down along me," he ordered.

Wandin and Nero squatted on either side of him.

"Who told you to bone the blackfeller p'liceman?"

"Jimmy Partner, Johnny Boss," replied Nero. "Y'see, Johnny Boss, that beeg feller blackfeller p'liceman him find tree and him find green hair from Anderson's whip feller. Bimeby him find Anderson. Then him make things crook for our Johnny Boss."

The final phrase, "our Johnny Boss," spoke a volume of affection. Gordon stared into the small fire, finding it too difficult to look up into the two pairs of appealing black eyes.

"Why you not tell me you bone detective feller?"

"You tellum no point the bone any more, Johnny Boss. Long time back you tellum that. You say bone-pointing no play fair, likeum you said one time me no hittem Wandin with cricket bat feller that time Wandin he hittem me with ball feller. You only little Johnny Boss then."

So for many days and nights these two, with others of the elder bucks to assist, most probably, had taken turn and turn about to squat over a lonely little fire and will another human being to death, because they thought danger threatened him, not themselves. They hated for him, not for themselves. By the white man's standards they might be children, but they had employed a weapon fashioned by ten thousand generations, whilst wearing the crown named loyalty. Was he not one of them? Had he not been initiated into the Kalchut tribe? Had he not been entrusted with secrets so zealously guarded by the old men? An enemy was trying to harm him. The enemy must be destroyed. Gordon stood up and they with him. Anxiously they looked into his eyes and were overjoyed to see that the anger had gone from him.

"You no point the bone again, eh?"

Wandin caressed his jaw and Nero certain portions of his plump body.

"No fear, Johnny Boss. We tellum Jimmy Partner git to hell outer it."

Gordon grasped Wandin by his left arm and Nero by his right arm, and drew them close to him.

"Me sorry feller I hittem you. You good feller black-fellers. You my fathers and my brothers, but me I'm Johnny Boss, eh?"

"Too right, Johnny Boss."

"To-morrow you all, lubras and children, go on walkabout Meena Hills. You stay out there till I tellum you come back Meena. Me, I take Jimmy Partner and Malluc. You bin tellum Malluc come along house. In the morning you tellum lubras come along store for tucker."

A gaunt face and a round one expanded in cheerful grins.

"Now you sittem down all night and drawum bones and eagle's claws outer blackfeller p'liceman. You tellum little pointed bones and little sharp claws come outer him."

"All right, Johnny Boss, we tellum so."

Gordon's hands squeezed hard before he left them and returned to the deserted camp, and then along the path back to the gate. Near the horse yards Jimmy Partner and Abie were unsaddling, and Jimmy Partner, forgetful of his enormous strength and wrestling prowess, left his horse and retreated.

"Come here, Jimmy Partner," Gordon ordered.

The aboriginal hesitated for a moment, then advanced slowly to meet Gordon. When they were near Gordon held out his hand and said:

"I'm sorry I hit you, Jimmy, but you did wrong to get Nero and Wandin to use the bone. The results might be bad, not to the detective but to the Kalchut. Shake hands."

Jimmy Partner grinned although to do so pained the bridge

237

of his nose. He grasped Gordon's skinned hand and Gordon did not wince.

"That's all right, Johnny Boss," Jimmy Partner said with surprising cheerfulness. "Your crack was only a fly tickler. I didn't think I was doing any harm—to you."

"To me, no, but to the Kalchut, the boning might have most harmful results. Don't you ever again persuade the Kalchut to act without my orders. Better see to your face before you come in for dinner."

"Me face! Oh, Abie did that when we were sparring out in the paddock. It was quite an accident, wasn't it, Abie?"

And with knit brows John Gordon left them to walk over to the house.

More Facets

BONY was to remember all his life his awakening on the morning of the second of November. During the night something wonderful had happened to him, and for some time he pondered on what this could be.

The white roof of the box tent was dully opaque, for the sun had not yet risen. It was delightfully cool, and the flies that had taken up their abode with him still slumbered on the sloping canvas panels. Perched on the topmost branch of one of the protecting cabbage-trees, one of Australia's leading songsters began its serenade to the new day, going through its range of four distinct tunes over and over again. This butcher-bird and two magpies had taken possession of the camp, greatly to the annoyance of the crows.

By degrees Bony took stock of the remarkable change within himself. He was astonished by the absence of pain from his body, for no longer did the darting pain-arrows shoot through him like white-hot comets. Timidly he moved himself on the stretcher bed, and instead of pain there was that delightful desire to animate muscles. And with this physical well-being had come the return of health to his mind. Gone was the heavy, cramping depression that like a dark fog had blinded his mental vision. His mind this morning felt free and illuminated by a radiance not of earthly day.

Something had happened away over at Meena Lake to interrupt the willing of his death.

For several minutes Bony's freed mind energetically attacked this thought, energetically because the new-won freedom delighted it. It was thus engaged when simultaneously the two dogs camping at the tent's entrance growled, and then, with nerve-torturing abruptness, broke into frenzied barking. Together, they raced to the skirting boundary fence, leapt over the barrier and sped away to a distant point to the north-west. The barking stopped as abruptly as it had begun.

The ensuing silence was unbroken even by the watching butcher-bird. A shaft of yellow light was laid along one slope of the canvas roof by the rising sun. Then to Bony's straining ears came the dull thudding of the hooves of a horse approaching the fence from the north-west. An iron-clanked, and presently the dogs returned to the tent. One pressed a cold nose against Bony's forearm, the other attempted to lick his face. Thus they announced the arrival of a visitor.

Bony softly ordered them to be quiet. They obeyed, one taking his stand beside the stretcher, the other sitting against the tent wall. Both listened with ears cocked. Then a not unpleasant voice shouted:

"Good day-ee, boss!"

It was the voice of an aboriginal.

Both dogs growled, but both tails wagged.

"Good day, there! What d'you want?"

"Me Malluc."

According to age-old custom Malluc had halted fifty yards from the camp, waiting for permission from the occupier to enter.

Malluc! Now what did he want here so early in the morning? Bony demanded his business.

"Johnny Boss, he sentum letter feller."

"You bring letter feller here," instructed Bony. A letter from John Gordon! It might be so, but it might mean an open attack by the people who had so persistently boned him. The small automatic pistol was drawn from beneath the pillow. He heard the light sound of boots crunching loose sand. Again Bony ordered the dogs to be quiet.

Into the triangle presented by the raised flaps normally hanging before the entrance to the tent appeared the figure of an aboriginal, tall and grey of hair and beard. He was wearing a suit of very old dungarees, and his feet were encased in elastic-sided riding boots much too large for them. He carried the white envelope in his left hand. There was no weapon in his right hand, nor was one attached to his person, and the boots on the feet precluded the possibility of a spear being dragged along the ground by his toes. He smiled broadly at Bony who had raised himself the better to see the visitor.

"Drop the letter feller," ordered Bony, who then, when the order was obeyed, urged one of the dogs to: "Fetch it, Hool-'Em-Up."

The dog, understanding that the order was for him, advanced to the letter and brought it to Bony. Malluc retreated but remained in view. Bony opened the letter and read:

I regret to hear that you are ill of the Barcoo sickness. I learned of it only yesterday. I am sending to you the Kalchut medicine man, knowing him to be an expert on gastric troubles. If any man can effect a swift cure, Malluc can do so. He has treated both my mother and me with great success.

The development was so curious that Bony could not at once decide what to do. That these aboriginal medicine men could effect cures for divers complaints he was well aware. Still, the process of willing him to death had been interrupted. Of that he felt sure. That John Gordon had stopped the boning was likely enough; but might the coming of Malluc mean a different kind of attack upon him, an attack of physical violence, since the attack of mental violence had been stopped? To permit a hostile aboriginal near him when he was physically weakened by the torture of the boning would be the height of stupidity.

The figure of Malluc disappeared from the triangle opening of the tent. The butt of the pistol was comforting to Bony's hand. If the attack was to be made it would not be delayed, but an attack appeared to be illogical in face of Gordon's letter. And then the figure of Malluc reappeared before the tent doorway.

He now wore the insignia of his profession. A human hair string tufted his long grey hair high above his forehead, and suspended from this hair string, so that they rested against the forehead, were five gum leaves. Through his nose was thrust a nine-inch stick with needle-pointed ends. He had discarded his white man's clothes and boots, now wearing only the pubic tassel of kangaroo skin. On his chest and abdomen, brilliantly white against the black of his skin, was emblazoned the Kalchut sacred drawing, an artistic masterpiece done in pigments that had defied the friction of his clothes.

He was indeed a medicine man, and Bony was induced to submit to treatment by the knowledge that no medicine man of the inland tribes may do evil. Their role is to cure. What probably assisted Bony in making his decision was his inherited respect for any aboriginal doctor, and his inherited faith in their power to heal.

"What you do, boss?" asked Malluc. "You crook feller all right. You full of pointed bones and eagle's claws. Me fine feller medicine man. Malluc him see him bones and him claws in your insides."

Bony was aware that, as the show of pointing the bone must precede the actual working of the evil, so the show of healing would have to precede the actual treatment. He understood, too, that although the boning had ceased he was still in a condition bordering on prostration and that it would take weeks for his body to become strong again. Often the curative effects of the medicine concocted for gastric complaints were astonishing in their swiftness. And so he said:

"You good feller blackfeller, Malluc. You make me strong, eh?"

Malluc grinned, nodded and again vanished. A few seconds later Bony heard the crackling of firewood thrown upon the still hot ashes of his campfire. Knowing that the medicine man would require his body outside, Bony slowly pushed his legs over the edge of the stretcher and sat up. Immediately pain entered him like swords of fire, to send him down upon the bed, groaning aloud.

Then Malluc entered.

"Too right you crook feller," he said. "You bin sung by the little pointed bones and the eagle's claws. Me see 'em in your insides all swim about like blackfish feller."

Slipping his arms under his patient, Malluc saw the small-bore automatic pistol but evinced no curiosity. He was now much more a doctor than an aboriginal. Without effort, he lifted Bony and carried him outside the tent, laid him down gently at the edge of the fire-heat and began to strip off his pyjamas.

After the terrible spasm of pain, Bony lay breathing fast, his "insides" feeling as though in the grip of a steel-gauntleted hand. The sweat of terror dampened his forehead. Hope engendered by his awakening that morning had gone from him, and while he watched Malluc he realized that if the boning did not stop he would die. His iron resistance was at long last beaten down, and only in a detached kind of manner did he observe Malluc take from a gunny sack a roll of thin bark and empty the handful of dried leaves it contained into a billy. Malluc then added water and placed the billy to heat at the fire.

Now Malluc walked round and round his patient, stepping absurdly high, alternately stretching out a hand towards

243

Bony and then jerking it smartly to himself. Meanwhile he recited in the Kalchut language :

"I am the medicine man of the Kalchut Nation.

"I am the great healer of the Kalchut Nation.

"I am the master of all good magic, and no evil magic can touch me.

"I am the child of Tatuchi and Maliche, the all powerful ones who dwell in the sky, who never were born, who never can die. They came down upon the earth. They saw Malluc, of the Kalchut Nation, and they said they would make Malluc of the Kalchut Nation a great medicine man. They took me into the bush and killed me with a magic spear. They cut me open and took out my insides and threw them away. They each took from their inside enough to give me new insides, and before they joined me together they put Atnongara stones among my new insides so that I could project them into the bodies of sick people." (Meaning to inject an anti-toxin.)

"So hear me, you little bones and you eagle's claws.

"I take you out from the insides of him who lies sick on the ground.

"No use for you to run about his insides like fish looking for a hole in the ground. I suck you out. I unsing you of the evil magic sung into you.

"I see you, little bones and eagle's claws.

"I am the medicine man of the Kalchut Nation.

"Like water running down a gully bag magic runs from me."

Suddenly Malluc ceased his prancing walk and arm jerking, and he fell upon his knees beside Bony and rolled him over on to his chest. He then applied his mouth to the small of Bony's back and began vigorously to suck. For many minutes this sucking continued, until venting a gurgling cry, Malluc sprang to his feet, went to Bony's head, and stooped, forcing Bony to look at him. And Bony saw him spit to the ground a small, pointed bone.

At the end of a full hour's sucking Malluc had "drawn from Bony's insides" six little bones and two eagle's claws, and, having rolled Bony upon his left side the better to observe, he pushed the bones and the claws on to a piece of bark with his nose stick. Then, taking the bark and stick some way away, he dug a hole with the stick and carefully buried the bark and the bones and the eagle's claws. That done, he pushed the stick into position through his nose.

Thus was the show completed.

Smiling triumphantly, Malluc returned to his patient. "You goodoh, bimeby," he assured Bony. "No little bones and eagle's claws in your insides now. You drink blackfeller med'cine, and bimeby, one-two days, you walkabout goodoh."

Fetching the steaming brew in the billycan, he squatted beside his patient and again assured him of certain return to health and strength. Now and then he blew upon the grey liquid in the billy, often testing the temperature with a finger. Satisfied at last, he offered the billy to his patient, saying :

"You drink-em-down."

Bony obeyed. The warm, thick liquid coursed down his gullet, entered his stomach. There it began to radiate a softly glowing heat. Bony could feel the heat creeping all about his "insides," creeping upward to his shoulders and down his arms to his hands, downward into his legs to reach the toes. Malluc squatted over him, watching. The glow brought sweat bubbles to Bony's face and arms and legs. It was so delicious that Bony sighed often with sheer ecstasy. And then Malluc lifted him nearer the fire, and entered the tent to bring out his day clothes and dress him in them.

Malluc remained with his patient a further two hours, leaving only when assured that Bony could stand and walk, albeit falteringly.

"You goodoh now," he said, immensely pleased with himself and his patient. Bony held out his hands and Malluc took them, gripped them lightly, and then began to spoil everything by donning the old suit of dungarees. He turned, when on his horse, and waved a cheerful farewell.

Bony trembled with weakness and yet wanted to shout aloud that he was freed of the pointing bone.

Blake arrived at the camp about noon. His worry concerning Bony was accentuated by the delay of Superintendent Browne's arrival, a delay caused by a forced landing near Windorah. His mind, however, was relieved to a great degree when he saw a decided improvement in Bony. Having heard the car approaching Bony had the tea billy on the fire.

"Well, how are things to-day?" asked the sergeant when, escorted by the excited dogs, he carried his tucker box from car to tree shade.

"I am feeling much better, Sergeant," replied Bony. "I awoke this morning conscious of a change. And then, I have been receiving medical attention."

"Good! Dr Linden come to see you?"

"No, Dr Malluc, M.O.K."

"Malluc! What do the initials stand for?"

"Medical Officer to the Kalchut. He performed a surgical operation on me and was able to remove from my insides, as he called my—er, insides, six pointed bones and two eagle's claws."

"And you feel better, eh?"

"I feel much better. The pains have left me and my mind is freed of the dreadful depression. Of course, I am excessively weak. I am like a man up from a sick bed where he has been lying for six months. I think to-day that I could drink tea."

"What about a pint of meat extract? Do you more good than tea. Then I've brought a chicken and fresh bread, and butter kept hard with wet cloths."

"Yes, the meat extract, now, and perhaps a little slice of bread and butter."

During the meal Blake craftily watched Bony, and was

delighted when it became evident that the sickness really had been conquered.

"What's behind Dr Malluc's visit, d'you think?" he asked.

Without comment, Bony gave him Gordon's letter, and then he described the visit of the Kalchut medicine man.

"Gordon, in his letter, refers to my illness as the Barcoo sickness," Bony pointed out. "But Malluc tells me that little bones and eagle's claws were darting about in my insides like blackfish, and he then produces six little bones and two eagle's claws to prove it. He knew, therefore, before he came what was wrong with me and he provided himself with the claws and the bones."

"It looks as though Gordon didn't know of the boning."

"I believe that he did not."

"And yet you think Gordon was mixed up in Anderson's——"

Bony was sitting on his petrol case, and now he leaned forward to stare at Blake.

"Let us assume a hypothetical case," he said. "You know Gordon, and you knew Anderson. Supposing Gordon slew Anderson in self-defence, when Anderson was striving to tie him to a tree and flog him as Inky Boy was flogged, what would you do?"

"Seek a warrant for his arrest on a charge of manslaughter."

"Exactly. And why would you do that?"

"It would be my duty."

"Again, exactly. You are the senior police-officer stationed at Opal Town. But, Blake, I am no longer an inspector attached to the Criminal Investigation Branch. Therefore, in such a case, I might not act as you would act in duty bound. Now then, let us assume that you were retired from the Force, and then learned the facts of our hypothetical case, what would you do, knowing Gordon and having known Anderson?"

"We're getting into deep water, don't you think?" Blake prevaricated.

"By no means—as yet. What about my question?"

"I might do nothing about it," answered Blake, after further hesitation.

"I think there would be no might about it, Blake. I have for some time been thinking that a little good has come forth from what Colonel Spendor calls the sack. As a member of the Police Force I should be bound to maintain the machinery of the law set in motion by Old Lacy when he wrote his letters to the Chief Commissioner. As an ordinary citizen I can commit a merely minor sin against society by declining to set the machinery of the law in motion. In its way the law is a fearful thing. Once its machinery is started there is no stopping the machine. As you would be bound to maintain the machinery in running order, I shall confide in you no further. When we are old, and should we meet, I will then relate the details of this case. What you know of it will permit you to guess with some accuracy those details which I am withholding from you."

Blake grinned, but there was no mirth in his eyes.

"I can guess so much," he said, "that I concur in your decision about not confiding further in me. Privately, I think that the penalties imposed on whites for crimes against the blacks are not nearly severe enough. By the way, you remember you asked me to find out if the officer in charge here thirty-six years ago was still living, and if so whether he remembered an Irish woman working on Karwir at that time. I have had a letter from him. He is now retired and living at Sandgate."

"Ah—yes," Bony murmured.

"He says that he does remember an Irish girl working at Karwir in the year 1901. Her name was Kate O'Malley."

Bony smiled.

"That small jotting of evidence may come in useful," he

said. "I wonder—I wonder if I might eat another thin slice of bread and butter?"

"Think you'll be able to master it?"

"I think so. And then you may leave me. You must be sick and tired of visiting me daily, and your office work will have accumulated. I have only to locate Anderson's grave, and now that will not be a difficult task."

After Blake's departure, Bony carried a sack to the boundary fence. Many days before he had been compelled to cut the two topmost barbed wires, to lay the sack over the third barbed wire and lever himself over. He was this afternoon so physically exhausted that, having reached the Meena side of the fence, he had to cling for a space to the barrier. But now, when he ought to have been lying down, he was energized by a crystal-clear brain. By a process of elimination, he had grown confident that Anderson could have been buried in very hard ground because less than two miles away, at Green Swamp hut, there were shovels and a crowbar.

Often accompanied by Sergeant Blake, he had spent hours fossicking about the lee slopes of the sand-dunes. Hour after hour he and the dogs had hunted for a body below the surface of the flat lands' west of the dunes and north of the northernmost depression. Now he began an examination of the wide line of claypans running along the foot of the dunes.

Claypans are invariably to be found skirting sand-dunes. Here they separated the dunes from the flat lands, forming a grey ribbon a hundred odd feet in width. In the centre of this ribbon grew the mulga-tree on the trunk of which Bony had found the wisp of green sewing silk and the human hair.

In size, claypans vary from a few square feet to many acres. These that Bony began to examine averaged about five hundred square feet. Somewhere far to the westward the prevailing westerly wind had gouged into the soft sandy soil and lifted billions of tons for many miles before depositing the sand grains in the form of these dunes. The top soil of sand having been thus removed, the wind set to work on the clay beneath, carrying particles of clay to deposit them on the dunes.

The wind's action on the dunes is to move them forward, leaving the heavier grains of clay to become waterholding bottoms of pools. In this manner rainwater is conserved in country as porous as a sponge; but as the sheets of water are seldom deeper than a few inches, the sun's heat quickly evaporates them. The wind constantly playing on the surface of the water during the course of the evaporation creates a perfectly level surface of clay, and the sun's heat bakes the clay to the hard consistency of a brick. Even heavily loaded trucks may pass across a claypan without leaving wheel depressions.

What eventually aroused Bony's interest in a particular claypan within a few yards of the solitary mulga-tree was the extremely faint ridging of its surface in the rough form of a giant star. So faintly corrugated were these marks that even Bony, with his inherited keen eyesight, would not have observed them had he not been looking for just such marks.

The claypan was one of the larger pans along this ribbon of claypans. Like all the other pans it was surrounded by a ridge of soft sand in which were two natural cuttings. One took overflow water from the pan nearer the dunes and slightly higher, the second cutting permitted overflow water to fall into the pan lower and nearer the flat lands, all the claypans representing shallow steps from the dunes to the flat country.

Accompanied by the dogs, Bony walked to the slope of the nearest dune where he sat down and rested his back against it. His investigation was complete. Again he had successfully solved a case.

"Yes, it was very cleverly done," he told Hool-'Em-Up. "A claypan makes a perfect grave, one never to be detected by man, by bird or ant or wild dog. One that will never fall in. One that nature itself will cover with stone almost as hard as marble. Beneath the surface of that cement-hard claypan lies the body of Jeffery Anderson and, most probably, his stock-whip and his horse's neck-rope.

"Ha—hum! I have the feeling that I am going to be sentimental. After all is said and done about justice, why should a dead man be able to do more evil to the living than he accomplished whilst he lived? And what sense would there be in arraigning men on a charge of justifiable homicide merely to acquit them? To do so in this case would be no tribute to justice. It would be opposed to the rightful interests of very many men and women, even little children. Yes, I am sure I am going to be sentimental."

The blue eyes were shining as Bony slowly and falteringly walked back to the fence, and so on to reach his camp where he brewed a billy of weak tea and drank it with the addition of fresh milk left by Sergeant Blake.

He lay down for an hour before shakily saddling the mare, and mounted her with the assistance of a tree stump. Once on her back he was rested, and slowly she carried him to Green Swamp well, where at the trough she took her fill of water. Bony was satisfied and quietly triumphant, and when the sun was westering and the first of the birds were arriving at the trough to drink, he became blind to his surroundings while he planned the dramatic *dénouement* of this case. The horse, instead of taking him back to his camp, followed the track to the main road leading to the homestead, and when Bony "awoke" he found himself opposite the southern corner post set in the middle of the southernmost depression.

This hot and still afternoon the mirage water lay deep over the depressions. Small bushes growing on the separating ridges appeared like giant trees and the ridges themselves like tall cliffs. It was strange water, this mirage water; it could never be reached. The walking horse, on its way to the camp, for ever walked on dry land, as though it were carried by an island, less than fifty feet across, from ridge to ridge. The fence before and behind ran back into the "water," then rose to an extraordinary height above it.

The horse was crossing one of these wide depressions when the detective's interest was abruptly aroused by innumerable lines of grey dust cutting the surface of the mirage westward of the barrier. All these growing dust lines were approaching the fence. They were not unlike the tips of shark fins.

In the far distance a peculiarly yellowish mist was rising from the mirage water, as though the sinking sun were sucking upward impurities from the heated ground beneath the "sea". Bony directed his horse to the fence the better to observe this phenomenon, and so the animal came to stand on an "island" bisected by the Karwir boundary fence.

Then, as though coming up out of a prehistoric sea, as though wading through the shallows to reach the dry land, there appeared dun-coloured sticks, all in pairs. High and still higher out of the "water" came the first of the twin sticks. On the surface of the shallows appeared dark things all moving towards the shore. Small brown heads appeared at the base of the sticks, and, astonished, Bony saw they were rabbits.

They swarmed to land on his "island," the first of them to run without hesitation to the netting, which flung them back. Again and again they dashed at the barrier dazed yet unafraid and determined.

Where, less than a minute before, there had been no living thing beyond the fence, now rabbits stood on their hind legs against the netting, some pushing their noses into the mesh, others savagely gnawing the wire. And without cease countless rabbits came swimming to the island to join in the onslaught on the fence.

Now above the mirage sea the yellowish fog was rising higher. The silence itself began to throb.

CHAPTER TWENTY-THREE

Life Gone Mad

THE migration of rabbits sweeping south-eastward from Meena Lake was the first Napoleon Bonaparte had seen. Once, beside a lonely campfire, he had listened to a man describing a rabbit migration that had ended against the South Australia-New South Wales border fence in a forty-mile-long rampart of carcases. And now the rabbits were piling into the V made by an angle of the Karwir boundary fence.

Normally rabbits are controlled by fear of their many enemies—men, dogs, foxes, eagles. Their lives are governed by caution begot by fear out of hereditary experience. Having no defensive weapons other than claws and teeth, which they employ ineffectively and seldom in time to be of service, they never attack other animals and rarely attack each other.

A host of rabbits had sprung into being over the miles of country bordering Meena Lake. Then came the first of the dry seasons when, moisture failing in grass and shrubs and herbage, the host had centred upon the drying water of the lake. When the water had vanished the host increased no more. Yet all the enemies of the rodent seemed to make not the slightest reduction of the total number. Then came that April rain during which Jeffery Anderson had disappeared, and, as soon as the new grass appeared over the uplands, like a giant bomb the host burst outward to take charge of deserted burrows, clean them out, and show the world how it could breed.

Every doe began to breed after reaching the age of nine weeks. Every litter ranged from five to seven young ones among which the females predominated. From April to the end of September every doe gave birth to about twelve young ones. And the does greatly predominated.

During October a fearful battle for existence had been waged against starvation and thirst as well as against the increase of natural enemies. Only the strongest of the young ones had survived, but even so those that died were as nothing to the number that lived.

About the hour that Diana Lacy and John Gordon discussed Bony's illness at the boundary fence, an order was issued to the rabbits massed on the shores of Meena Lake.

What issued the order no man can tell. The order impelled the host to move away from the place that had given it birth to some mysterious place far to the south east and in obedience to the order nothing could halt its progress except a river of water or a netted fence.

Natural caution and fear were in a flash of time driven out of these Meena rabbits. They became controlled by one mass idea like the people of a totalitarian state. Formerly each individual unit lived independently of other units, swayed by fear and governed by hunger; now they had no desire other than to obey the order. Even the primary instinct of self-preservation had been taken from it. From a shy and docile creature, self-willed and possessing a degree of cunning, it had become an automaton in a mass relentless in purpose, irresistible in movement, entirely fearless.

Close though Bony was to the bush and its varied and often hidden life, he sat his horse entranced by this unfolding drama of the wild. Compared with it his human dramas were petty and ridiculous.

Normally the mirage lying so deeply over the depressions

culminating at Green Swamp would have drained slowly away as the sun set; but this late afternoon the rabbit host rushing upon Karwir quickly dispelled the mirage water beneath the surface of which it moved. On the Karwir side of the fence the "water" remained long after it had vanished on the Meena side.

In the van ran the leaders, big strong grey bucks, their teeth bloodied in many a combat, their rumps scarred and scabbed, their ears bearing honourable wounds. Without halt they advanced to the barrier, dashed against the mesh as though blind, and were flung back in dazed astonishment. The manner in which they then behaved clearly indicated that the impact had momentarily awakened their minds. Then the mass hypnosis controlled them again, and again they charged the fence. After several defeats, they stood against the netting with nostrils scenting the wire and sharp teeth testing its strength.

The does forming the main body of the horde had not yet reached the fence. They were advancing on a front miles wide, until the left flank struck the barrier eastward of the northern corner post of the two mile north-south section, and ran along the fence past Bony's camp and the mulga-tree. The right flank met the fence somewhere westward of the gate spanning the Karwir road to Opal Town, and from this point ran along it eastward into the V of the angle.

Bony's frenzied dogs sprang to the fence, clambered over the topmost barbed wire and jumped down to slaughter rabbits. There was no chasing the rodents. They ran straight to the dogs' slavering jaws, ran between their legs as though unconscious of them. In less than three minutes the dogs wearied of the killing. One lay down pantingly and rabbits leapt over it. The other slunk towards the fence to gaze up at Bony, and rabbits bumped against its legs till, suddenly prompted by fear, it leapt over the fence, followed by its amazed companion.

Now when Bony urged his horse northward along the barrier he met rabbits running the fence southward, following the line of least resistance to their general advance to the south-east. Rows of rabbits were standing against the netting testing it with their teeth. From the north-west countless others were arriving every second to join those running the fence southward, and now among the arrivals were black, blue, white, fawn, and piebald rodents, rarely seen in normal conditions.

Bony had forgotten the triumphant conclusion of his investigation. He was unconscious of his physical weakness. When his horse desired to leave the fence to walk direct to the camp, he reined her back so that she kept alongside the barrier.

The sun was low to the distant horizon, now hidden by the faint red dust-mist raised by the horde. The sun itself was an orb of scarlet. So still was the evening air that this mist did not extend eastward of the fence.

At the northern corner post, Bony was interested to see how the rodents followed the line of least resistance when reaching the fence. Those that arrived south of the corner post proceeded southward and those that were met by the fence eastward of the corner ran to the east past his camp and over the sand-dunes. As far as he could see, west and north, uncountable rodents were advancing from the north-west.

The dogs slunk to camp with him and, having yarded and fed his horse, Bony made a pint of meat extract and drank it with bread broken into it. And then, having fed the dogs with grilled rabbit, he stood for a moment in the gloom of early night listening to the march of life gone mad beyond the fence. It was not unlike wind among mulga leaves.

He was up again at break of day, feeling stronger, but still far from normal. In the silence of early morning, he again heard the sound not unlike wind among mulga leaves, and when the light of the sun reached the earth he saw at the foot of the fence a thick line of fur, tipped with little sticks moving endlessly up and over the sand-dunes to the east.

Still unable to mount his horse from the ground, Bony led her to the tree stump. Breakfasted, he was indeed a vastly improved man compared with the tortured wreck from whom Dr Malluc had sucked six little pointed bones and two eagle's claws. His new-found mind was hungry to feed on the impressions offered by this extraordinary manifestation of life. His dogs did not attempt to climb the fence again. They trotted behind the horse, evincing lordly disdain of the scurry of rodents barred back by the nettting.

As Bony advanced southward over the depressions, the risen sun striking hotly on his left side, the stream of rodents beyond the fence widened. Every second, dozens of rabbits coming direct from Meena Lake swelled it more. From a trickle at the northern fence post, the flow of fur became a stream when horse and man and dogs began to cross the last depression in the centre of which stood the southern corner post. Into this angle flowed the stream accompanying Bony. Into it, too, flowed a greater stream along the fence coming eastward from the main road gate.

The V of the angle presented an astonishing sight. Like wind-driven snow, rabbits were piled in a solid mass against the barrier for fifty yards back from the corner post. The mass had been suffocated, and now up this mound of fur ran living rodents to reach the top of the netting and to jump down into Karwir. They were like a brown waterfall, the lip of which extended along the two sides of the V for ten or twelve feet. Once over the fence they streamed on and away to the south-east, raising a wide ribbon of greyish dust upon which the sunlight of early morning thickened to hide the animals running below it.

Within the angle itself the mound sloped down to a moving sea of fur covering several acres, a sea in which were many eddies and cross currents. Here and there the sea was ridged and humped by the living rodents on top of those that had died of exhaustion. And into the sea footing the mound poured the two streams coming from the west and the north along the fence.

Bony could observe no slackening in the tide of fur sweeping towards Karwir, but he did observe that among the rodents was a goodly proportion of does. There were no half-grown rabbits; all were adult and strong. The number of those already arrived could not be estimated; their weight in tons could not be guessed. There was never a break in the procession coming directly to the angle or in the streams coming along the fence.

It was shortly after ten o'clock when Bony heard the hum of a motor engine, and he noted the time by the sun's position, thinking that it was early for Sergeant Blake's visit. The car was coming along the branch track from the Karwir-Opal Town road, and, expecting to see a Karwir car or truck bringing him horse feed and probably fresh meat and bread, Bony was surprised to see a yellow utility truck appear on the road where it began to skirt the south edge of the depression. The truck left the road there and came directly towards him. He saw Gordon driving it and two aboriginals perched on top of a load of wire netting.

Welcomed by the dogs, Gordon and the blacks reached ground, and the aboriginals at once began to unload the rolls of netting while Gordon walked towards Bony. Bony slid from his horse to meet the Meena squatter, now wearing khaki drill trousers, open-neck shirt and a wide-brimmed felt hat. He looked hard. He walked with the mincing step of the horseman. A smile was upon his face but not in his eyes.

"Good day, Inspector!" he said, in greeting. "I hope you are better to-day after Malluc's services yesterday. He seems quite confident that his beastly medicine will have effected a cure."

"Good morning Mr Gordon," Bony returned, smiling. "Yes, Dr Malluc is a great medico and something of a surgeon, too. He operated on me successfully, removing from my insides six little pointed bones and two eagle's claws."

"He *would* have to go through with his picturesque performance," complained the young man. "Well, I am very pleased to know you are better. It's a dickens of a mess here, isn't it? The migration moved faster than I anticipated. Didn't expect it to arrive here before this evening, but we knew last night it was headed into this angle and so brought the netting to top the fence. We'll have to cut poles to string it on, and you'll excuse me for not talking more just now."

"Of course. Perhaps if you left your billies and water and the tucker box over there in the shade of that leopardwood I could act as camp cook. You'll want plenty of tea, and I'm useless for hard work."

"That's decent of you. We'll do that. It's going to be a snorter to-day and we'll want all the drink we can get. Malluc says you ought have another dose of his medicine. He can get the fire going for you and brew the stuff while Jimmy Partner and I go off for a load of poles."

Bony laughed, saying :

"I'm a willing patient, and Dr Malluc's medicine doesn't taste so badly."

"Righto !"

Gordon hurried back to the now unloaded utility and, with the blacks beside him on the running-boards, he drove to the tall leafy tree standing where the road began to skirt the depression less than a quarter of a mile from the corner post.

Within the shade of another tree Bony neck-roped his horse, and then joined Malluc who had made a fire and was filling the billies with water from several four-gallon petrol tins.

"You goodoh, boss?" he inquired cheerfully.

"Much better, Maliuc. You fine feller medicine man all right," Bony said, flatteringly. "Are those the herbs in that billy?"

"Herbs?" Malluc questioned.

"Med'cine."

Malluc laughed, saying:

"Herb feller no belong Kalchut." Then he remembered the rabbits and pointed to the mound of fur at the point of the V. "Bimeby plenty stink, eh? All no good feller. Skin-em-feller no good. Now no fish in Meena and now no rabbit feller at Meena. Blackfeller him do a perish."

This appeared to be a joke, for he laughed uproariously, both hands pressed to his flat stomach. It was a joke with a lasting savour, for he continued to laugh while he attended to the brewing of his medicine and afterwards when he stood with the billy in one hand and tested the falling temperature of the liquid with the point of a dusty finger.

"You drink-em-down," he urged when satisfied.

Bony drank without hesitation, and again he experienced that ecstatic glow spreading throughout his entire body.

A large billy of tea had been made when the utility returned with a load of poles, and Malluc and Bony carried the tea and pannikins and a loaf of brownie to the scene of the coming work.

"Get it down your necks quick," Gordon ordered the men. "We have got to stop that leak as soon as possible. What a shot for a movie camera! Nothing like that down in Brisbane and Sydney, is there, Mr Bonaparte?"

"No, not even in the zoos," agreed Bony. "It is the first migration I've ever seen and I shall never forget it. Have you seen one before?"

"Never. But my father and mother did years ago. Mother says that the rabbits then were not so numerous, but they left the lake country as suddenly and they came this way, too. This fence wasn't up in those days, and when it was and this angle was created, the dad predicted this mess if another migration happened along. Now then, you chaps, let's to it. You take the truck for another load of poles, Jimmy Partner. Come on, Malluc, you give me a hand wire-twitching poles to the posts."

Bony felt regret that his physical condition barred him from taking a share in the labour. Gordon and Malluc lashed a twenty-foot pole to each fence post back from the corner for a hundred yards. With a brace and bit, Gordon bored a hole in every post to take one of the supporting wires, and, when Jimmy Partner returned, he stood on a case on the tray of the truck and was driven from pole to pole to bore holes in them at higher levels.

Fencing wire was run through the holes and then fastened to strainer posts. Rolls of wire netting were run out along the ground and then lifted to be suspended from the new-run wire while the lower selvedge was wired to the top of the netting in the actual fence. And so the waterfall of fur was stopped from splashing in brown foam down into Karwir.

The stoppage was effected shortly after twelve o'clock, by which time Bony had taken the billy back to the campfire and had made more tea for lunch. He shouted that lunch was ready.

The men drove across in the utility, and Jimmy Partner obtained a wash basin, soap and a piece of bagging. Hands were washed. On a length of American cloth Bony had set out the pannikins, the sugar tin, the tomato sauce, the meat and bread. A bag covered something laid down beside the American cloth.

"Feeling hungry, Jimmy Partner?" Bony inquired mildly.

"Too right, Mr Bonaparte. I could eat a whole sheep."

Jovial, his round face was expanded in a hearty smile, and one never would have thought he had instigated the boning of a man to death.

"Well, here is the sheep," Bony said invitingly, and stoop-

ing to the bag, he lifted it away to uncover three dead rabbits. Even Gordon chuckled.

"You eat-em-down," urged Malluc, again pressing both
his hands to his flat stomach.

"Too right, next year," countered the aboriginal wrestler.

"Oh no," objected Bony. "You eat them now, fur and all.
Remember, you said you would when I was leaving your
camp that time you were footing the fence."

The smile faded from Jimmy Partner's face.

"I said—" he began and stopped. "I said I would eat three
rabbits, fur and all, if you found Anderson within ten miles of
this boundary fence."

"Well, keep your promise. I've found Anderson, and he is
not even a mile away from the boundary fence."

Bony stepped back. Jimmy Partner slowly stiffened his huge
body and a scowl spread over his ebony features. Gordon had
bent to reach down for a filled pannikin of tea, but now he
became like a statue. Malluc appeared to be mystified. And
then Jimmy Partner's arms became bowed and slowly he
advanced upon Bony. The movement continued until the
automatic pistol halted him.

"Sit down!" came the order like the crack of a stock-whip.

Slowly the great athletic body went to ground.

"It is as well for you, Jimmy Partner, that I am not a
vengeful man," Bony said, quietly. "When I tell you that I
found Jeffery Anderson buried beneath a claypan, you will
not, I think, demand to be shown which claypan. And I will
relieve you of the task of eating three rabbits, fur and all, in
consequence of the work still to be done. Do not again be so
rash when meeting Napoleon Bonaparte.

"Now, Mr Gordon, let us begin lunch. Do not permit my
little revelation to spoil your appetite. I am happy to assure
you that, being in possession of all the vital facts concerning
the Anderson affair, I am not going to make any official
move against you or Jimmy Partner."

Gordon flushed, and came alive.

"That's very decent of you, Mr Bonaparte. Knowing the facts, I'd like to explain why I acted as I did."

"Not now, Mr Gordon," urged Bony, smiling. "There is still more work to be done at the fence. Later, I should like to hold a conference when all matters can be explained and settled. Having completed my investigation, I must leave Karwir to-day. For the wonderful service you Gordons have rendered to the Kalchut tribe, I am going to make reward. Hullo, I hear the Karwir aeroplane!"

"Car, I think," Gordon said listening.

"Plane all right," said Jimmy Partner.

"Him motor feller," voted Dr Malluc.

CHAPTER TWENTY-FOUR

A Mountain of Fur

HAVING written his letter to the Chief Commissioner, in which he stated the blacks' bone-pointing as a fact and not as a suspicion, Old Lacy considered that he had done his duty. He continued to worry about Bony, however, and Diana came to understand that her father had been captivated by the man in spite of the stigma of his birth. When Old Lacy suggested that she should spend the afternoon in the open air, she sought her brother and persuaded him to take her in the aeroplane to visit Bony and then—if it could be managed—-the Gordons at Meena.

At one o'clock brother and sister were in the air, at the girl's feet a box of comforts specially ordered by Old Lacy. At four thousand feet the air was cool and invigorating, making her face glow, her eyes sparkle.

The sun-heated world so far below was bisected by the subdivision fence and the road to Opal Town that skirted it. The horizon was sharp against the cobalt sky and broken only in the north-west by the Meena Hills, lying like blue black rocks set upon a black sea.

Diana delighted in these air trips, and she adored her pilot brother, so different, immediately he left the ground from the seemingly carefree man whose laughing eyes so effectively concealed thwarted ambition. Never had her confidence in his flying skill been shaken, and up here, so high above the heated earth, she thrilled to the sense of freedom from material bonds.

Young Lacy turned round in his seat in the forward cockpit to draw her attention with a hand to something ahead of them. For nearly a minute she could not determine what it was he wanted her to notice. There was nasty looking whirlie staggering towards where Pine Hut was hidden by the timberbelt, and there were several eagles beyond the boundary fence. The edge of this timber, in which ran the boundary fence, momentarily revealed individual trees as the belt slid over the curve of the world to meet them. She saw the road running more plainly through the scrub to the white painted boundary gate which, from a pinhead, was growing magically into a perfect oblong.

Now she saw the abnormality to which Young Lacy had drawn her attention. Over the gate, and where the fence ran towards Green Swamp, hovered a tenuous red haze, so fine and so still that it could not have been made by sheep or cattle. Then she saw that this haze extended far back from the boundary fence, and her interest was increased to astonishment by the extraordinary number of eagles flying above it.

The road gate passed under them. The red haze was more dense at the gate, the road beyond was hidden by it and the usually sharp outlines of the trees were blurred. When over the border, Diana saw, partially obscured by the dust, what appeared to be a muddy stream of water.

Abruptly the earth swung upward on her right side. The engine roar almost died. The earth swung to for'ard and now there was the blur of the propeller between her and the scrub. The gate swung into her radius of vision, remained there for a little while, swung away and returned to appear ever so much bigger. Then the fence took position on her left side, and remained there with the tree tops only five hundred feet below. The ship rocked in the air pockets, but Diana did not notice this.

Down there against the fence the muddy water had resolved

into animals. Rabbits! Rabbits running as close as sheep in a yard race. Outward from the fence the ground was alive with running rabbits, rabbits all running the same way. The rabbits had left Meena Lake!

The engine burst into its song of power, and now they were flying low along the road to Pine Hut and Opal Town. The girl could see beneath the red haze the army of rabbits crossing the road in the direction of Green Swamp, marching like an army without a van or a rear.

So absorbed was she by the animals on the ground that she failed to notice the birds until the machine almost collided with an eagle. There were hundreds and hundreds of eagles, like aeroplanes engaged in a titanic battle. Many came so close to the machine that she could see their unwinking agate eyes, and beyond the countless near ones could be seen countless others all the way to Meena Lake.

Young Lacy passed back to her a hastily scrawled note:

Too many eagles for my liking. They're following the rabbit migration. Rabbits must be running into the Green Swamp fence angle. If the prop. isn't smashed by an eagle you are going to see something that Hollywood can't put on the screen.

The machine was now following one of the depressions. Like a main track it unwound to pass under them, and then Diana wanted to stand up the better to see that which opened her eyes to their widest. There was the fence angle up from which was rising a thick grey mist. The wings of the angle appeared to run into a dun-coloured quarter-circle. Then she saw the fence leaving the timber to cross the depression to the corner, and the river of fur flanking it, a river that poured like sluggishly moving mud towards and into a dun-coloured quarter-circle.

She saw the utility truck standing beside the campfire, and the men waving up to them. She saw John Gordon, and noted no one of the other three, before the world spun round and they were landing bumpily, rushing along the depression towards what appeared to be a great brown rock. Between this rock and the truck the plane stopped for a few seconds, while the pilot searched for a safe position in which to tie the machine. He taxied to the timber edge near the truck, close before a fallen box trunk to which a light line could be fastened to prevent a whirlie wrecking the machine.

In the silence so pronounced after the roar of the engine, Gordon's voice was very small. He was looking up at Diana.

"Good day! Come to have a look at our rabbit drive?"

"Yes. It seems to be quite a successful one," said Young Lacy. "Must be more than a dozen brace in the bag."

"It—it's terrific, John," Diana exclaimed. "Why, look at the corner! They are piled in a solid mass!"

"A few birds about, too," remarked the pilot.

"They have only just begun to arrive," Gordon said, assisting the girl to the ground. "I brought Jimmy Partner and Malluc over with me, and the rabbits were then falling over the dead into Karwir like a waterfall. We've put up one line of netting above the fence netting, and it looks as though we'll have to put a third line."

Diana was so entranced by the spectacle that she failed to note the strained expression in her lover's eyes. Speechless, as he seldom was, Young Lacy stood with the mooring rope in his hands, staring at the massed rodents and the mound surmounted by a frieze of living animals frenziedly searching for escape through the wire.

The task of mooring the machine was hastily accomplished, but Diana could not wait. She walked over the flat bottom of the channel to the fence, there to stand and stare and marvel. She heard Young Lacy talking to Bony and Gordon, but she was unable to turn to greet the detective so mastered was she by this drama of life gone mad.

There at Diana's feet passed one of the endless streams of animals, hurrying, jostling, biting for space. They were flung from one kind of death to rush into another—the two arms of netted barrier. Farther out, tens of thousands milled and flowed like eddies in a steamer's backwash. They completely covered the ground. They formed a cloth of fur, ridged here, humped there, reaching to the foot of the gigantic mound, crushed and suffocated at the apex of the angle where the topmost living layer was already nine feet from the earth.

Countless eyes glared upward at the girl and the two men standing on either side of her. Teeth worried at the wire. Teeth bit rumps and the bitten squealed. Mercilessly the sun beat down and heat generated by the massed bodies killed and killed. Like the plopping mud in the mud-lakes of New Zealand, units of the mass leapt high, screamed, and fell dead with heat apoplexy, to sink into the mass like stones. Death was busy among these animals so passionately desirous of life, and Diana felt strongly the urge to tear down the barrier, to give life with both hands.

"We'll have to put up more topping, John," Diana heard her brother say. "D'you notice any difference in the tide?"

"No," replied Gordon.

"I don't think the last of 'em have left Meena Lake yet, according to the dust haze we could see from up above," Young Lacy said. "That topping will have to go higher and be brought farther out on both sides of the corner post. Is there enough netting on the job?"

"I think not. We'd better get busy. Even if only half the rabbits from Meena run into this angle . . ."

Diana was conscious that the men left her, save one, but she did not look round. Something of the hypnotic condition of the rabbits seemed to be controlling her. There were other sounds besides the death shrieks of sunstruck rabbits. The whirring of giant wings was increasing. The excited cawings of countless crows created pandemonium. Even the wires of the fence on which she leaned vibrated from the constant shock of alighting birds.

The birds appeared to have no fear. Great eagles planed low to ground, their legs extended. Others stood upon the ground and thrust forward their cruel beaks at rabbits running past them. Others flew labouringly, low to the ground, their talons sunk deep into living rodents and chased by a brigade of crows blaring out their massed caws. The fence top was lined with birds. They strutted outside the angle, eagles surrounded by crows, eagles gorging, crows fighting in black masses for the crumbs left by the eagles.

The sky was etched in whirls, by the heavy bombers and the funeral-black fighters. And from the north-west still further fleets were coming to plane in great circles lower and lower to join the groundlings. When the utility truck was moved from pole to pole the sound of its engine did not reach the girl and Bony who stood beside her. Bony spoke and she did not hear him. He had to raise his voice.

"One would never think that Australia could stage such a marvel," he said.

"No one would believe it unless he saw it. I wouldn't." Diana became aware of Bony, and her eyes tightened a little when she added: "Hullo, Inspector! Are you feeling better?"

"I am a little better, thank you, Miss Lacy," he replied. "I am expecting Sergeant Blake at any hour, when I shall ask him to take me to Karwir for my things and to thank your father for his great kindness to me."

The girl's eyes did not so much as flicker.

"You are leaving? I think you are wise. Away from the bush you will be able to have proper treatment."

"I have been receiving treatment from Dr Malluc," Bony told her. "He has worked wonders with me. I am really going because there is no longer reason to stay. You see, I have completed my investigation."

She stared at him, and in her violet eyes he saw tears. She

spoke one word so softly that the birds' uproar banished its sound.

"Indeed!"

Then she saw the aeroplane. She was standing westward of Bony and she saw it over his shoulder, a big twin-engined machine flying straight to land on the depression beyond the corner post. So loud were the birds that the noise of the engines did not reach them. Bony turned to gaze in the direction of her outflung hand. The machine rocked badly when about to make a landing, but the landing was effected with hardly a bump.

Now with their backs to the fence, they watched two men climb down its fuselage, and over Bony's thin features spread a soft smile when he recognized the first as Sergeant Blake and the second as Superintendent Browne. There could be no mistaking either. A third man appeared, small and dapper, whose movements on the ground were sprightly. Bony recognized him. Captain Loveacre, one of Australia's leading aces, had been associated with him on the Diamantina River.

The slight figure of Napoleon Bonaparte appeared to become a little more upright, a little taller. From watching the newcomers cross to the men at work with the netting, Diana turned to look at Bony. She was aroused by the look on his face, the look of a man seeing a vision.

So Colonel Spendor hadn't deserted him because he dared to disobey orders! The all-powerful Superintendent Browne himself had come to Karwir to ascertain why he, Bony, had not reported for duty. They must want him badly down in Brisbane, for the Super to have come in Loveacre's aeroplane.

They watched Young Lacy shake hands with Captain Loveacre and Superintendent Browne. They saw Loung Lacy point to them, and then they watched the three men advance, Loveacre slightly in the lead. He had donned a straw panama, and now he was raising it to Diana although he continued to gaze at Bony.

"Good day, young feller-me-lad!" he cried to Bony before he could hold out his hand to grasp the one immediately offered. "Every time I happen to meet you you manage to stage some kind of a wonder. Last time it was a flood of water and now it's a flood of animals. And birds! I had to make a detour east, to prevent smashing a propeller. You are looking peaked."

Bony smiled and the birdman was shocked.

"I have been indisposed, Captain. Allow me to present you to Miss Lacy."

"Happy to meet Eric's sister, Miss Lacy. Does Karwir often put on a show like this?"

"Only for Mr Bonaparte's entertainment, Captain Love-acre," the girl replied, laughing.

"Now, Miss Lacy, meet Superintendent Browne, my brother-in-law, who is having a flying holiday," interposed Sergeant Blake.

Bony's eyes went cold. He was, after all, not so important to the Criminal Investigation Branch. A flying holiday it was, not a special mission to plead with him to return to duty, the Commissioner giving him another chance.

Gruff and hearty, Browne acknowledged the introduction, nodded to Bony a little too casually, and then the party turned to watch the drama being played beyond the fence. And Bony was smiling, for he had recalled that Browne's salary would not meet the expense of such a holiday and, moreover, that Browne was known to be a careful man married to a still more careful woman. He remembered his self-imposed task of acting camp cook, and, without a sign, he walked slowly and still falteringly across to the temporary camp where he filled the tea billies and set them on the fire. He was seated on Gordon's tucker box waiting for the water to boil, when Browne detached himself from the group at the fence and came across on his tracks.

"Well, how's things, Bony? Heard you were very ill."

"I have been so, but I am round the corner and on the road to recovery. Why have you come?"

"That being a straight question, I'll give a straight answer. The Old Man sent me."

The large man, dressed in tussore silk, seated himself on the ground and rested his back against a tree up which ants were running. He began to fill a pipe. Bony smiled, wondering how long the ants would permit the Superintendent ease.

"Why did Colonel Spendor send you for me?"

"He reckons you would be of greater service to the Branch alive than here at Karwir under the ground. From information received we learned that you were desperately ill, that you were being boned by the local blacks, and the Old Man sent me to take you back. You coming quietly?"

The question was absurd. Browne weighed sixteen stone of bone and muscle, Bony weighed in the vicinity of eight stone and could not have resisted a child of twelve.

"And your informant—who was it?"

"In police practice the informant's name is never divulged, as you well know," Browne remarked casually. "When the Old Man heard about you he showed that he has a soft spot for you in his heart. If the Chief Sec objects to the expense of this plane trip the Old Man will be paying for it." Browne knew how to deal with Mr Napoleon Bonaparte. "It's going to be a wicked day for the Force when Colonel Spendor retires, Bony, and you and I will be losing a good friend."

"I concur in that," murmured Bony.

"Good! I didn't doubt that you would. Now you pack up right now and we'll start back. Loveacre says we can camp the night at Opal Town, using the Karwir private 'drome. You let up on this disappearance case. Not finishing it can't be held against you. Then we'll talk to the Old Man who will, I think, reinstate you without loss of pay."

"You think he will?" asked Bony, his eyes shining.

"Sure to. Can't do without you. Knows you're a tiger once

you begin an investigation, knows you haven't any more respect for authority than a crow, but in his big heart he thinks a lot of you."

Bony sighed. He was quite serious when he said:

"Very well. I'll relinquish this investigation. You see. I am a sick man, and it is most difficult to work longer on it. I should like to write a line of thanks to Old Lacy for his great kindness to me. Have you writing materials?"

"Yes, on the plane."

"And I have a few words to say to Miss Lacy and to Mr Gordon. After that we might wait here while Mr Gordon or Young Lacy goes to the homestead for my things. It is only twelve miles away and it will not take long. I shall be glad to leave Karwir."

"D'you think you were really boned by the blacks?" asked Browne, his grey eyes small.

"Oh, yes. But you will do nothing about it. The blacks have made me well by un-boning me. Their medicine man has done me a very great deal of good and I am infinitely better than I was yesterday morning. Now you get me the writing materials while I make the tea.".

From this task Bony looked up to observe the broad back of the Superintendent walking towards the big machine. He smiled, for there were several ants on that broad back. A minute or two later he beat an empty water tin with a stick, attracting the attention of Captain Loveacre and Diana, and the party working at the fence corner. When they had all come into the shade for afternoon tea he was busy writing his letter to Old Lacy. It ran:

Dear Mr Lacy—The Chief Commissioner has chartered an aeroplane and sent my superior officer to take me back to Brisbane. I should much like to have paid another visit to Karwir and thanked you in person for the great kindness you have shown me during this investigation into the disappearance of Jeffery Anderson. I owe more to you than you may appreciate, and I am happy to say that the Kalchut medicine man visited me yesterday and to-day and has begun to send me along the road to full health and strength.

Miss Lacy will inform you of the details of my investigation which will, I think, completely satisfy you as to the fate of Jeffery Anderson and the reasons why I intend taking no action against any persons. Anderson's fate and the manner of it is better forgotten, and in this I am sure you will agree.

I have the honour to announce to you the engagement of your daughter to Mr John Gordon.

I am confident that you will be overjoyed by this announcement, for Gordon is a splendid young man and they are very much in love. I look forward to receiving notice of the wedding, when it is arranged, and to adding a piece of cake to my treasured collection of wedding cake. We are both getting old, and it is good for us to be sentimental sometimes.

And so, good-bye, or it may be *au revoir*.

I have, indeed, the honour to be,

Most sincerely yours,
Napoleon Bonaparte, D.-I., C.J.B.

P.S.—I was nearly forgetting. During the course of the investigation, I learned that Jeffery Anderson was your son by a woman named Kate O'Malley. It puzzled me why you kept him at Karwir, why you treated him as you did. It was strange that his mother's love for the Irish national colour was shown by your son in his choice of cable silk for his whip crackers. It is a sad chapter better closed. Remind Miss Lacy to send me a piece of the cake, won't you? Hope you will be up and about long before the cake is cut.

This letter containing a hint at blackmail Bony placed in an envelope in his pocket-book with those five envelopes marked "Exhibits" from one to five. The men had finished lunch and were smoking, the girl was talking animatedly with them as she smoked a cigarette. Bony rose, saying to them all:

"I am going to ask Mr Lacy to fly to Karwir for my things, as Superintendent Browne wishes me to return with him and Captain Loveacre. While Mr Lacy is away, I should like to talk privately with you, Miss Lacy, and you, Mr Gordon. Please convey my thanks to Mr Lacy senior, and say that I am writing to him to express my gratitude for his kindness to me."

"Righto! I'll get going now. I'll come back on the truck. We'll want more netting out here and more men," said Young Lacy cheerfully.

"We'll go along and see him off," suggested Bony.

Loveacre and Browne remained in camp. After Young Lacy's machine disappeared over the scrub, they watched the girl, Gordon and Bony, walking towards the shade cast by a robust leopardwood-tree. Bony walked in the centre, each hand holding an arm.

"Looks like he's taking 'em for a little walk," remarked the Superintendent.

"May be hanging on to them for support," Blake said. "He's worse than he looks. You can have no idea what he's gone through."

"He looks terrible to me," asserted Captain Loveacre, "this boning must be a pretty dreadful business. What's he doing now? Making a fire over there. Hang it, isn't it hot enough without a fire?"

A spiral of smoke rose from the group of three. They could observe Bony inviting the girl and Gordon to be seated.

"I'd like to know what he's up to," growled Browne. "I feel that it was too easy persuading him to give up this case. You know anything about it, Sergeant?"

Despite the fact that the question was officially put, Sergeant Blake brazenly lied:

"Nothing, sir."

Captain Loveacre rose to his feet, saying:

"Well, I'm going across to the fence. There's much more of interest over there."

Superintendent Browne frowned at the three seated about the little fire, then he grunted and followed the others to the netted barrier.

Hool-'Em-Up and Sool-'Em-Up stood regarding the retreating broad back, then they slowly walked along the depression's bank to the party of three and went to ground close behind Bony.

CHAPTER TWENTY-FIVE

Bony is Sentimental

LIKE Captain Loveacre, neither Diana nor John Gordon could understand why Bony made his little fire when a breath of cool wind would have been a relief. Dusty and begrimed, the man appeared in striking contrast to the girl who was wearing superbly fitting riding kit and knew how to sit gracefully on the ground. Bony was sitting on his heels making a number of cigarettes, and only now did his companions clearly see the physical effects of the pointed bone. His face was almost fleshless. His eyes were sunken and lit with blue gleams. Neither Gordon nor Diana Lacy had spoken a word since Bony had brought them from the lunch camp, and now they waited for him to speak with such anxiety that the extraordinary scene at the fence angle was forgotten.

"You two need not fear me," he told them almost pleadingly. "No one fears me except evil-doers. Had you known me in the beginning as well as I hope you will know me after I leave Karwir, you would have been spared a load of worry and I a dreadful experience. Now listen to my story, and do not interrupt, for we haven't much time.

"On the eighteenth of April of this year, John Gordon and Jimmy Partner left Meena homestead to work in the Meena East Paddock and Jeffery Anderson left the Karwir homestead to ride the fences of Green Swamp Paddock. It began to rain about two o'clock, and at this hour the three men were able

277

confidently to predict a heavy fall. They also knew—a fact known possibly only to a fourth man, Young Lacy—that John Gordon and Diana Lacy were in love and met secretly at points on the boundary fence. Two matters, therefore, they were all agreed upon : the love affair and the prospect of an excellent fall of rain.

"When it began to rain Anderson decided to he need not visit Green Swamp itself. He continued riding the paddock's fences. Gordon decided that, because the Channels become sheep traps in wet weather, he and Jimmy Partner would ride the southern boundary of the Meena East Paddock and muster northward any mobs of sheep they found.

"They came upon a mob of sheep and Jimmy Partner was asked to drove them well away from the danger zone while John Gordon rode on looking for others. Thus it was that he and Anderson met on either side of the boundary fence. It was raining steadily and the sky promised a continuance of the rain.

"We know that Anderson wanted to marry Miss Lacy and that he regarded John Gordon as his successful rival. We may also assume that he disliked Gordon for another reason, namely Gordon's indignation and actions following the atrocious treatment of Inky Boy and a lubra.

"Well, there he was this wet afternoon miles from the homestead and without protection from the rain. His mood was evil before he saw John Gordon riding towards him on the far side of the fence. The man's record proves the ugliness of his temper when aroused. His anger, already sharpened by the rain, was whipped to fury by the sight of his rival.

"It is likely that at once he began to insult Gordon. Probably he threatened to reveal the secret love affair to Old Lacy. More probable still, in order to taunt Gordon into furious action, he referred insultingly to Miss Lacy. My reading of Gordon's character leads me to think that he would not quietly ride on, that he would resent insults to himself and violently protest against insults to his sweetheart. Angry words were flung to and fro across the netted barrier.

"Early this day, Anderson had what is termed 'taken the sting' out of The Black Emperor, and no doubt his subsequent riding had further subdued that great horse. He dismounted and secured the end of the reins to a fence post. The use of the neck-rope for this purpose seemed to his angry mind an unnecessary delay. Over the fence he vaulted, and John Gordon also dismounted from his horse.

"We know that Anderson was a big, strong man, much heavier and stronger than his rival. He smashed Gordon, knocking him partially unconscious, and then, before Gordon could recover, Anderson decided to treat him as he had treated Inky Boy. With the horse's neck-rope he secured Gordon to the tree by passing the rope round the trunk and the victim's neck, and knotting the rope in such a position that Gordon could not release himself.

"Without doubt, Gordon recovered his senses to find himself at the mercy of a raging sadist who delighted in outlining the programme before executing it. Gordon realized that once his knees relaxed in a struggle to escape the whip the rope around his throat would take the weight of his body and suffocate him.

"From what I have learned of Anderson, it is probable that he gave his victim an exhibition of his dexterity with a stock-whip, and at about this time Jimmy Partner rode back to assist in the muster of further sheep. Anderson, governed by sadistic rage, did not see Jimmy Partner dismount from his horse some distance away, and approach as an aboriginal does when stalking a kangaroo. Every time Anderson turned his way, Jimmy Partner froze into immobility and the unwary man received the impression that the blackfellow was a fence post or a shortened tree trunk.

"Now Anderson came to stand at the exact distance from his victim at which he could use the whip effectively. When he made a trial cast with the whip, the cracker made with green cable silk smacked against the trunk above Gordon's head. Gordon jerked his head back in an effort to avoid the whip lash, and his head came in violent contact with the trunk, the rough bark of which retained at least one hair from his head.

"Whether or not Anderson had time to make another cast I am unable to determine, but Jimmy Partner now rushed him. We all know that Jimmy Partner is superlatively strong and an expert wrestler. It was comparatively easy for him to master Anderson, and during the struggle John Gordon shouted to him not to kill Anderson. He knew what many of us know, that once an aboriginal is thoroughly aroused he is a terrible person. Having Anderson at his mercy, Jimmy Partner recalled the treatment of Inky Boy, and a lubra, and the treatment about to be meted out to a man dear to him and to his people. It is not surprising that he killed Anderson with his hands.

"Leaving the dead man, he ran to the tree and released John Gordon. I am inclined to assume that during his struggle with Anderson one of Jimmy Partner's hands was wounded and bleeding, and that when he was releasing Gordon, blood from the wound stained the neck-rope."

"That's quite right," interrupted Gordon. "In fact, so far you are remarkably accurate."

"Good!" Bony said, with great satisfaction. "But to proceed. John Gordon was a quick thinker and clever. He realized that other than Jimmy Partner and himself, who were directly concerned in the tragedy, there were no witnesses whose evidence would prove justifiable homicide, and that inevitably the law would arraign Jimmy Partner for murder, and, probably, himself as accessory. The effect of the tragedy, however, would reach out far beyond himself and Jimmy Partner. Miss Lacy would be brought into it. Anderson's history would become public property, and the affair with the lubra, and that with Inky Boy, would be broadcast. There would be an outcry because those affairs had been hushed up, and the Kalchut tribe would be drawn into the limelight.

"We know that three generations of Gordons have followed a splendid idea, which is to preserve one aboriginal tribe from the evil shadow of civilization as long as is possible. We know that three generations of Gordons have, by wise overseership, maintained the Kalchut tribe in its original state. The Gordons have encouraged the Kalchut people to maintain their rites and customs; they have frowned on anything tending to destroy the practice of those rites and customs. They have shielded the Kalchut tribe from Government officials and from missionaries, in fact from every kind of white and yellow men. And so this people has remained happy and healthy, while neighbouring tribes have become debased and wretched. That the shadow of civilization will eventually fall on the Kalchut tribe we are agreed; but its blighting effect can be deferred as long as is humanly possible.

"And so, with the dead body of Anderson lying at his feet, John Gordon clearly saw the threat to the ideal handed down to him by his father. He realized that this man, who when alive had delighted in sadistic cruelty, would in death thrust the shadow of civilization upon the Kalchut aborigines and thus hasten their de-tribalization and ruin. Public bodies would demand what is called 'official protection,' and religious bodies would demand a different kind of interference that would have the same fatal result. I concur earnestly and without reservation in the decision made by John Gordon, the decision to hide the corpse so that the disappearance of Jeffery Anderson might not be associated in any way with the Kalchut tribe.

"As I have said, fortunately for many, John Gordon was a clear and a quick thinker. He and Jimmy Partner had with them no digging tools, but they knew that at Green Swamp hut there were shovels and a crowbar, and that no stockman was living there. Gordon sent Jimmy Partner on The Black

Emperor to fetch the crowbar and a shovel, and while Jimmy Partner was away he selected the site of the grave. He is to be complimented on his choice.

"He decided to bury the body beneath one of the ribbons of claypans skirting the dunes. Already water was collecting on those claypans, and, selecting one but a few yards distant from the solitary mulga-tree, Gordon dammed back the water gathered in the pan above it. When Jimmy Partner brought the tools, he, being the stronger of the two, used the crowbar to crack the surface of the claypan as though it were a sheet of thick ice. The cement-hard surface blocks thus created were carefully removed. Then the grave was carefully excavated, the soil being shovelled out and on to the claypan lower down the slope. Into the grave were placed the body, the stockwhip, the neck-rope and the dead man's hat. The removed earth was then solidly packed about and over the body until the grave was filled to the proper level to take the surface material. Like the pieces of jig-saw puzzle the blocks were fitted together over the grave, like tiles laid and fitted on a cement hearth bed. The interstices were filled in with water-softened clay, human fingers doing this work. Finally the water from the claypan higher up was released, to flow into that beneath which was the grave, and so to the one below whereon was still the residue of excavated earth, which was carried away on to the flat, porous land.

"The rain eventually filled all those claypans, but in due time the water was evaporated by the sun's heat and the wind, and during the last stages of evaporation the cement-like clay of the pan beneath which Anderson was buried settled into its natural level and became so hard that the wheels of a ten-ton truck would have made no indentations. It remained only for me to see the infinitesimal abnormality in the surface of that particular claypan, and I would not have seen it had I not known for what to look. Is my reconstruction correct?"

Gordon nodded. Diana continued to stare down into the little fire.

"By the time Jimmy Partner came back from returning the tools to Green Swamp hut it was early evening," Bony went on. "The Black Emperor was let loose, the end of his reins being permitted to trail upon the ground, and we know that several hours afterwards he reached the homestead gate.

"On the way home, John Gordon instructed Jimmy Partner to inform Chief Nero of all that had happened. The tribe was to go on walkabout being the tale that a lubra at Deep Well was dying. Jimmy Partner was to accompany the tribe. The aboriginal attached to the police at Opal Town was to be recalled, the method of communication with him being the age-old one of telepathy. Abie at once obeyed the summons, and so when the police were called in to investigate the disappearance there was not one black tracker available for several days. When they were employed, they had been carefully instructed.

"I am not going to weary you by detailing how I found where you two met that day I arrived, and how I found that traces of the meeting had been removed. That was a secret you wanted to keep from me, not knowing that Napoleon Bonaparte has a soft spot in his heart for lovers. I haven't time to explain how I learned that I was being tracked and watched by men whose feet were covered with feathers, or how I came to suspect that you, Miss Lacy, knew something concerning Anderson's disappearance and were opposed to me, fearing for your lover. In my inner heart I never believed that you, John, instigated the blacks' boning of me, and I am delighted that you did not and that you stopped it when you learned of it.

"However, your stopping of the bone-pointing resulted quickly in my completing this investigation, for immediately my mind was freed of the terror created in it by those other minds, I reasoned that only the claypans had not been examined, that one of them would provide a perfect grave, and that over at Green Swamp hut was the ideal tool ready for use. I regret that you will have to replace the battery jars in the instrument at Pine Hut, smashed by my order to interfere with Miss Lacy's communication with you."

Bony now produced from his pocket-book six envelopes. That addressed to Old Lacy he put down on the ground beside him. The remaining five he held as though they were playing cards, saying :

"Exhibit One, the strand of green cable silk found attached to the rough bark of the mulga-tree to which John Gordon was tied.

"Exhibit Two, a cracker removed from one of the whips owned by Jeffery Anderson, and manufactured from green cable silk similar to that of Exhibit One.

"Exhibit Three, a human hair found on the bark of the tree to which John Gordon was tied.

"Exhibit Four, hair from Anderson's brushes.

"Exhibit Five, hair from John Gordon's brushes all similar to that one named Exhibit Three.

"These envelopes contain sufficient proof for the indictment of Jimmy Partner and John Gordon. It has not been a difficult case, and I should have solved it weeks ago had not the boning blurred my mind. The grave I have not disturbed, nor have I marked its position. As for these exhibits, well, what shall I do with them ?"

The question was asked directly of Diana Lacy. Looking up, she encountered his feverish blue eyes.

"Do you really mean that you would do with all that proof just what I might ask ?" she said.

Slowly Bony nodded his affirmation, and when she spoke her voice was barely heard above the cries of the birds.

"Burn them."

Now Bony smiled, saying :

"That is why I made this little fire. Burn these envelopes

and their contents we will. Then you will be free, both of you."

Silently, they watched the envelopes become black and grey ash. Then the girl's eyes again sought the blue ones so deep-set in a softly smiling dark face.

"I think you are a rather wonderful man," she said earnestly.

"A large number of people think that, Miss Lacy," Bony told her gravely. Then: "I asked you once to be frank with me. You then found that you were unable to be frank. Would you be frank with me now?"

"I couldn't be anything else, Mr Bonaparte."

"Then, tell me, why are you afraid to announce your love for John?"

"Because father doesn't like John."

"Only for that reason?"

"No. Were John and I to be married it would mean leaving Karwir, and father is growing old and has no woman to look after him."

"To announce your engagement would not mean having to marry immediately, even next year," Bony said, as he took his letter to Old Lacy from its envelope. "I want you to read this letter. Afterwards, you may deliver it to your father, or you may burn it now."

While she was reading, Gordon watched her and Bony stared down into the now smouldering fire embers. Gordon saw her face flame, saw her teeth press hard upon her lower lip. Then she stared at Bony, and he said:

"Well?"

"I don't know what to do. Perhaps John—"

"Yes, perhaps John could assist you."

Gordon was given the sheet to read. He said, unhesitatingly:

"Deliver it. Old Lacy will read as much between the lines as we read. Even if we can't marry for a long time, dear, it would be good to shout to all the world that we are lovers!"

"That is what I have been thinking," Bony told them. "Do not let your father know that you know the contents of my letter to him, but hint that you suspect I know something concerning the parentage of Jeffery Anderson. You, Miss Lacy, and I are experienced lion tamers, and we know that sometimes we need assistance. Your father does not really dislike John. He only thinks that he does." Diana was presented with the letter, sealed within the envelope, and then Bony struggled to his feet and they stood with him. "Tell your father all I have told you. Omit nothing. He will agree with my handling of the case, and with my disposal of it."

Involuntarily Diana held out her hands to accept his.

"I—I wish you were not leaving to-day," she said, her voice trembling. "I wish you were staying for a week or so, so that I could show you that I am not naturally hateful."

"I saw that when I first met you at the Karwir horse yards that afternoon I caught The Black Emperor. I shall not quickly forget your loyalty to a man needing it so badly as John did. Now let us go across to the others watching that extraordinary spectacle."

This time they each slipped an arm round his, and he was glad because the action not only bespoke full hearts, it assisted him to walk when he wanted to lie down. He was very tired.

The sun was low when the Karwir truck arrived loaded with rolls of netting, coils of wire, swags, rations, and men among whom was Bill the Better. The sun was now a huge scarlet orb floating in a scarlet mist that stretched from the apex of the fence angle to its couch of leaping flame. The eyes of the birds were winking scarlet lights. The tips of the fur streaming along the fence footing were varnished scarlet, the glossy plumage of the crows flying in the mist was tinted mauve.

From under the scarlet mist, the units of the mighty migration continued to come in endless procession, but there was a slackening in the tide of fur, indicating that the procession must have an end, and that the end might arrive before the scarlet sun rose again.

Everywhere were eagles perched motionless on trees and on the fence itself, birds gorged and tired of slaughter. Countless others stood on the depression eastward of the fence, unable to fly. At most they could only hop over the ground. The crows on the wing were like flakes of a black snowstorm. They chased eagles and each other for no reason except that it was their nature to want something others possessed.

Jimmy Partner, assisted by Malluc, had used the remainder of the wire netting brought by John Gordon to raise the netted barrier for fifty feet outwards from the corner, and Bony estimated that the height of the fur mountain at the apex of the angle was almost twelve feet. The surface was still etched by living rodents frantically searching for ingress to Karwir.

"I've never seen anything like this before," Captain Love-acre said for the hundredth time.

"Nor I," stated Superintendent Browne. "I'm glad that Bony is a bit of a rebel, otherwise I wouldn't have seen this show."

Gordon drove away on his truck to Bony's camp to fetch the detective's few personal belongings. Young Lacy and the men he had brought unloaded the Karwir truck and began the work of extending the fence topping and raising it still higher.

Gordon returned with Bony's effects from the camp, and these few articles were placed in Bony's case and the case in the aeroplane. Captain Loveacre required all hands to turn the machine so that it might have a clear run along the depression towards Green Swamp. He was the first to say good-byes to the Lacys and to John Gordon. Bill the Better came to Bony and asked in a strained voice:

"I understand you're leavin', Inspector. Have you found the body?"

287

Bony shook his head. Bill the Better looked glum.

"Well, I don't win me two quid, but I don't lose no two quid, either. So long!"

John Gordon and his sweetheart came to Bony, for whom Browne and Sergeant Blake were waiting patiently. Gordon took Bony's hand, and he said only one word:

"Thanks."

Diana took both his hands and squeezed them as she looked up into his wasted face.

"Thank you, Inspector," she said softly.

Bony smiled and bowed over her hands, saying:

"My friends all call me Bony."

"Bony—our friend," she cried.

Bony waved a special farewell to Jimmy Partner, to Dr Malluc and to Bill the Better. To Young Lacy, he said:

"Good-bye, Eric. Please remember me kindly to your father and convey to him my wishes for a speedy recovery."

"Good-bye, Bony. We'll all be glad to see you should you ever come to this part of Queensland."

Bony smiled at them all.

"You know, I really believe you would."

Browne and Blake had to lift him up into the 'plane, and they waved to the small crowd before they disappeared inside the machine. The crowd ran back towards the timber to escape the dust. The scarlet mist and the scarlet sun painted the machine with glowing colour, and made scarlet searchlights of its windows.

She did not seem to know it, but Diana, clinging to her lover's arm, was crying. They saw Bony waving to them from behind one of the windows as the engines broke into their thunderous song of power. They waved back to him as the machine glided away towards Green Swamp, to rise and turn in the direction of the town. They continued to wave while the machine dwindled in size to an eagle, a fly, a dust mote.